DISCO BOY

DISCO BOY

DOMINIC KNIGHT

BANTAM

SYDNEY AUCKLAND TORONTO NEW YORK LONDON

A Bantam book
Published by Random House Australia Pty Ltd
Level 3, 100 Pacific Highway, North Sydney NSW 2060
www.randomhouse.com.au

First published by Bantam in 2009

Addresses for companies within the Random House Group can be found at
www.randomhouse.com.au/offices

National Library of Australia
Cataloguing-in-Publication Entry

Knight, Dominic.
Disco boy.

ISBN: 978 1 74166 626 7 (pbk.)

A823.4

Cover illustration by Jasper Knight
Cover and internal design by Christabella Designs
Typeset in 12.5/17 Bembo by Midland Typesetters, Australia
Printed and bound by Griffin Press, South Australia

Random House Australia uses papers that are natural, renewable and recyclable
products and made from wood grown in sustainable forests. The logging and
manufacturing processes are expected to conform to the environmental regulations
of the country of origin.

10 9 8 7 6 5 4 3 2 1

For Lindsay, John, Isabelle and Jasper,
with thanks for the encouragement and yum cha

★ NOTE TO THE READER ★

This is a work of fiction. While certain names of individuals or businesses used in this book may also coincidentally exist in the real world, there is no connection or affiliation between any such real individuals or businesses and the fictional ones in this book. Any friends or family members of mine who think I've based any character on them should reassure themselves that I would never dream of doing such a thing. Please note that the author is not a trained DJ, and bears no responsibility for any adverse consequences that may result from playing any of the songs referenced herein in a public place.

#40

★ CELEBRATION ★
KOOL AND THE GANG (1980)

I looked out across the dancefloor at the punters bathed in refracted mirrorball light, clutching at one another to avoid collapsing onto the garish carpet, and asked the question every low-rent DJ asks themselves near the end of a gig. Were these people ready to shake their tailfeathers?

They were. Some of them, I regret to say, even loop de looped. But hey, I didn't make the rule that every playlist has to feature *The Blues Brothers*. Just like I didn't decide that Ricky Martin's 'Livin' La Vida Loca' was still fit for public consumption, or that anyone should ever be asked to do the 'Time Warp' again. I just learned what people like and played it to them. Because DJing at the shabbier end of the social spectrum is ultimately about democracy. Which makes a great argument for dictatorship.

I'd chosen a twenty-first birthday at the Waverton Bowls Club, the premier registered club in one of Sydney's sleepier harbourside suburbs, because my other option was a fiftieth at the Gordon Rugby Club, and I generally preferred being humiliated because some of the guests were friends of mine as opposed to friends of my parents. Also, being twenty-five myself, twenty-firsts weren't such a distant memory that I had difficulty choosing what to play.

I'd learned a thing or two in six years of DJing. Sure, it was mostly stuff like which Ace of Base songs people remember, but there's a time and place when even that dubious knowledge is useful. So I followed up 'Shake Your Tailfeather' with 'All That She Wants', and they loved it. My skills wouldn't have helped in a pumping superclub on the fair island of Ibiza, but you could give me – well, not two turntables and a microphone, as Beck put it. But give me two CD players and a box of greatest hits compilations, and I could pump up the jam, pump it up, while your feet are stomping.

Besides, pumping jams is an easier way to make a buck than pumping gas, and it's not much harder, if you know what you're doing. It turned out to be a textbook gig – and yes, there is a textbook. My boss Phil wrote it, and it's the musical equivalent of *The Anarchist Cookbook*, the legendary internet publication that teaches aspiring terrorists how to make pipe bombs. Phil's expertise wasn't in throwing Molotov cocktails into a crowd, though; it was in knowing when to chuck 'Footloose' into the mix at an office Christmas party. The impact was almost as lethal.

Shortly after the party started at eight, I kicked off with the Run-DMC version of Aerosmith's 'Walk This

Way' to get the braver guests dancing. Then I lured the shyer patrons to join them with Dragon's 'Celebration', Madonna's 'Holiday' and 'Come On Eileen' by Dexy's Midnight Runners. I can't speak for Dexy, but that song would make me run away from a dancefloor at any time of day. Nevertheless, the crowd ate it up.

Phil had taught me that the art of DJing is all about alcohol consumption. Not for us, unfortunately – I rarely dared to sneak a beer while I was on the job, as much as it improved it – but for the punters. So I gauged the crowd's intoxication by how raucously they cheered when they recognised each song, how raunchily they danced, and how many of them had actually fallen over. When around half the guests were well on the way to loaded, I started bringing out my black-label selections. Sure, no one wants to hear the daggy old '*Grease* Megamix' when they're sober, but with enough VBs under their belts, even the most self-consciously cool partygoer will sing 'Tell me more, tell me more'. And what's more, they'll actually mean it.

I hate to quibble with Robbie Williams, but being a Rock DJ didn't always make me feel all right. The music was an issue, sure, but my biggest problem was with the patrons, and specifically the young guys who'd had too much to drink. Time and time again, I've seen that serving unlimited alcohol packages to twenty-first guests produces much the same result as serving mogwais food after midnight – wanton destruction set to a cheesy '80s soundtrack. Fortunately, like Gremlins, dancefloor dickheads also tend to disappear when you shine a bright light on them at the end of the night.

A good DJ watches the crowd carefully, and throughout the gig I'd been keeping a disapproving eye on a posse of posers who'd spent most of the night propped up against the bar, looking contemptuously at the dancefloor. But by midnight, it was a different story. One guy with expensively messy hair and designer stubble, who'd put more time into his wardrobe than the birthday girl, sang along with 'White Wedding' like he was auditioning for *Australian Idol*. And suddenly his crew started getting into the dancing instead of sneering at it, and took over the middle of the dancefloor for some ironic posturing, pushing the regular kids over to the fringes.

A few songs later, stubble boy headed ominously in my direction.

'Hey buddy, this retro stuff is shit,' he leered. 'Got any real dance music?'

'Like what, exactly?'

'Like, I dunno, Ministry of Sound or something.'

'That's a club, pal, not an artist.'

'We want to hear bangin' tunes, mate, not this retro crap.'

Crap? My selection of songs was *crap*? Yes, correct — ten points. But I wasn't taking that from a guy wearing sunglasses at midnight.

'So you've come to request something cooler, but don't actually *know* anything cooler?'

'Steady on, we just want . . .'

'Well look, I'd love to play something tossy for you and your pals. But I'm busy playing the birthday girl's favourite songs so she can dance with her *friends*.'

He threw up his hands, dimly realising he was being a dick.

'Geez, no need to be so goddamn touchy. Play that crappy music then, white boy,' he replied, staggering off to sit down with a 'too cool to talk to the DJ' vibe I felt was somewhat undermined by the fact he'd just quoted Vanilla Ice.

I'm not exactly Eminem in *8 Mile* when it comes to a dissing battle, but intoxicated jerks are always easy fodder. To celebrate my victory, I fired up 'You're So Vain'. He and his mates sang along with gusto. And I hoped, like the guy in Carly Simon's lyric, he thought the song was about him.

#39

★ IN THE STILL OF THE NITE ★
BOYZIIMEN (1993)

It was a relief when the Waverton Bowls staff switched on the lights, sending the stragglers scurrying into the night, their eyes smarting from the sudden burst of fluorescence. I always relish the moment when the couple pashing uninhibitedly in the corner are suddenly forced to take a decent look at each other. No fewer than four drunken liaisons were interrupted by the cold light of closing time, making it a good party by any client's yardstick, if not my own. It wasn't long before the last wobbling reveller tottered off in search of a cab, leaving us to pack up. I welcomed the relative peace even after they started vacuuming.

I carefully boxed away the hardware, coiled up the last of my cables, and lugged the gear to the beat-up silver Volvo stationwagon that my parents had given me so I wouldn't die in a car crash. Or impress women – they were considerate like that.

Packing up was the least glamorous part of my unglamorous job. Occasionally, when a dancefloor greeted every one of my selections with whoops, and girls were flirting with me because they thought my taste was cool, I felt a little like an alchemist, weaving the base, base metal that was the MobyDisc catalogue into pure partytime gold. But even on the few nights when I'd successfully chatted girls up, the need to wait around for an hour while I put my gear into roadcases quickly evaporated their interest.

The birthday girl's father slipped me a hundred bucks on my way out the door and thanked me for making his daughter's night. I thanked whoever'd given him a few too many drinks. And before I walked away, I handed over his receipt.

'MobyDisc,' he said, reading the name of Phil's company off the tax invoice. 'That's funny.'

He was wrong, of course, but I smiled anyway as I shook his hand and said goodbye. In fact, MobyDisc is a whale of a crappy pun, beating even 'The Foam Booth' near my old school, and a BBQ chicken shop near my house, 'Nick's Hot Chicks', which offers neither attractive women nor adequately heated poultry. Phil came up with the name, and he loves it because – make sure you're seated, folks – while most people think it's a pun only because 'Disc' sounds like 'Dick', from the Herman Melville novel, 'Moby' is also an abbreviation for 'mobile'.

'I love it because it has so many levels,' Phil was fond of saying.

'And so does hell,' I was fond of replying under my breath.

But I did allow myself the pleasure of telling him that while it was a legendarily good pun, it seemed a shame to lose so much business because everyone thought we only played Moby.

Before I drove off, I took out Miles Davis's *Round About Midnight* from my definitely-not-for-DJ-use stash. It sure beat the last song I'd played at the party, 'Nutbush City Limits'. My own personal limit for Nutbush City was down to about five seconds.

MobyDisc killed my love of pop music because even when I love a song the first twenty times or so, I get heartily sick of it by about the fortieth. I read that the Americans used music to torture – sorry, interrogate – people at Guantanamo Bay. It makes sense – honestly, play me Aqua's 'Barbie Girl' enough times, and I'll confess to anything.

Every time I drove home from a gig, I wondered why I was still doing this, two years after finishing law school. I always insisted it was temporary, but as my parents pointed out, it was beginning to look a lot like a career. I'd developed a whole range of justifications to defuse the question, from the socialist – 'I like being an ordinary worker, not a member of the elite' – to the artistic – 'It's about *creating* something, you couldn't possibly understand' – to the downright preposterous –'I just do it for the babes'. But the truth was that finding a regular job just didn't appeal. What I really wanted was to work with another kind of music – my own. MobyDisc was vastly different from being a singer/songwriter, but it was a hell of a lot closer than corporate law.

Although my musical career has historically been confined to law revue bands and my bedroom, I've been learning guitar since I was a kid, and writing songs since I was an angst-ridden fifteen-year-old, kind of like Daniel Johns without the fame, fortune, critical acclaim or ridiculously hot ex. (Or the talent too, probably, but the jury is out on that.) In my more optimistic moments, I dream of having a career like Beck's – in terms of the eclecticism and consistency rather than the Scientology.

Many's the night I'd sat fading the Spice Girls into Shaggy, and wished I'd brought along a guitar to see if my own songs couldn't do a better job of entertaining the crowd. But I'd never had the guts, so instead I continued to sit there serving up the same stale hits as always.

I'd studied law only because my parents had told me I'd be wasting my marks otherwise, and I'd hoped spending five years at uni would keep them off my back while I got my music going. (It hadn't.) I'd even tried a clerkship at a big firm one summer holiday, and while I found the work manageable, we'd put in a lot of hours making foreclosures easier for our bank client, and it didn't exactly make me feel I was contributing positively to society. By contrast, as daggy as it was, my DJing made other people happy. Or rather, when alcohol had already made them happy, I gave them music to jump uncoordinately around to.

The other thing was that MobyDisc paid me $800 a week plus tips – not all that much less than a graduate solicitor wage, for the relatively low cost of four evenings and my dignity. And it gave me even more time than I'd had at university to theoretically work on music. My friend Zoë often goaded me about how little I'd produced – certainly nothing I was ever brave enough to play to her. But I still believed I'd get around to producing an EP eventually, and if I joined the 'real world,' it would be as good as admitting I'd never do it.

Plus, as Phil never tired of pointing out, our job had

'fringe benefits of the lady variety'. Scarily enough, it was true: despite his burgeoning beer gut, handlebar moustache and fondness for funny-guy novelty waistcoats, it was a lean month when he didn't get at least a pash. Sure, to the casual observer he may have appeared well north of forty, balding and a bit of a dork. But come the right hens' night harbour cruise, Phil was The Man.

Whether through lack of opportunity or effort, I hadn't gotten any action in a long time, and that night was no exception. As I cruised back through North Sydney, which was mercifully empty at one in the morning, I told myself it really was time I did something about that.

At a red light, I switched my phone on and found a text message: 'DRINKIES @ STRAND WL GO L8, COME AFTER GIG NIGE.'

A typical offer from my friend Nigel. While I felt like some company, a quiet drink was what I would've opted for, not more noise, smoke and alcohol-fuelled boisterousness. But heading home wouldn't have helped me with my chronic singleness, so somewhat against my better judgement, I headed over the Harbour Bridge to meet him. It was time I got out more. That is, to places I wanted to be.

#38

★ THE LADY IN RED ★
CHRIS DE BURGH (1986)

The later a Sydney pub stays open, the worse it is. The genteel, quiet, pretty pubs are all in residential areas and have to close at midnight for the residents' sanity, which forces their tipsier patrons to relocate to dives like the Strand, where the clientele is even uglier than the decor. Judging by my nights drinking with Nige, I've deduced that the inspectors only issue 24-hour licences to sticky-floored hellholes that happily serve up doubles to punters too drunk to order them coherently. Which pretty much sums up my mate's taste in pubs.

The Strand is in Darlinghurst, a suburb that ranges from irritatingly trendy to seriously downmarket, and the pub is definitely at the latter end of that spectrum. It's located on

William Street, Sydney's premier kerb crawled by transvestite prostitutes, who often stagger into the bar to feed their earnings into the pokies. It doesn't have quite the grandeur of London's Strand.

Inside, it's one of many CBD establishments decorated in the hope that a couple of tatty brass railings, fake wood panelling and some grimy stained glass equate to the charm of a traditional English pub. The interior does equate to traditional English backpackers though, and as I entered, the usual dozen were sitting in a corner, shouting unintelligibly in response to the Premier League football on the big screen. Honestly, the more English people I meet in pubs, the more I wonder why Australia ever had a cultural cringe.

Nige saw me before I could spot him, which gave him a chance to bellow 'JONO!' at me, informing every single patron of both my name and how much he'd had to drink. It wasn't the most creative nickname — just my surname, with the obligatory ocker 'O'. But it was enough for the six other tipsy people at his table to cheer my arrival, even though I'd never met any of them. I guess they figured anyone with such a dinky-di nickname simply must be a top bloke.

Nige is a good-natured, loud-voiced larrikin who's immediately mates with anyone he meets. We've been friends since Year Seven, when we were randomly assigned to share a desk, and we'd gone on to law school together. While our social circles diverged somewhat at uni — his revolving around college and rugby, and mine around the law student scene — we remained close, and as an undergraduate I'd spent more of my nights than I care to remember crashing on an air mattress on the floor of his room at college.

To my envy, Nige's charisma always attracts women whose quality exceeds what I privately think his oafish, beefy looks merit, and as I shook his hand and headed to the bar to buy a round, I noticed more than a few in his orbit. There was no way of telling whether the ladies were from his work crew or just random barflies who'd decided to come and check out the loud, funny guy in the corner. Like Rupert Murdoch, Nige always boasts an abundance of satellites.

He works at a big commercial firm and was recently admitted as a solicitor. Nige's life, or at least sixty hours a week of it, is mired in the minutiae of financial regulations. Which is why he needs to compensate by spending as many hours of the weekend as possible drinking. Nige's life is a corporate T-shirt saying, 'Work hard, play hard'.

I sat down next to him and finally started to relax as I got into my schooner. It turned out all his friends were work colleagues from Morphett Jackson, the firm that had snapped up most of the smartest kids at our law school. Not uncoincidentally, they were often also the dreariest. Nige is an exception, which is why several of his colleagues had followed him to a genuinely horrible pub at one on a Saturday morning.

'We've just come from the firm trivia night,' Nigel informed me.

'Really. The life you Morphett's kids lead.'

'Just because you go to at least four *awesome* parties every single week.'

'Against my better judgement.'

'I've known you long enough to know you don't have any. Nah, Jono, trivia's great. An athletic contest for the mind. Separates the wheat from the chaff.'

'And which are you?'

'Oh, the wheat, mate – we were runners-up. These are our victory drinks, and I just knew you'd want to be part of the celebration.'

So he'd invited me here for his own amusement, knowing that if there was one kind of success I wouldn't want to celebrate, it'd be trivia. I've always hated how it brings out the hideous competitiveness in the most placid person. Even easygoing Nige is an absolute shocker when there's some petty intellectual glory on offer.

'Wouldn't have missed it for the world. Unless you'd told me what it was.'

'C'mon mate – they can take away your security pass but they can't take away your place in the Morphett's family, hey?'

Nige was referring to the laboured attempts at friendliness made in the managing partner's welcome speech when we'd clerked there together. All the 'family' had required of its newest members, in ascending order of importance, was photocopying, filing and sucking up to the fulltime staff. And we were always getting trapped in conversations with HR flunkies, who were like those unwelcome relatives you get stuck next to at family functions. Their job was to constantly pretend we were all having fun so we'd sign on the dotted line. Nige knew that I'd threatened to throw myself out the window of their anchor tenancy in a chic new office tower if I ever went back.

'And hey, you know you could come back on board in a second if you ever decide to retire from your high-flying musical career, mate.'

But Nige's attempt to make fun of me went well over the head of the woman sitting on my other side.

'Did you work at Morphett's, then?' she asked, her prior

efforts to ignore me temporarily suspended at the sound of the magic M-word.

'Sorry,' Nige said. 'Paul, this is Felicity; Felicity, Paul – one of the most promising summer clerks ever to have served in the Banking and Finance trenches.'

Felicity was quite promising herself – so much so that my chest instantly constricted as I took in her long dark hair, intimidatingly sleek figure, and pretty alabaster face. Even without Nige's introduction, I'd have guessed she had some kind of corporate job from her groomed appearance and general air of privilege – neither of which made me think she'd have much interest in a lowly party DJ.

Still, for the moment, her intense brown eyes had locked onto mine so I thought I might as well have a crack at keeping them there. Nige helpfully left me to it, turning to entertain the rest of his acolytes while I attempted to provide her with something resembling entertaining conversation.

'I was barely there. Just the clerkship,' I clarified. 'Although I'm sure my filing skills are still the talk of Level 35.'

'Banking and Finance is a really great section,' she gushed.

No, it really isn't.

'I'm on rotation there at the moment, I'd love to stay,' she continued.

Why on earth? The firm practically had to apply thumbscrews to make me work in that section in the first place. I'd only given in on the understanding that I could spend half my time in the section that actually interested me – intellectual property.

She asked why I'd left the paradise on earth that was MJ's banking department. 'God, it's the best firm for bank work in Sydney,' she said, a smirk flickering across her lips. 'You must be a very accomplished musician to have given up such a great opportunity.'

Cheers, Nige, for mentioning it, I thought.

'Well, not exactly; I'm more in the DJing game.'

'Wow! Have you played any of the big clubs? Do you know Kid Kenobi or Goodwill?'

No, I only knew that they were famous club DJs of exactly the kind I was not. And that left me with few options. I could have admitted that I was just continuing with a student job because of inertia, and that no one had dangled superior alternatives in front of my face, but that was generally where my conversations with beautiful girls like Felicity ended. Especially as she would probably have shared my parents' inability to understand how I'd resisted the siren song of banking and her alluring sidekick, finance.

But I was saved from having to admit that I hadn't played in a single non-RSL club and that the most pre-eminent DJ I knew was Phil because my stubbly-faced friend from the party walked in with his trendy mates. I should have known. Given his level of intoxication, the Strand was the perfect end to his night. Most of the city's flotsam and jetsam washed up here, and that night he was very much in the drink.

It took him all of five seconds to spot me, demonstrating surprisingly accurate perception given how blurry his eyes must have been.

'Hey, it's Mr DJ. He's crawled out from under his rock,' he said. 'His daggy '80s rock.'

His pals liked that one a whole lot more than I did.

'And who's this lovely lady, then?'

'Aren't you going to introduce me, Paul?' Felicity cooed.

Great, so she liked drunk pretty-boys. I wouldn't have done the honours even if I'd known his name.

'Harris,' he interjected.

'Whoa, you're so cool you've got a surname for a first name.'

Not my finest conversational gambit, and he ignored it appropriately.

'Have you heard Paul here play his little tunes, then?' he asked, smirking.

'No, I was just asking him . . .'

'Well, we had the pleasure earlier tonight at a twenty-first. And I must say, he's got a magnificent Bryan Adams collection.'

She was as unimpressed as I'd been when the birthday girl had told me her favourite singer.

'"Can't Stop This Thing We Started", "Summer Of '69", even "All For One" with Rod Stewart and Sting,' Harris said, displaying an incriminating amount of Adams knowledge. 'In fact, this guy's got it all for one *awesome* party.'

Having had well above a trafficable quantity of Adams songs in my playlist that night, I had no comeback.

'You get *paid* for playing that stuff, Paul?' Felicity asked. 'As opposed to a restraining order?'

She was beautiful, witty and she hated the right music. But this scumbag was hitting on her right under my nose, and using my stupid job to do it. Was I going to stand for that?

I did what any honest, red-blooded Aussie male would've done. I gave up and, to pretend there were no hard feelings, I bought a round. I would rather have gone several rounds with Harris, but that would only have made Felicity even less impressed. Besides, with that quantity of alcohol in his system, he probably wouldn't have felt a punch to the head.

When I returned with the drink that my new buddy definitely did not need, he was still regaling Felicity with tales of horror about the twenty-first. OK, so she didn't like Bryan Adams. But if she had such impeccable taste, I asked myself, how could she stomach Harris's effete clothes? His ludicrous facial hair? The prominent, sickly sweet cologne?

But I knew exactly why she could. The beautiful people have this innate super-confident way of communicating that we mediocre-looking types can't understand. So, realising that I couldn't have interrupted their growing rapport with anything short of a fire extinguisher, I slunk away to talk to Nigel instead. He was in the middle of a long work anecdote which had his colleagues in stitches, but that I couldn't comprehend, let alone find amusing.

It didn't distract me sufficiently from Harris, unfortunately. So I wasn't at all surprised when about forty minutes later, just on the off-chance I hadn't been watching him intently out of the corner of my eye, he brought Felicity over. With a grin that was even firmer than the wax he'd smothered into his hair, he pumped my hand and announced they were leaving.

'See ya mate, we're outta here,' he said. 'And thanks for introducing me to Flea.'

'Oh, my pleasure.'

Was evidently going to be a whole lot less than his.

'It was lovely to meet you, Paul,' Felicity said, a little sheepishly, since her rejection of me was so clear it could've been written on the sodden coaster in front of me. 'I hope we run into each other again. Maybe you can spin some Bryan for me sometime?' she said.

And with that, they took themselves off for what I sincerely hoped would be terrible sex.

#37

★ LADY MARMALADE ★
LABELLE (1974)

There was only one way to react. Well, except for going home, but I wasn't anything like sensible enough to take that option. No, I had more to drink – so much more that I calculated it wouldn't be legal to drive home until about two the following afternoon. I matched Nige for loudness and crudeness, laughing boisterously to prove that getting barred in front of everyone hadn't bothered me in the slightest. It didn't convince Nige though, and he took me over to the bar for a debrief.

'What the hell happened there? I really thought you'd like Felicity. She hasn't had a boyfriend in quite a while. Not as long as your drought, sure – what is? But she seemed interested.'

'She obviously prefers tossers.'

'Ah, you just gave up at the first sign of competition. What do I have to do, serve them up on a platter? Actually, don't answer that, I don't want to know what sick shit in your head is fucking you up so much that you can't do this stuff.'

Really, his psychoanalytical skills put Dr Phil's to shame.

'You've got to stop being so embarrassed about your job,' he continued. 'It's a funny story – an *angle*. You do barely any work and earn nearly as much as I do. Half the time, I'm jealous of you. Then I go to one of your gigs and realise I wouldn't do it for twice the money. But c'mon – you can't tell me the chicks wouldn't love that shit.'

'Yeah, maybe.'

'Don't look all despondent, get back into it. Plenty more fish in the sea and all that, you know – especially at places like this. In here, you're shooting them in a barrel.'

'A barrel of gin.'

'Vodka Cruiser, more likely. But my point is: stop moping and get yourself some loving.'

Now, one-night things aren't my style, through both principle and a general lack of opportunity. And an even firmer rule with me is never to follow Nigel's advice. I would've taken Felicity out to dinner or something – you know, shown a bit of class. And ordinarily, after having been knocked back by a young lady, there would have been no second-chance draw. There would only have been a self-pitying ride home while I tried not to weep in front of the cabbie.

Perhaps it was my frustration, my drinking, or Nige egging me on that made me do it. More likely, it was finding myself talking to a cute member of Harris's gang, who'd been at the party and had stayed out after his triumphant departure. Well, if I'm honest, the real reason was that she was Harris's younger sister.

Surprisingly, given her genetic heritage, Emily was a lovely girl. And she was gratifyingly complimentary about my DJing. Sure, this was based on the large volume of Kylie and Britney I'd played – but still, it made a nice change from her brother. She was the birthday girl's best friend, she explained, with the precision of someone young enough to draw up a league table. Which also explained why Harris's crew had gotten invites. In other words, it was her fault he'd been at the twenty-first. So it seemed only fair that she make reparations.

I could chalk it up to the battering my self-esteem had taken at the hands of her brother. Others might share my friend Zoë's observation that drinking can make me unpleasantly sarcastic at times. (Although she puts it more succinctly, as 'a cock'.) When I get knocked down, as a rule, I don't generally get up again, Chumbawamba-style. I tend to try and drag others down with me.

Talking to Emily, I outdid myself. And she ate it up, thanks either to the booze that she herself had put away or her nineteen-year-old naiveté (yes, that number again is nineteen, folks). A lot of the stuff that came out of my mouth was so ridiculous that Nige had to put his hand over his own to avoid laughing.

I told her that the MobyDisc thing was just a bit of fun, helping out a mate, because I wasn't flying around playing superclubs in New York and Ibiza this month. I even told her I'd DJed at the after-party for Kylie's most recent Sydney concert. She was gobsmacked by that, and even more when I said I'd probably be able to get her a backstage pass for Kylie's next show.

'Oh my god, really? I love Kylie! Oh, that would be, like, the best thing ever. I mean, *ever*.'

'It's no trouble.'

She grabbed my arm and bounced up and down in her seat so excitedly that her long blonde hair flew into her face. Gee, I thought, I should lie outrageously to women more often.

'Oh, you are so *sweet*! I would owe you forever. I mean, I would *so* owe you. Forever.'

Whoa, enough with the 'forever', I told myself cockily, or cockishly, as Zoë might have put it. No way was this going past one night.

'Shucks, it's the least I can do for a fellow fan. I'm sure Kylie'd love to meet you.'

'God. No way, you *can't* introduce me to Kylie. I'd be – I'd be – GOD!'

In my defence, she was the one who invited me back to her place. In her defence – well, it's not easy to defend anyone who gives it up to a guy who pretends to know Kylie.

No, in her defence, it was completely, irrevocably my fault. She couldn't help that her brother was a jerk. Like I had been, in fact; only substantially more attractive.

The drink-driving laws dictating that my car would have to survive Darlinghurst overnight, we left to get a cab, to Nige's great amusement. I still don't know how she didn't see the absurdly theatrical wink he gave me as we left together. Once in the back seat, it took all of five seconds before Emily was all over the famous, well-connected music industry figure she imagined she was taking back to her grungy arts-student sharehouse. That's right – she was only nineteen and had her own place, while I still lived with my parents. And didn't *that* make me feel like less of a loser?

I won't go into the precise details of the night. After all, a gentleman doesn't kiss and tell. Especially when that gentleman has had a bit to drink, and may not necessarily have been capable of putting in a virtuoso performance. And while I'm evidently no gentleman, I have to start pretending somewhere, so let's just say that the rest of the night was entirely satisfactory.

Well, except morally.

#36

★ HELLO, I LOVE YOU ★
THE DOORS (1968)

When I eventually unglued my eyes the following morning, I realised that Emily's bedroom didn't quite constitute the groovy student pad I'd been expecting. Virtually everything in the room was pink, even a desk that was covered with university course readers and chaotic piles of paper. Lamps decorated with frilly pink bits of lace abounded, and there was even a stuffed toy collection, just in case I'd forgotten how young she was. But most striking were the posters she'd crammed onto every available square-centimetre of wall space – to the extent that the actual colour of the walls was a complete mystery. But I was definitely tipping pink.

The largest wall, opposite the bed, was

reserved for the pert buttocks and flawlessly airbrushed skin of one K. Minogue. The biggest poster, from the period just after she'd been made cool by sleeping with Michael Hutchence, said 'Impossible Princess'. Which was pretty much what the rest of the room was telling me as well.

I asked myself what on earth I was doing there. And then an embarrassed glance at the condom wrapper on the bedside table brought it all shuddering back. My head may have been sore, but it was clear enough to calculate the implications of going out after work, getting disgracefully drunk, and bullshitting my way into bed with a girl who'd heard me DJing.

I had become Phil.

★ ★ ★

Emily awoke, and what had been a peaceful sleep-smile flipped up into high beam when she saw me. I was relieved she was glad to find me there.

'Why, hello,' she said, stretching out her arms and arching her back, setting her mass of blonde ringlets quivering. 'I hope you slept well, I sure did!'

Right, so this conversation was only going to be awkward for me.

'No complaints here,' I ventured.

We made a little small talk, and then she suddenly sat upright and fixed me with an intense gaze.

'Just so you know, I don't usually do this. Like, I'm not out every weekend picking up guys,' she said. 'Although this time, I'm glad I made an exception.'

'Well, I *am* out every weekend picking up guys, and I'm glad I made an exception this time as well.'

'Really? You're bisexual? Cool, I've never been with someone who was that before.'

Was it too early in the morning for sarcasm?

'I was kidding.'

'Oh. Well, all I'm saying is, if you want to introduce other guys into our relationship at any point, I'm fine with that. In fact, I think it'd liven things up a bit.'

'Relationship? Look, I –'

She laughed and poked me.

'I can kid too, you know. Don't worry, Paul – from my perspective, your age just about adds up to two guys anyway.'

'You can kid? You *are* a kid. But look, if you really need multiple guys to make it exciting enough for you, I know a charming football team who could –'

'One senior citizen was quite enough, if my memory serves me correctly.'

'Oh, thanks. Although to be honest, if your memory was really serving you correctly, you'd kick me out on the street.'

'Hey, don't be modest,' she said. 'Which is not to say I won't be kicking you out on the street in a little bit. Unless you want to try and change my mind?'

And so, without even the excuse of inebriation, we repeated what was already beginning to seem less like an error of judgement.

★ ★ ★

I always enjoy that half-hour or so afterwards when two sweaty bodies lie close, deferring the awkward, fumbling moments of clothing and cleaning up. Which is why there could not have been a worse time for a loud rap on the door to inform me that Emily shared her groovy student house with her brother.

'Oi! What are you doing to my sister in there? Do you need me to kick him out, Em?'

'Piss off, Harry!'

Harry. I filed it away for future use.

'We're going down to Well Connected, come and join us if you can drag yourselves out of bed.'

He had company? Felicity? Far too well connected for my liking.

The teenager and I shared a long, hot shower that must have been a special treat for the mould on the crumbling plaster roof of her bathroom. I kept trying to amorously prolong matters in an attempt to defer the horror of breakfast. But eventually I was forced to put on my now foul-smelling work clothes, which rendered me obviously overdressed and indicated exactly what had happened between us. So I was feeling self-conscious as we slowly wandered down to the café Harris had nominated.

Emily lived in the student enclave of Glebe, and Well Connected is as stereotypical an undergraduate dive as you can hope for on a lazy Saturday morning, right down to the Goth waiters and the hand-drawn posters offering reiki services from which, depressingly, most of the little phone-number strips had been torn.

We ordered eggs Benedict and elaborate fruit whips, and then sheepishly shuffled upstairs to the large balcony overlooking the street where Harris was stretched out in the twin radiance of the midday sun and Felicity. She had on those big 'god I had a hard night' sunglasses, and wore a T-shirt whose ostentatious designer label would have told me it was his even if it hadn't been too big for her. She looked great, really great, which made me resent her all the more.

'Well, look what the brat dragged in,' Harris quipped, his face all too smug with delight at the fun he was planning to have with this. 'If my little sis hasn't bagged herself the disco boy.'

There wasn't going to be a good way out of this, I realised. So I opted to go down gallantly, and gave a little mock-bow.

'Harris, Felicity; delightful to see you again.'

'Phil, wasn't it?' Harris asked, inadvertently reminding me of the depths to which I'd sunk.

'Paul,' Felicity said. At least she remembered.

'Awesome night last night, wasn't it?' he said.

'Yeah, it was. Paul was awesome,' Emily interjected.

'*Was* he now?' Harris grinned, having produced the sought-after blush from Emily.

'At the *party*,' she clarified unnecessarily. 'Abi had such a brilliant twenty-first — he played every single one of her favourite songs. Literally.'

'Kylie *and* Jason, eh Paul?' Harris said, winking. Felicity tittered, covering her mouth demurely and then meeting my eyes slightly apologetically. If that earned a laugh, I thought, he was welcome to her.

'You're *very* good at it, we all thought so,' Emily said firmly, defending her man; or more likely her standards. 'I wouldn't be surprised if you get more work from Abi's friends. And you can play my twentieth if you like.'

'And he'll do it for free, won't you Paul?' Harris said, laughing. 'Least you can do, judging by what I heard last night.'

'Harry!' Emily blushed again, her usual confidence wilting under her older brother's teasing.

'I'd be happy to, of course,' I said, only partly masking my reluctance.

'Ah c'mon, you shouldn't be DJing at her party,' Felicity said, mercifully interceding. 'You should be out there dancing.'

Emily cheered up visibly. 'Yeah, dancing with *me*.'

Out of the frying-pan, into the fire.

* * *

For the rest of the meal, Harris didn't miss a single opportunity for a sly dig at his sister. And each time, she turned as pink as our rashers of bacon. But after the fourth wisecrack, I'd gotten over the embarrassment for the time being. This was just a normal situation for us inner-city hipsters, I told myself. It was even a normal situation for Phil. And that got me wondering whether perhaps one of the reasons I resented him was that very success with 'the ladies'. He'd always found the game surprisingly easy, aided by a convenient lack of both standards and shame. Regular work entertaining Sydney's tackier class of revellers and then taking one of them home for some sweet, sweet lerve were about all Phil asked of the universe. And its tendency to deliver so consistently on both fronts was a major source of the self-satisfaction that irritated me even more than his '70s pornstar moustache.

'So, I imagine you'd often attract the groupies when you're out DJing then?' Harris couldn't resist a smirk at Emily who, on this occasion, varied her blushing routine with a scowl.

'No – and I don't generally try, to be honest,' I replied, and then decided to try and return some of his serves. 'If you can imagine that.'

'No, Harry can't imagine a situation where the ladies aren't interested,' Emily said. 'I know – it's my bedroom door they slink past the following morning.'

'I meant he might have difficulty relating to not trying,' I clarified, Felicity tittered.

'Are you calling me a try-hard?'

'Of *course* not.'

Of *course*. Fifteen-love.

'I just meant – you're a heckuva suave guy, *Harry*. And very well turned-out, I thought, last night. Nothing wrong with putting in a bit of effort, especially when it yields results.'

A glance towards Felicity, who deserved at least a little hassling for going home with this piece of work.

'And Harry's metrosexual look's very in at the moment, Paul,' Emily said, contributing a neat volley to the rally. 'Just look at David Beckham.'

'Oh I do, Em; I do,' I said, backing her up. 'Personally, my response is generally to laugh at him, rather than signing up for my own dreadlocks and sarong. But each to their own.'

'Yes,' Emily giggled. 'Harry had a sarong a few years ago with lovely hibiscuses on it, didn't you, darling? Kept saying it was now OK for men to wear them, but no one believed him.'

'So I'm fashionable. So sue me,' Harris said, demonstrating minimal familiarity with the grounds for civil litigation that Felicity and I had studied so carefully at our respective law schools. Being an MJ girl, Felicity couldn't resist.

'Oh, don't worry Harry, there's no action in tort for being trendy,' she said. 'Although there might be an issue of misleading and deceptive conduct!'

I chortled appropriately at the ever-so-droll Trade Practices Act reference. That's the sort of thing that passes for a joke at Morphett's. It would have fitted perfectly into one of their unfeasibly cheerful staff newsletters.

'Oh, there's nothing misleading or deceptive about Harry,' I interjected. 'You get immediate notice he's a fashionista as soon as you clap eyes on him, wouldn't you say? After that, it's *caveat emptor*,' I said, raising my eyebrows at Felicity to emphasise exactly what I thought of her *empt*ing.

'Buyer beware,' she clarified for the two non-nerds. Returning my arch glance, she said, 'And what makes you think I'm buying?' Interesting.

'Don't worry, a beautiful girl like you doesn't have to pay to be with me,' Harris said, turning on the suaveness again. 'I'm like J. Lo,' he added, and then inadvisedly broke into a falsetto version of the chorus from 'Love Don't Cost A Thing', before relapsing into his regular tones. 'But of course, if you want to, I won't argue . . .'

'How about I shout your breakfast?' Felicity said, 'Given I'm the one on the evil corporate wage, as I'm sure our bohemian muso friend here would put it.'

Of course, I could do no less than offer the same to Emily, what with her being a struggling student and all. Which led to the biggest grin she'd produced since we'd arrived at the café. Sometimes even the clumsiest piece of chivalry can go a long way.

We paid a languid, long-haired emo type wearing the sort of gear that would have gotten him beaten up anywhere other than this kind of café in this kind of suburb, and went back to their place to get our stuff. Not for the first time during this whole episode, I found myself wishing I had a little more experience in the amorous arts. I bet Casanova was never terrified about what to say to a girl with whom he'd had a great time but wasn't particularly serious about.

What's more, I bet Casanova never had to play Kylie at a bowls club, the bastard.

But in keeping with the little I'd learned of her character, Emily was more direct.

'Paul, give me your phone so I can put my number into it,' she said as I was up in her room collecting my jacket and tie. 'That way, if you want to call me, you can. As you haven't asked for it yet.'

Ouch. Embarrassed, I handed over the phone.

'Em . . . I think you're great . . .'

'But. Don't say it, I know there's gonna be a but. Don't worry, I've got one too. Mine is that I only broke up with a guy last month, and I'm not particularly over it.'

'Phew.'

'Plus, you think I might be too young for you.'

'Was I that transparent? Sorry. But yeah, it's an issue.'

'But I just *know* I'll see you again – you promised me those backstage tickets to Kylie, right?'

I made a few noises that sounded vaguely like the beginning of a coherent sentence, but then gave up.

'That's OK,' she said, laughing at my embarrassment. 'I was flattered. I figured you must've liked me a lot to go to such lengths to bullshit me.'

'Yeah, I did; and I was just being a drunk show-off, really. I'm sorry.'

'Ha! I knew last night that you didn't have a hope in hell of getting backstage passes. If anything, I'd be the one giving them to *you*, bucko.'

'Is that right?'

'You're talking to the reigning New South Wales president of the *official* fan club – Klub Kylie.'

She pulled out her membership card to prove it. And yeah, it was spelled with two Ks.

'I knew there was something distinguished about you. Presidential, even.'

'So if you ever want to go to one of her shows, let me know. I can hook *you* up.'

'You're too kind.'

'Oh come on Paul, you're too trendy for Kylie? Hey, it's your loss: she's been trendy since *Fever*. Anyway Paul, the bottom line is, hang out with me again or don't, it's up to you.'

'Of course I'd like to see you again. I'll give you a call.'

She frowned. 'Oh, don't promise that. That's just what everyone says so they feel less guilty when they leave.'

'Hey, I actually will.'

'Good. But you do feel guilty, I can tell.' She grabbed my arm and looked at me intently. 'Don't be thinking you just used me for sex. Or at least if you did, I used you just as much, OK?'

'I must say, you're wise beyond your years, young Emily.'

She laughed. 'Bugger off, grandpa!'

So off grandpa buggered.

#35

★ THE POWER OF LOVE ★
HUEY LEWIS AND THE NEWS (1985)

Felicity was waiting for me downstairs. We'd agreed to share a cab because she lived quite near the Strand – albeit in a new apartment block designed by a trendy architect – and I needed to retrieve my sorry excuse for a car.

'So, I gather you had a pleasant evening,' she grinned as we lolled on the grey vinyl of the back seat.

'And yourself!'

'Harris is a nice enough guy, but I told you, nothing happened.'

'Hey, it's no business of mine,' I said. 'And like I can talk.'

'Oh you weren't talking, I know. I think the whole neighbourhood heard what you did to that poor innocent girl,' she grinned. 'But seriously – I know what guys are like, and I don't need you telling Nigel, and thereby our entire floor at MJ, that I shagged Harris, OK? They already saw us leave together, and I'd hate for them to get the wrong idea. That place is an absolute echo chamber for gossip.'

She had that right. The uneventfulness of most young lawyers' personal lives is no bar to the constant discussion of them. And I knew Nige's antics had fuelled many a break-room chat session. It was just another one of the invaluable social services he provided to that firm.

'My lips are sealed.'

'That's a change,' she said. 'No, actually, I don't even want to *think* about what your lips have been doing recently.'

'And yours?'

'OK, fine. I'm not going to deny I kissed him. Although *you'd* better if Nige asks you. But just to be clear: he is *so* not my kind of guy. Really.'

'Deal, as long as you don't give our mutual friend any details about Emily either. He'll give me shit for months.'

'And that's supposed to convince me not to do it?'

'No, I'm counting on the threat of mutually assured destruction. Besides, Nige probably won't remember anyway; he'd virtually passed out by the time Emily and I left. And as for Harris – I don't know, you seemed pretty keen on him last night!'

'Hey, it's been a while, you know?'

'Really?'

'Yeah. I'm fussy.'

'*Really?*'

'Ah c'mon, he was quite charming, and I'd had a bit to drink. But by the time he tried to convince me to come upstairs, I was over it – and so was he, as a matter of fact, after all those beers. And I slept on the couch downstairs, I'll have you know. In fact, you woke me up when you came in.'

'Oh god.'

'Don't worry. I admired your . . . enthusiasm.'

I couldn't sink down any further into the seat, so I was relieved that we'd reached the gate of her chic compound. But at the same time, I was sad to be saying goodbye. Although I could scarcely believe it, we seemed to be developing a rapport.

'I'll see you round,' I said. A man with no shame like Nigel would've gone for the phone number anyway, but I was in no mood to be rejected by her twice in 24 hours.

'It was so nice meeting you. See you soon.'

'I hope so.'

'Well, I'm having a barbecue at my place in a couple of weeks' time. You should come along with Nige, he's got the details.'

'OK, that'd be fun.'

But then, as she opened the door to jump out she added, 'And of course, bring your new girlfriend.' And then slammed the door before I could offer the obvious Harris-related comeback.

Felicity was smart, beautiful and had a great sense of humour. A little out of my league on the attractiveness scale perhaps, but it doesn't hurt to aim high. And otherwise, I told myself, she was definitely the sort of girl I ought to be dating. We were from the same little law enclave – we probably had a whole lot of friends in common who'd be surprised to hear we'd hooked up, but would understand completely. The overlap might save us a fortune on wedding catering one day, I thought, smiling to myself.

Ridiculous ideas, of course, but that's the fun part of being attracted to someone – your imagination runs out of control. Absurdly presumptuous scenes pop up in your head and you can't stop them even if you want to.

It had been a much more interesting night than I'd been expecting when I'd walked through the doors of the Strand. I'd met someone I found attractive, which was rare, and I'd gotten some action, which was even rarer. If only both incidents had involved the same girl.

#34

★ FUNKYTOWN ★
LIPPS INC (1980)

I've always been one for mulling things over with a coffee, even when nothing is happening in my personal life. So now that Emily had given me something that genuinely required thinking about, I knew I'd better book in a serious session of sipping hot drinks. My list of coffee companions isn't long. When it was about women – and it usually was, unless I was complaining about Phil – I made my friends so sick of my passivity that they offered to ring up my target themselves to ask her out for me. After a few drinks one night at the pub, one of my friends actually followed through on the threat. She misinterpreted and, well, I'm going to be his groomsman next year. Thanks, Fitzy.

Nige's isn't my first-choice shoulder to cry

on, since his solutions always involve dodgy pubs, dodgier liquor and palming off some girl he'd tired of onto me. At times, when he'd found me particularly exasperating, he'd offered to rent me a hooker so I could bloody well get my end away for a change and stop taking myself so damn seriously. He was certainly generous. To a fault.

Besides, he wouldn't have seen anything wrong with the Emily escapade, and would have mocked me mercilessly for having had scruples. And so my regular need for a good heart-to-heart whinge was best fulfilled by Zoë.

At the time she was my only close female friend, which is an indictment on me, of course. I generally find it tough to just hang out with girls when I'm single because I'm always terrified they'll think I'm hitting on them – cultivating a friendship so I can clumsily and unwelcomely shift gears to asking them out. Little do they know I wouldn't dare. My patented approach to seduction involves sitting back and hoping the girl will realise I'm interested and make the first move. It doesn't recommend itself through results.

That whole issue wasn't a problem with Zo, though, because while she's certainly attractive, we had the perfect basis for a strong, indisputably platonic friendship – a drunken pash on first-year law camp. When we had the mandatory painful conversation the following day and discovered that neither of us wanted it to go anywhere, the mutual relief – along with a shared taste for self-deprecating jokes about the incident – was enough to turn us into instant friends. Apparently we were right about the having lots in common and enjoying hanging out together bit, and wrong about the wanting to stick our tongues down each other's throats bit. But as Meat Loaf so insightfully observed, two out of three ain't bad.

Since discovering that the romantic road was a cul-de-sac, our friendship had blossomed. Guys often asked me how I could put up with it – right after they'd asked whether she was available and been disappointed. Zoë was very much taken in those days, so I always explained that while of course I knew abstractly that she was attractive, we were friends.

There was quite a bit to be immune to, if I'm honest. She has a petite, pale body, dark hair cut in a bob and high cheekbones – a hint of Audrey Hepburn, particularly given her similarly intense, dark eyes. Sometimes they sparkle with a lively wit and sheer overabundance of brains, but on occasion they crackle with genuine fire.

Her default mode is playful, but the intensity of her manner sometimes proves devastating for the male of the species. She focuses so intently on every conversation that guys are convinced she finds them fascinating. They start to delude themselves that there is something special there, or even that she's coming onto them. Invariably she isn't; she's just really invigorated by meeting people. I was often reminded that I'd made the same mistake when I'd met her.

The other thing that put Zoë completely off the agenda was that her boyfriend Josh is an old school mate of mine – in fact, they met at my twenty-first. Since they were one of those rare couples who didn't make outsiders feel like a vestigial limb, the three of us spent a lot of time together. Josh and I had never been all that so close, but I often joked that since I'd brought them together, it was only fair that I get the best man gig.

Zo's response was that I had to be her maid of honour instead – one of her little witticisms about my lack of manliness. I always replied that as long as it didn't involve a dress or in any way render me unavailable for some primo bridesmaid-scoring opportunities, I was there. To which she replied she knew I was there, but there was still no way I was scoring with the bridesmaids.

People often assumed that a friendship like ours couldn't be completely platonic. And since I was the single one, I got accused of holding a candle. My reply was always that sure, she was attractive, but after we'd kissed, I'd been the first to say I didn't think it was going anywhere. And that generally put an end to the ribbing.

★ ★ ★

Zoë showed up shortly after I did, only slightly grumpy about being dragged away from bed and boyfriend. She'd quickly thrown on some jeans and, judging by the Asian beer logo, one of Josh's T-shirts. Her eyes were hidden underneath a voluminous pair of sunglasses. Not a skerrick of makeup, but then she doesn't wear much anyway. Even so underdressed, she looked a whole lot better than I did, clad in last night's stinky semi-formal clothes.

We usually met at Bill & Toni's in Darlinghurst's Little Italy. It's only a short stumble away from her terrace, and conveniently near where I'd dumped my car the night before. The décor is so ugly it's charming – exposed red brick, shabby grey tiles, wood-veneer Laminex tables and vinyl chairs whose plastic backs have been misguidedly moulded into a cane pattern. No one would dream of designing it like that now, but it'd break everyone's heart if they renovated so much as one shabby tile, or added anything more to their menu than foccacia, gelato and coffee strong enough to keep even my struggling eyes open.

Zoë invariably tried to speak Italian with Marco, the barista, and it annoyed me every time. '*Ciao Marco, come stai?*' she'd ask. He'd unleash a stream of rapid Italian she couldn't understand. She'd laugh, nod and say '*Molto bene, grazie.*' It was their little joke.

I usually threatened to ask Marco the Italian phrase for 'show-off', but never dared. This was because he never let us pay for our coffees, unless I was foolish enough to go there without Zo. Marco's another one, I think, who misinterpreted her friendliness as flirtatiousness. I always told her she should start wearing a wedding ring just to save me time on the clarifications.

After I filled her in, she made an effort not to laugh at me, but not much of one. Evidently my little melodrama was absolutely the funniest story Zoë had ever heard, or so she kept telling me in the rare moments she wasn't too busy giggling to actually speak. I'm not sure whether she was more entertained by the actual details, or my humiliation in the retelling.

'I hate to ask, but could you run me through the whole Kylie thing again?'

'You know what? I think once was embarrassing enough.'

'Oh please? I really need to hear it again. I'm still deciding whether it's more tragic that you tried to get her into bed by promising her a backstage pass to the Kylie tour, or that she subsequently turned out to be the president of the fan club.'

'That's Klub with a K, I'll have you know.'

'See, Paul? Now you're enjoying it too. We both know that in a week, you'll be dining out on this story.'

'Really, I won't.'

She grinned wickedly. 'Yeah, you will. At the McDonald's Playland where all the pre-school girls hang out.'

'Hey! That's a bit below the –'

'Nappy?'

'C'mon, gimme a break, she's over the age of consent by at least three whole years.'

'OK, OK; I know you're a bit frazzled, but c'mon – this happens so rarely that I want to enjoy it.'

'Fine, but once you've stopped revelling in my embarrassment, you might like to tell me what I should actually *do*.'

Realising I'd had enough, she switched gears into her more familiar wise-counsel mode before she cost herself a hypothetical maid of honour, and flipped up her sunglasses to look piercingly into my eyes. 'See, this is where I thought you'd go wrong.' She waggled a finger. 'You don't have to do anything.'

'How's that going to work?'

'See, this isn't actually a crisis, Paul. It's normal. It's what people *do*.'

I snorted.

'Not you, babe, sure,' she said. 'But regular people.'

'Like Phil.'

'Ah, come on. Phil doesn't have a monopoly on being a ladies' man, you know. Even at MobyDisc nowadays, apparently . . .'

'Well, it just seems sleazy.'

'No, *Phil's* approach is sleazy. Look, if Emily had recently gotten divorced or become a grandmother, you'd be like Phil. But all you are is a single guy, going out and having a good time with a single girl, right? And I use the term "girl" quite specifically.'

'I know, I feel awful –'

'Yeah, evidently; but you shouldn't. God, lighten up about it! That's the only problem here – how you're feeling, not the situation itself. Personally, I'm relieved you're finally getting out there.'

'But what about Felicity? She's far more my type, and I blew it.'

Zoë winced a little. 'She's far more your *age*, by the sound of things, but *type* I'm not so sure about. Do you really want to be dating a corporate lawyer? Or at least a corporate lawyer who's totally into it?'

'Well, she'd probably get the logo tattooed on her wrist if the right partner asked her. But I feel like we've got a real rapport, and that hasn't happened for ages, as you well know.'

'That's true. I'm still in shock. You've exceeded your yearly average for both crushes and random shags within one 24-hour period. You'd better let me know if this is going to continue, because I'm going to have a bit of adjusting to do.'

'Felicity's got a great sense of humour, she's gorgeous, and she seems to like me, at least to some degree. Maybe slightly out of my league, but I can really see the two of us together, honestly.'

'Fine, well I'm willing to take your word for it, in lieu of other evidence. I'm not sure the Emily thing was necessarily an error, though. Perhaps you'll have made this Felicity jealous? That might work in your favour . . .'

'Oh, come on.'

'No really. You said she'd been single for a while, right? And it's pretty clear you showed Emily a – how can I put this – somewhat better time than she had herself. This new alpha male thing of yours is very alluring. Hey, I kind of find you more intriguing myself.'

I blushed, and was quick to cut her off. 'I'd have thought that after all these coffees, we didn't have much left in the way of intrigue.'

'*You* certainly don't. But really, some girl's gonna find a lot to like about you someday Paul, trust me. You've just had bad luck.'

I couldn't help but smile sheepishly and look downward. Coming from a woman who knew me so well, it meant a lot.

'I hope you're right about Felicity, Zo,' I continued after a moment. 'Maybe she'll decide she picked the wrong guy? I've got to tell you, that Harris character really is something.'

'You should have been more confident, Paulie. I always tell you: beautiful girls do it tough. Nice guys like you never approach them. They're too intimidated.'

'That sounds like me – the intimidated bit, anyway.'

'I've met a million Harrises. Look, if a guy's good at picking up girls, if he enjoys it, he'll want to keep on doing it. And he often won't value the one he's got because it all came so easily. You know, thrill of the chase and all that.'

She sat back and folded her arms, having convinced herself, and grinned at me.

'Whereas for you, the whole process is sheer torture, and you're so relieved when you actually get anything happening that you treat the poor girl well, right?'

'Out of terror she'll find someone better and bugger off, yeah.'

'Exactly. And I'd hate to change that about you Paul, it's part of what makes you a good guy.'

'Aww . . .'

'No, really.' She smiled, and I felt I might have a chance with Felicity, if she could only come to see me in a similar light.

'But while you're working on that – and I suspect progress will be slow – you may as well keep chasing Emily, if you like her enough. Maybe even some other girls, now that you're such a ladykiller. It'll do you good.'

'Do you think my current state can in any way be described as "good"? I've been a wreck all day.'

She laughed at me again. 'Not entirely, Paul. As big a wuss as we know you can be, you're still a *guy*. You've been swaggering a little bit this whole time, pleased by what a stud you are.'

'OK, so I'm a tiny bit glad to finally be back in the game. I admit it.'

'And I'm sure all the girls here are *terribly* impressed. Hey, that one over there's right in your demographic too.' She pointed to a baby in a stroller.

'Thanks Zo, that's real sweet.'

'Ah, come on, you're not cut up about all this at all, are you? You just got me down here so you could boast, didn't you? *Ohhh, Zoë, I'm so confused, too many babes* . . . and some of them are literally babes . . .'

I blushed again, and felt dismayed. It had occurred to me that she might be somewhat impressed by my new-found prowess.

'Oh come on, enough with the whole crestfallen thing. All right, I've listened to you crapping on for twenty minutes about something I refuse to agree is even a problem, so now it's time for me to bore you with the trivial details of *my* life.'

And so she proceeded to fill me in on the goings-on at the law faculty where she'd been working since we finished uni. She had seamlessly moved to the other side of the lecture theatre while finishing a Ph.D, like the academic superstar she's always been.

I always enjoyed hearing gossip about the nutcases we had as lecturers. By the time she'd finished telling me about the contracts lecturer who'd hated me in second year getting a nose-hairball and spraying Earl Grey tea all over himself, I had completely forgotten about my predicament. Which was undoubtedly the point.

#33

★ OUR HOUSE ★
MADNESS (1982)

While I know it's important to be independent, I'd never really seen the point in making the transition from freeloading at my parents' place to paying outrageous inner-city rental prices for a dump. And like the countless other times I'd visited a student dive, Emily's terrace hadn't exactly encouraged me to rush out and rent a fleapit I could call my own. She had so much rising damp that it really should've kicked in something towards the rent.

Nige had often talked about getting a place with me before he'd bought his own apartment, but it was exhausting enough being his friend on a part-time basis. I had shuddered to think of the awkward morning conversations I'd have been obliged to conduct with random girls who couldn't quite understand why the carefree, jolly fellow they'd met the previous night had gotten up so early to go into work on a Sunday.

Besides, I was doing practically nothing with my life, and some days even that was a huge effort, so I suspected that taking on responsibility for a full-blown household was well beyond me. Consequently, I kept living in Cremorne Point, a suburb equally renowned for its genteel water views and the wealth of the residents who get to enjoy them.

Of the two richest quadrants of Sydney, the Eastern Suburbs are known for trendier European migrants while the North Shore is more an enclave for conservative Anglos. Our suburb is kind of a cross between the two – it's technically on the North Shore but has the water views directly opposite the glamorous east. So the locals go to church, but probably also to the opera. The area's probably best known for Taronga Zoo, which is a few bays around in Mosman. It's the only thing remotely wild about it.

We aren't quite so well-heeled – the real estate ad had optimistically described our place as having 'water glimpses'. Which realistically means that from one upstairs bathroom you can glimpse a sliver of the harbour if you stick your head dangerously far out the window. I'm sure my parents paid an extra hundred grand for it nevertheless.

I turned into our quiet leafy avenue, fired up the remote control roll-a-door and parked my lower-bourgeois second-hand Volvo alongside the spot reserved for my parents' upper-bourgeois late-model Lexus. Its absence meant they were out, which was welcome news. Given my tiredness and the hangover I still hadn't quite shaken, I was glad to defer the awkward questions about where I'd spent the night.

Without making my usual fridge detour, I headed straight downstairs and into the comforting embrace of a brown leather sofa my folks had paid far too much for because it happened to have been made in Italy. I put my feet up, but hung them over the edge of the armrest so that if my parents came in, I wouldn't get into trouble for leaving my shoes on. And yes, that was as independent as I got.

The architect had shunted the kids away downstairs, our bedrooms branching off a communal den so we could fight over the remote far away from the spotless, designer-minimalist 'adult' areas reserved for entertaining guests. I'm the youngest of three by a considerable margin – five years younger than my brother Andrew who's a trader in London, and three years younger than my doctor sister, Rachel. The moment she'd left, I'd grabbed her big room that opens out onto the garden, arguing I'd need the space to spread out during my HSC. And I'd commandeered Andrew's old room as my 'studio'. It was full of my music gear – a few guitars, a fancy keyboard and a computer I could use to record songs, if I ever actually got round to it. In practice, it was mainly used for aimlessly browsing the internet. As Zoë – who'd moved out at nineteen and never looked back – liked to mockingly point out, I had my own suite. So really, going out on my own wasn't really at the top of my crowded transition-to-adulthood to-do list.

My parents work far too hard to really enjoy the fruits of their labour. Dad's a gastrointestinal surgeon at Royal Prince Alfred, which is Sydney University's main teaching hospital. His days are long and stressful, and his phone's always on in case there's an emergency in the middle of the night, which happens roughly once or twice a week. My mum's an English academic at the same uni, which seemed like a cushy job before the government slashed tertiary funding and classes got overcrowded. I'm amazed Mum even gets any of her own research done, given the time she has to spend with students. Sydney Uni's always been a big part of their lives – they met at the student bar back in their undergrad days, cutely enough, and they've never bothered to leave the campus. I guess inertia runs in the family.

They met in 1968, the year of all the great student revolutions around the world, but their personal insurrection extended only as far as moving in together in the days when that was still slightly scandalous. That pretty much used up their lifetime's supply of rebellion, and since then they've dedicated themselves to never doing anything so controversial again, unless you count my mother's early neo-Marxist scholarship.

Oh, and she'd taken great pride in telling us she'd voted Green in the last few elections, as if it would somehow achieve anything beyond a fat parliamentary pension for an eccentric former feral. Like so many baby boomers, she is still looking for the scanty evidence that she hasn't sold out. But she doesn't burn bras anymore, only rubber as she fangs across the Harbour Bridge in the Lexus, with the salve to the inner-city-elite conscience that is ABC talk radio blaring out through all eight speakers.

My dad is a man of science, interested only in arguments and evidence. Even though he's in a tax bracket where he probably should vote Liberal, he's always been a Labor man. Which is fortunate, as voting for John Howard would have led my mother to instantly divorce him. Nobody hates our former Prime Minister with quite the same level of bitter, yet fundamentally passive, rage as the inhabitants of university arts faculties.

I trawled through the cable channels. My first sweep unearthed a *Police Academy* film festival, a special on Richard Clayderman – about whom there is nothing in the least bit special – and a bunch of shonky-looking guys in Unabomber sunnies who were unsuccessfully pretending poker was a legitimate sport.

You know you're a bit down when even the hundred-odd channels of the deluxe cable package can't distract you. So I really didn't need to stumble upon a Kylie video on MTV. Especially one as aptly titled as 'Can't Get You Out Of My Head'. Although the thing I couldn't dislodge from my cranium was not so much Emily as my lingering sense of – I think the word is 'Philness'.

Still, it was progress of a kind. I'd been dangling a line for a long time, and received barely more than nibbles; and that can make you start to doubt the quality of the bait. Emily hadn't seemed to feel the least bit bad about what we'd done, and Zoë had been pretty adamant that there was nothing wrong with it; that it was normal – fun, even. If Nige had been here, he'd have been high-fiving me. It was only me who was worried it might have been a mistake, and I wondered why.

And then I thought back to when Zoë had walked into the café that morning. She'd taken herself away from her nest, the little world she'd set up with her partner. And ultimately, I wanted the same companionship she and Josh had – that assumption that you'll be together every night, every weekend, whenever. The stuff you take for granted when you're with someone, and miss so terribly when you're not. All that stuff Sting sings about in 'We'll Be Together', which I used to think was corny but now realise says it perfectly. When you're with someone, he contends, you can swim the seven seas. (Susie Maroney must've had one hell of a boyfriend.) But when you're on your own, you can barely dip a toe into the water.

Emily was too young, and too incompatible. As a brief, casual thing it was fine, but it got me no closer to what I really wanted. And that was someone I could go to arty movies with, discuss books with, split a bottle of wine with, who wouldn't think I was a wanker for doing any of these things. Someone who'd be impressed by my clever ideas and indulge my stupid ones. Someone who'd one day fondly remember when my breakthrough song had been just a bunch of scribbles on a notepad that I'd nervously shown her for feedback. Someone I could think about moving in with, and maybe one day marrying. Even though everyone was advising me that it was cool to have flings with the Emilys of this world, the experience hadn't made me any happier.

I'd written lots of melancholy songs about girls I'd missed out on, but unless I was comfortable limiting my fans to the emo crowd, there was no way I was ever going to perform them in public. What I needed was someone to lift me out of a minor key once in a while.

I lay there on my parents' sofa with my thoughts, worsened considerably by their Kylie backing track – another reason, incidentally, why Emily and I couldn't be together. There was no way I was walking down the aisle to 'Especially For You'.

Being with her had left me feeling more alone than I had before. So if I'd been consulted about my schedule, I would definitely have nominated another time for my mum and dad to get home and start giving me shit.

Shortly after 'Can't Get You Out Of My Head' had given way to both 'Spinning Around' and the distressing realisation that I'd stumbled upon a Kylie marathon, my self-flagellation session was interrupted by the booming voice of my father, who was halfway down the stairs and keen to take his turn with the whip.

'Well, look who's finally taken time out from his girl-friends to come and drop in on his old mum and dad!'

I gathered my dear father wasn't going to reach quite the same heights of supportiveness as Zoë.

'Hi Dad.'

'I'm not going to ask where you were last night. Sure, some people might have sent a text message or something to reassure their mothers, but we understand you never have a moment free from the attention of the ladies.'

'How do you know I didn't just crash at Nige's?'

'Maybe you did, the two of you and a bevy of exotic women? I know how these things go, my boy. You know, back in '68 your mother and I were at a wild party in the basement of St Paul's College when . . .'

A lot of my friends have painfully conservative parents – law school will do that to you. But sometimes I'd rather have hidebound, judgemental parents than ones who seize every opportunity to show you how goddamn *hip* they still are. I'd always been something of a disappointment to them because I didn't take advantage of their relaxed, permissive attitude to things like sex, alcohol and even soft drugs. They'd been big drinkers at uni, by their own admission, and even tried a little 'ganja', as they were endlessly reminding me. And judging by the fond way they spoke about those days, it was a wonder they'd found time to attend lectures what with all of that blissing out. Whereas university as a partner-swapping, chemical-fuelled miniature Woodstock was a million miles removed from my experience – and I suspect, in truth, from theirs as well.

Dad was joined by my mother, his charming reminiscence cut short by yet another of her reminders of their permissiveness.

'You can bring girls here Paulie,' she said. 'You know we're OK with that. Really.'

They persisted in assuming that the reason I didn't constantly have girls at the house was because I didn't feel comfortable directing my endless stream of women through their front door, rather than because there weren't any. That's the thing about people who meet the love of their lives young: they never understand how hard it can be for those who aren't so lucky.

'I know. Thanks Mum, that's very hospitable of you.'

'I wish you would, maybe I'd worry about you less.'

And she really does, sweetly enough. Dad, by contrast, views much of my life as an elaborate pantomime staged entirely for his entertainment.

'Oh, you don't need to worry, Helen. For a man of the world like our Paul here, the only concern is which of his harem to grace with his favours next.'

I snorted. 'Very droll, Dad. Spot on.'

'No need to be sarcastic, son. I think it's classy, very *Raise the Red Lantern*. Although I expect these days you'd announce the lucky girl by SMS, wouldn't you?'

Mum arced up at this, switching gears into her pop-culture academic mode.

'Oh yes, I've seen that on *Dr Phil*! A "booty call", I believe it's called. Or a "booty text". Have you been sending booty texts, Paulie?'

Unbelievable – a respected English scholar, and she never

misses *Dr Phil*, even when she's at uni. Actually, it probably counts as uni these days, for one of her trendy cultural studies subjects. I wish pop psychologists would stop passing our generation's slang onto our parents – it's ruining our youth.

'Well, as long as you know you can bring your booty back here, Paul.'

'Oh, I do, Mum. As in, my arse. Which is parked on this sofa, alone, pretty much every night, in case you hadn't noticed.'

'Just as long as you know we're . . . *cool* with it', Mum continued, putting far more emphasis on 'cool' than was, well, cool. 'You know we view you as more of a flatmate than a son these days.'

This unlocked a whole new flank for Dad.

'Ah yes, meaning he should start paying rent. Excellent.'

'Hey, I –'

'Oh, your father's just teasing you. Is there anyone special you'd like to bring back to meet your parents, Paulie? We don't bite, you know.'

'Well, not our guests, anyway!'

'Please, if we can just get through this conversation without any allusions to whatever you guys get up to in the bedroom, seriously . . .'

Dad grinned. 'Come on, Paul, we're all adults here. We can talk about this stuff.'

'That's right, it's nothing your old mum and dad haven't done in their day, you know.'

'No, really, I don't. I'm aware you guys must have had sex at least three times, given us kids, but really, that's all the information I need.'

'Don't be so *prudish*, Paul. You might be able to pick up a few tips from your old dad, you know.'

'It's true, Paulie,' Mum added far too enthusiastically for my liking. 'He certainly knows how to make a woman stick around.'

Part jibe at my sexual conservatism, part opportunity for a sickeningly lovey-dovey inter-parental glance – a devastating combo. By this stage, this felt like cruel and unusual punishment. I made a note to ask Zoë whether there was a UN convention that covered parenting.

I could come up with no better response than burying my head in a cushion, which I did, ever so subtly indicating that the interview was over.

'Come on Liam,' my mother said. 'We've teased Paul enough.'

From underneath my cushion, I could hear them clomping up the staircase, chuckling indulgently to themselves. I found myself remembering Madness's song 'Our House', which sounds like it's full of fond family reminiscences – which Suggs then undercuts by singing about his need to move away from it. And it occurred to me that my friends who paid so much to live away from home were getting an absolute bargain.

#32

★ SAILING ★
CHRISTOPHER CROSS (1980)

My job, as some have noted, was pretty adolescent. But within its limited bounds, I was the consummate professional. So even though I would have rather spent three more hours discussing my parents' sex life while simultaneously doing my tax return than face another night of drunks and retro, I knew that my people needed me.

After all, I had responsibilities. If I took the night off, there would be no one to deftly fade Queen's 'We Will Rock You' into Toni Basil's 'Mickey'. If you really know what you're doing – and folks, I do – you can make Toni start that famous cheerleading chant right in sync with Queen's iconic drumbeat. So as much as I'd have liked to, I wasn't about to abandon our paying customers to someone with less experience. They deserved the P-Man. That is to say, if you're unfamiliar with rap-style big-upping yourself, they deserved me.

By 5.30, said P-Man was donning his work gear. Proper DJs generally wear T-shirts with obscure hipster record label logos, Asian characters or ironic, semi-humorous slogans like 'Porn Star' on them. But, paradoxically, we at the lower end of the musical food chain have to dress more classily. So when the dress code insisted on formality, as it did that night, I tended to go with a black suit, white shirt, perhaps a skinny black tie. A touch pretentious art-rocker, perhaps, but what I liked about it was that nobody could possibly mistake it for a corporate suit.

It was a Code Red in the MobyDisc calendar, a really big earner. Phil and I were going tag-team on a swanky harbour cruise. Well, as swanky as an event can get when the major social activity is vomiting over the side of a boat. It was a fortieth birthday party on a cruiser so large that there would be no fewer than two dancefloors pulsating to our dubious beats – yours truly with his involuntary specialty, the 1980s; and for the main attraction, the big kahuna himself, Philip Trelawney, Esq. He'd be spinning pop classics from the '60s and '70s for the middle-aged to jitterbug to, or whatever it is they do.

It was a big deal for Phil. Which is why, as I was peering at myself in the mirror, checking that the thick, wiry curls on my head were as controlled as possible, my mobile rang.

'P-Man,' I said. 'How's it going?'

Phil had also insisted on assuming the P-Man moniker since he'd overheard me using it on the phone. But unlike me, he didn't use it ironically.

'Just wanted to check you're OK for tonight.'

'You're sounding a touch nervous there, *el capitan*. Don't worry, I am pumped boss. Pumped.'

'Have you got the '80s box?'

'I'm packing enough Bros to tranquilise a small elephant.'

'Attaboy. And that new Wham! compilation I bought specially?'

'Woken up and ready to go-go, boss. And you've got enough golden oldies? The music from your deprived childhood?'

'Yep. See you down there.'

'OK. P1 over and out.'

Once I'd established the P-Man label, I also developed P1 and P2 for us, as a form of homage to the Bananas in Pyjamas. Phil was a little hurt by my claim to be P1 when he ran the show. So I always signed off with it, and then hung up before he could dispute my claim to P-primacy. Sure, it's petty, but Phil's buttons were easier to push than a Fisher-Price telephone. It's kind of a bit like picking on a five-year-old. Well, a 45-going-on-five-year-old. And yet, I was in the entertainment business, and I was my own favorite client.

On cue, my phone beeped with a text message from the man, a common response when he couldn't think of a natty comeback immediately. 'Dude,' he began, not realising that the term had dated, 'if you're P1, I'm P-Zero, OK?' He evidently thought it was OK, because he signed off 'Cheers, P0.' I couldn't resist replying that he was welcome to it, as long as he didn't mind people addressing mail to him.

★ ★ ★

The cruise ship was a monster, in that it was both enormous and terrifying – a custom-built pashing stadium for university social clubs and the dodgier workplace function. Festooned with multicoloured lights and dominated by a giant neon sign that flashed 'Party Ahoy!', everything about the not-so-good ship *Croozr One* promised a truly messy night.

From the dock, it was clear that the one part of the boat's fitout that wasn't cheap and nasty was the sound system. And equally clear to everyone for miles around, as a crew member had fired up a Gwen Stefani CD, and her denial of being a Hollaback Girl was booming out across the water. With that much musical firepower, we stood a good chance of making ourselves unwelcome in pretty much every harbourside suburb. I liked the idea that Phil and I would be lobbing musical half-bricks into the tranquility of those who'd shelled out big bucks for a peaceful water view. Especially since that included my parents.

The host greeted us nervously as we boarded. And fair enough: I'd have been worried too if I was hosting a party aboard this floating Schoolies Week. Tony was his name, and he and his wife ran three thriving car dealerships. What remained of his hair was slicked back to within an inch of its life, and his shirt was unbuttoned to the point where it left far too little of his paunch and chest hair to the imagination. His mint-and-brown checked jacket was so loud that it was going to give the PA serious competition.

I don't give Phil enough credit for being good at his job. It isn't easy, and the boss was really earning his hefty fee that night, charming Tony and the crew, enthusing about how fantastic the boat was, how sharp he and his lovely wife looked, and just how awesome the party was going to be.

After a few minutes of high-wattage Philling, both of them looked far more relaxed.

'So Paul, you've got the disco room sorted out, right?' Tony asked, wanting reassurance from the sidekick as well.

'Absolutely, sir. Phil can play the smoochy stuff for the couples while I'll have the folk downstairs partying like it's 1999.' And here came my favourite cheesy line: 'Or more precisely 1982, when Prince wrote that song.'

'Ha, you know your stuff!' the client said. 'Excellent.'

'I take pride in my work, sir.'

'I remember 1982. I was sweet sixteen, never been kissed,' Tony went on.

'I soon sorted that out,' his doting wife interjected. 'Me and half of Caringbah High, if I remember correctly!'

'Paul's the best man I've got, Tony,' Phil said, clapping him on the back like the great mates they were fast becoming.

I did know what I was doing on a harbour cruise, having been on far too many of them. Some would say that 'too many' kicks in at about one, but I reckon my tally would be in the low sixties. I even clocked up a bunch in my student days because they were a particular favourite of an unimaginative Law Society social committee. And, against my better judgement, I went on a few organised by such idealistic student organisations as Beersoc and the Victoria Bitter Appreciation Association – which enjoyed almost identical objectives and membership lists, but cleverly extracted double the funding from the student union.

Zoë dragged me along to a VBAA event in first year because she was interested in one of the organisers who was, unsurprisingly, a college boy. The crush rapidly subsided after she'd drunk enough to lower her inhibitions and started pashing him, and he spewed all over her after about three minutes. And of course lucky old Paul was the one who had to clean her up and look after her for the rest of the cruise. Everyone cheered me as I left with her, an arm around her waist so she stayed upright, because they assumed I was taking her home. And I was, but only to install her safely in a spare bedroom so her mum wouldn't find out.

She would have done the same for me, but she never had to. I didn't really get close enough to any girls at those events for vomit or even saliva to be exchanged. And even though I did my share of drinking until I spilled my guts, I'll have you know that I retained enough control to make it to a toilet or bush every single time.

I've placed a strong emphasis on the chundering element of the harbour cruise experience, I know. But there isn't actually much more to them. I've never understood the rationale behind getting people drunk and making them dance aboard vessels that lurch violently from side to side. And while I'm the first to acknowledge Sydney Harbour's aesthetic qualities under normal conditions, no one on a harbour cruise ever looks twice at the view. You can hardly see it from the dancefloor, or the bar, or even that one quiet bit of the deck where you've gone to shove your tongue a dangerously long way down someone else's throat, given how much they've drunk.

To most revellers, the only real attraction of the water is that you can spew into it with impunity, unlike those horrible little sticky-floored nautical bathrooms that reek of people's guts within about half an hour of leaving the shore. I reckon the boats could stay moored to the wharf for the duration without detracting one bit from most people's enjoyment of harbour cruises.

So I knew exactly how Tony's party would play out, because they're always the same. The same preening, overdressed guests whose superficially dolled-up appearances quickly give way as the shirts are unbuttoned, the cheeks redden and the makeup runs. The same surly waiters in cheap white shirts serving gooey seafood canapés in the most minimal attempt to comply with the Responsible Service of Alcohol rules. The taste of the same bargain-basement acrid chardonnays and leathery reds they serve in an all-you-can-drink package. And above all, the increasing obnoxiousness of the guests as they get louder and wobblier. The couples obliviously pashing on the dancefloor while people around them point and laugh because it temporarily seems like the funniest joke in the world.

And for me, the endless series of irritating, inappropriate requests, of middle-aged Harrises coming up to ask whether I can 'play some Acca-Dacca mate, go on, this stuff's shite'. Or women flirtatiously asking me to play Celine Dion so they can sing along and bawl. Always the same equation: Australians plus boat plus alcohol equals disaster.

My familiarity may have bred contempt, but the flipside was a peculiar sense of comfort. The sheer predictability of these events made me grin with cynical foresight every time some aspect – a rambling, incoherent and sexually inappropriate speech, for instance – met my expectations. For me, it was like falling off a log – which was exactly what my audience would have done if they'd tried to walk along one. Which brings me to the final flaw in the harbour cruise concept: the guests' exit, when they're at their drunkest, is via a slippery, shifting plank of wood.

However, I know exactly what drunk people on a harbour cruise want to hear. Really, it's like playing a violin, if the violin's breath reeked. It's not rocket science to DJ at a party – not much is, other than rocket science itself, I imagine – but there's more to it than just putting a bunch of CDs on shuffle. It's all about experience – that is, it helps if you've previously suffered through dozens of similar events.

Grandmaster Phil has what I like to call his Furious Five categories of song. In fact, he's even colour-coded them. Starters (green) are designed to get people onto the dancefloor. Given that Tony had requested I stick to the 1980s, I kicked off the set with one of Phil's suggestions: Wham's 'Wake Me Up Before You Go-Go', which went down a treat. Then there are lifters (orange), which boost the mood when things are going well. Ray Parker Jr's 'Ghostbusters' proved popular with this crowd, and so did good old 'Dancing In The Street'. Some funster changed the lyrics to 'Dancing On A Boat' and soon everyone was singing rapturously along.

The next stage in Phil's formula is that when things are cooking – well, microwave-reheating – you whack on a keeper (yellow) to maintain the vibe – Lenny Kravitz's 'Are You Gonna Go My Way' is pretty reliable. Then, after forty good minutes or so, you vary the mood with downer ballads (blue) which get people a little smoochy, like 'Total Eclipse Of The Heart'. And then it's back to the keepers, interspersed with starters and lifters.

If you've got one of those crowds that just doesn't seem to want to dance, you pull out a filler (red) that pretty much serves as background music, like Womack and Womack's 'Teardrops', for example. But I had no need for the Womacks because it was all going really well. Of the 250 or so people on board, I had a fairly consistent eighty to a hundred dancing on my lower deck. In particular, Tony's teenage daughter Angelica – whose name, I'd thought on meeting her, was highly optimistic – was tearing up the dancefloor. She was absolutely trashed, and 'shaking her thang', as she put it. In practice this meant rubbing her body up against anyone foolish enough to come within five metres of her. She kept climbing up on the bench seats that lined the edges of the deck, hitching up her skirts and bending forward to show exactly how far beyond the confines of her low-slung party dress her breasts could bulge – which, I had to concede, was pretty darn far.

As the night went on, her sweaty gyrations became progressively desynchronised from the music, and the frequency of her whoops increased to about once every thirty seconds.

But she was making my task simple. As long as the daughter was happily boogying with her friends to a-ha's 'Take On Me', all was well on Planet 1980. So it wasn't really necessary for Phil to keep sticking his head down the stairwell every few songs to check on me, like a moustachioed jack-in-the-box. After the fifth time or so, I beckoned him over for a quick word.

'It's going fine boss, relax! Really.'

'You know me, Paulie. Perfectionist.'

'Oh, I know. And I must say, you've achieved perfection tonight with that Astroboy waistcoat.'

'Really? I bought it especially. It's '80s, you know? But in such a cool way.'

'Absolutely. I particularly like the little picture of Astro firing lasers out of his arse. Very you.'

'I guess I am a sharp shooter! Look, you know this cruise is kind of a big deal for me. And for you as well.'

'Why's that?'

'Well, Tony said that if tonight goes off – you know, really kicks some behind – he'll use us for the Toyota dealers' conference he's organising. He's got a lot of dealer mates here, and he'll refer us right across their network. And they're constantly holding functions, these guys. This could mean like fifty plus bookings a year, he reckons.'

'That's great, mate. Oh what a feeling, huh?'

'So you know, don't hold back, take it to the max.'

'I'm all over it, Phil. Leave it to the P–Man.'

'The other P–Man.'

'Yeah, the other P–Man.' And yes, that is as charitable as I get.

'OK, I'd better head back up, "Unforgettable" is probably finishing and I want to take things up a notch with "The Bird Dance".'

It spoke volumes about this function that someone with Phil's professional experience felt that 'The Bird Dance' would improve it.

'Knock 'em dead, maestro.'

So Phil gave me a high five, as though we were a tag wrestling team, and darted up the stairs to get the assembled company to flap their arms like chickens. They probably didn't know they wanted to do that. But we were a couple of hours into the cruise, so they would. Oh, how they would. About halfway through the song, the more inebriated ones would even start clucking. And the notion made me think I wouldn't mind seeing some demeaning actions myself. So, shortly afterwards, I had my patrons contorting their bodies to spell out 'YMCA'. I felt some of their As left a little to be desired, but they enjoyed it.

After the Village People's tribute to the Young Men's Christian Association, I decided it was time for some fresh air. So I whacked on 'Bohemian Rhapsody', which I knew would guarantee me no fewer than five minutes and fifty-eight seconds of refreshing night breeze. But I'd only just sat down to watch the twinkle of Rose Bay's luxurious lights when my attempt at a relaxing break was ruined.

#31

★ FAT BOTTOMED GIRLS ★
QUEEN (1978)

'Paul, is that you?' asked a strangely familiar voice. I whirled around to find Brent Fraser, my former boss from Banking and Finance at Morphett's. 'Shit,' I thought to myself, approximately eighty times. But what I said was, 'Brent! Great to see you.'

'How do you know Tony? Friend of the family?'

'Not exactly, I'm working.'

'*Working*? Don't tell me you turned us down for a gig as a *waiter*!'

His shock was genuine. Brent is the son of a judge, impeccably connected, and as loaded as you'd expect of someone who made partner at thirty-three and has spent the following decade capitalising. And I mean literally capitalising –

his house would make many an English country club jealous. If I'd answered yes to his question, it would probably have been the first time he'd ever known anyone with a low-level hospitality job.

'Um, well, I'm working part-time as a DJ at the moment. Just while I'm saving up to go overseas.'

A lie, although not as big as when I'd said it was great to see him. I had to use this 'overseas' line a lot because saving up for travel is one of the few socially acceptable reasons for having such a casual, non-career-oriented job.

'Paul, you know we regard you highly at Morphett's. So if it's part-time work you're after, my department's run off its feet at the moment . . .'

'Thanks Brent, that's very kind of you. I'll give it some thought.'

'And I'm confident we can pay a little better than . . . DJing.'

'Oh, you'd be surprised, it's not bad at all.'

'Well, if you keep this going on the side, you'll be winging your way abroad in no time.'

'Yeah,' I conceded, for the sake of my fib. 'Every little bit helps.'

Recruiting at law firms is a bit frenetic these days – interest has dropped off as law graduates have started to reject the punishing hours and pressure to climb the ladder. So I knew what would come next: the time-honoured matey invitation.

'Tell you what, why don't you drop in for a coffee this week? Love to catch up and see if we can't work something out.'

We'd just done all the catching up I deemed necessary. But he'd engineered things such that it would have been rude of me not to accept. After all, no one ever says no to a sociable coffee. And I knew there was no point in burning bridges, especially since I'd definitely have preferred to list him over Phil as a job referee. So I acquiesced.

'I'll get my secretary to give you a call and line something up.'

'No problem, you've got my number,' I said.

Trapped by a web of civility into an awkward tag-team with Brent and some HR flunky. The occasions where the MobyDisc and Morphett worlds collided weren't exactly frequent, so I couldn't resist asking how he knew Tony.

'Paul, Paul,' he laughed. 'Everybody knows Tony!'

What, was his surname Soprano?

'Toyota's a big client, we handle their auto finance department now. And we've recently assisted Tony on a number of transactions. I was very pleased he invited me.'

Yeah, but only because with a stronger personal relationship came more opportunities for lucrative work. A guy like Brent is only too glad to be your best mate, but good luck getting him to turn off the time-clock when he asks after your wife and kids. And so he'd fronted up in a tailored, subtle grey suit, with only his slightly daring pink shirt betraying that this was a party. Everything about him implied reliable professionalism, and hinted at his own wealth and good taste. And yet here he was, trying to tap a lucrative source for some more work. Pimping his services, in fact. Which made him just a more expensive version of Phil. Because like his Danza namesake, Tony was ultimately the boss.

'You'll be wanting to get back to the music, I'm sure,' he correctly guessed. 'And who knows – I might just see you on the dancefloor later.'

Brent Fraser, dancing? That sight alone would be worth the

awkwardness of the trip I'd booked in to his gleaming corporate headquarters. As I strolled back down to my post, I smiled to myself at the resumption of the old game. It's not easy to say no to law firms — their entire recruitment strategy revolves around making themselves the path of least resistance.

And yet, even though I knew all this, I was flattered they still wanted me.

I walked back down towards Queen. But right at the point where I should have been hearing Freddie Mercury, my ears picked up only an ominous silence. Just half an hour earlier, Lionel Ritchie had vowed to rock the party All Night Long. But now, the party appeared to be very much unrocked. Which constituted a code red MobyEmergency.

I burst into the room to see Angelica sprawled out face down on the bench, sobbing and being comforted by two female friends. A third came up to me accusingly.

'I suppose you think that was funny?'

'What?'

'Playing "Fat Bottomed Girls"?'

Shit, I thought — it must have been the next track on the Queen compilation. Damn Brent for pressuring me into small talk when I was on such a tight schedule!

'Sorry, I hadn't realised, I was outside.'

'Bullshit, you put it on and ran away. I saw you. Bastard.' She was slurring her speech terribly, but another girlfriend added a somewhat more coherent explanation.

'Ange jumped on the bench and started shaking her arse and singing along with it, but then everyone started laughing at her, and she got upset.'

'If you knew how hard she's tried to lose that weight . . . all the Pilates classes . . . you're a real dickhead, mate,' Drunk Friend #1 chipped in.

As tempting as it was to just keep on playing and ignore her and her friends, I figured I probably ought to restore order, for Phil's sake at least. So I went over to see if I couldn't convince Angelica to snap out of it.

'Hey, what's wrong?'

'I can't believe you played that song. You hate me.'

'It was an accident, it was the next track on the CD after "Bohemian Rhapsody" – which you requested.'

'How convenient. How *convenient*! You guys are all the same.'

She buried her head in her hands again, and Slightly Less Drunk Friend #2 tried to soothe matters.

'It's a sensitive subject for her because her last boyfriend dumped her. He said he just didn't find her attractive anymore. She was really upset.'

A fresh peal of tears from Angelica.

'C'mon, it was just a mistake. Come back to the party, I'll play any song you want.'

'You think I'm *fat* . . .'

'No I don't, Angelica. You look fine, really.'

'Prove it. Give me a kiss and I'll come back.'

She sat up and bent towards me, blasting me with boozy breath in which my trained nose could detect a soupçon of vomit.

'No, I'm sorry, I really can't. I'm working.'

And the client's daughter flopped petulantly back onto the bench. She had no interest in me, of course, other than that somewhere deep within the haze of her brain she felt I'd humiliated her, and that a slobbery pash was the only acceptable reparation.

It was not to be, since a red-faced, furious-looking Tony chose that precise moment to walk in, having been fetched by Drunk Friend #1. His wife and Phil followed in his wake, and he strode up and jabbed me in the chest.

'What have you done to my daughter?'

'Nothing, sir, really; she just got a bit upset.'

'The way I heard it, you deliberately insulted her.'

'No, I –'

'And then abandoned your post, am I right?'

'I was having a quick break –'

'I am not paying you to take breaks!' he screamed. 'And I am most certainly not paying you to upset my daughter. In fact, Mr Trelawney, I am not going to be paying him at all.'

My spineless boss acquiesced without even asking for my side of the story.

'And you will also pay for the water taxi I'm going to call to have him taken off the boat this instant,' Tony continued. 'Son, get out.'

'But I –'

He grabbed at me to start frog-marching me onto the upper deck. But I easily shook him off – his coordination wasn't what it might have been if he was sober, and by that stage I was beyond furious.

'I can fucking well walk myself, you fucking arsehole.'

I'd aced English Expression in high school, but those powers had temporarily deserted me.

'If you *dare* touch me again, I'll be pressing assault charges,' I went on, my irritatingly officious lawyer training kicking in. 'And I'm *delighted* to leave your shitty party, but if you don't pay my bill, in full, I'll fucking sue you faster than your idiot of a daughter got smashed tonight.'

I really should have left his daughter out of it because despite my pompous legal threat, I succeeded only in making him take a swing at my head. I got out of the way, fortunately – he was a big guy – and he staggered off to one side. Finally becoming involved, Phil grabbed Tony's shoulder and tried to hold him back.

'Don't, Tony, he's not worth it, really,' he said forlornly.

'I'll throw the little cocksucker overboard!' Tony screamed. But the little cocksucker was halfway up the stairs, and had his mobile out, ringing for a water taxi.

★ ★ ★

By the time we approached the shore, I had calmed down a little. My flush of rage had been replaced with a numbing fury.

My phone beeped with a text. Philip, of course.

'PAUL SORRY M8 HE JUST LOST IT. HE'S CALMED DOWN NOW. WILL CALL U LATER.'

'Don't bother,' I texted back. 'I resign, effective immediately.' That's right, lower-case and everything. I can be very cold when I want to be.

Seconds later, he rang. I let it go through to voicemail, and texted him again.

'A decent boss supports his workers. I'm not interested in discussing it further. And I will be billing you for tonight, and also this taxi.'

'RIGHTO THAT'S FAIR. TALK SOON OK?'

I would have rather he tried to argue the point, but my now-former boss was always weak, even in dealing with me. And when the fare for my waterborne escape came in at an outrageous $85, I wasn't exactly displeased.

I jammed my hands deep into my pockets and trudged up the hill to my car. Phil would have to spend the rest of the cruise running between the rooms. It would be a huge pain for him. Good.

I felt strangely liberated, like you do right after you break up with a girlfriend and a world of fresh opportunities is suddenly open to you, offering promise that rarely eventuates. Perhaps I'd just sit and write music all day? Or perhaps I'd relocate to some exotic overseas destination, a mystical land without retro?

What I wouldn't do, I told myself, was rush into another stupid job that was ultimately a waste of time. I'd take the opportunity to figure out what I actually wanted to do. Perhaps I might finally get around to playing at a few open-mic nights, road-test a few songs with my acoustic? I could do anything I wanted now. Of course, I could easily have done the exact same things while I was working for MobyDisc. But one crucial thing was different: I felt optimistic.

Maybe I would cloister myself in my room and record an album where I played all the instruments myself which would later be hailed as a masterpiece, like Shuggie Otis's *Inspiration Information*? Or, I begrudgingly admitted, like Paul McCartney's *McCartney*? I couldn't play the drums, but what the hell – now I had time to learn. And I'd make sure I threw in a song about Phil. Or more specifically, Phil's moustache. And it would be so popular that he'd be forced to play it at every MobyDisc gig. That'd show him.

My phone beeped again as I was sitting behind the wheel. Not even Phil could ruin this mood, I thought. But it was Emily.

I was a swinger now, I told myself. Of course I got text messages from tha young babez. Well, one of them.

'U OUT?' she asked.

Why, yes I was.

#30

★ TEQUILA! ★
THE CHAMPS (1958)

I didn't meet up with Emily, though. Not the night after. Feigning indifference is the unspoken male rule in these situations, as I'm embarrassed to say I learned from Zoë's copy of *He's Just Not That Into You*. (She claimed to have bought it, as a feminist, for 'opposition research', but I think she secretly enjoyed it.) In this case, my hesitation was authentic. So I texted Emily to say I was out with friends, and that I'd give her a call midweek. Playing it cool. Maybe I was out with another woman? Perhaps a supermodel, or a soapie star? I wanted her to wonder.

'OK SURE SAY HEYA TO NIGE FOR ME.'

So maybe she wouldn't be wondering. I left my attempt to cultivate a man-of-mystery façade for another day, an did exactly what she'd predicted. Nige was out himself, so saying 'HEYA' was very much an option.

I could have predicted where he was without calling him, for he is a creature of habit. And his Saturday night regular is The Oaks – a massive pub in Neutral Bay, just up the hill from my house. And yes, Neutral Bay is as bland as the name would suggest. As is The Oaks, which is one of those watering-holes that has sporting memorabilia on the walls, European beers on tap and a tartan carpet. Comfortingly bourgeois, and splendidly indifferent to the whims of fashion that dominate the southern side of the harbour, it's the kind of place where Nige's T-shirt saying, 'My drinking team has a rugby problem' is the height of wit.

He loves it not because they show live rugby – everywhere he drinks does – but because they let you cook your own steaks. Like so many Australian men, he considers scorching a bloody hunk of meat into a vaguely edible state the only acceptable culinary art for a bloke. I found him sitting outdoors with his feet up, dressed like the majority of people in the pub in a Wallaby jumper in honour of what turned out to be another loss to the All Blacks.

He'd been watching the game with half a dozen of his usual friends-who-wouldn't-be-friends-if-they-didn't-work-together, and once he'd forgiven me for my evident indifference to yet another Australian footballing capitulation, I'd told him about my altercation on the boat.

'So, the great scam is over,' he said.

'It's not a scam, it was –'

'The career of your dreams? Look, Jono, I'm not saying it wasn't a good bit of fun while it lasted, but really, it's time you started getting your shit together. Get into the game and leave the kiddies' league behind, you know? Although you haven't quite managed that on the lady front, eh?

'Oh god, did Felicity tell you I went back to Emily's place?'

'Geez how trashed were you? Mate, I saw you climb into the back of a cab, and then little Emily climb all over you! Still, it's about time you dusted those cobwebs off your goddamn balls. Was she good?'

'Oh, I don't really want to —'

'It's OK, you can be a gentleman about it. I respect that. All I want to say is that if you didn't bang the *shit* out of that little hottie . . .'

Nige and I, we don't always speak the same language. Especially when he's had a beer or two.

'Let's just say we had a pleasant evening.'

'Oh, you did, you dog; you can't hide that damn grin of yours.'

Evidently my international-playboy toolkit needed to include a poker face.

'But hang on a sec. How would Felicity have known about you and Emily? Hang on, don't tell me she shagged the brother . . .'

'Hey, I'm not saying —'

'Hey boys,' he announced to his colleagues. 'The ice queen finally melted last night.'

'No fucken *way*! You did Felicity? Oh my god, that'd make you a *legend* at Morphett's, no one's been there.'

'No, of course he didn't, Paul's useless with chicks. Well, chicks over twenty. That other bloke, the dickhead with the stubble, put one away.'

'She slept with that dipshit? No wonder none of us MJ guys had a chance, if she only puts out for funboys.'

I tried to deny it on her behalf, as I'd promised, but in typical dickswinging corporate fashion, they weren't having a word of it. She was going to kill me.

As crude as Nige's banter with his mates could be, it took my mind off Phil. And shifted it onto Emily roughly every five minutes, when Nige made a joke about her. But I was starting to get used to it.

By 2 am, when most of the regulars had staggered off in search of cabs, Nige's gang was still encamped in the beer garden, getting louder as the place became emptier. We were doing our best to act out another of the comedy T-shirts that's a perennial favourite at The Oaks: 'One tequila, two tequila, three tequila, floor'. Nige's frankness – which is never exactly inhibited – tends to increase in relation to his drunkenness, and after his third shot he told me how he saw it. Hazily, as it happened.

'The answer's simple. Two birds with one stone, mate. Or rather one bird. But one stone. That's you. You're the stone. Rock-hard. For Felicity.' And he laughed uproariously.

'Do you want to try that without the hilarious metaphors, mate? There's an outside chance I'll actually understand you.'

'You've gotta stop mucking around and come and work at Morphett's. Get off your stupid high horse. It's a good place, you whingeing bastard. Lots of people'd kill for an opportunity like it.'

'Lots of people'd kill themselves after taking an opportunity like it, Nige. But I still don't see how the bird thing works. If Morphett's is a bird. As opposed to a pile of bird *crap*.' OK, so my repartée wasn't exactly sparkling either.

'Felicity, you idiot. If you go back to Banking and Finance' – and he held up a hand to stop me protesting – 'you'll be in the box seat. For *her* box.'

'Mate, really, these metaphors aren't working for you . . .'

'Especially now that we know she's up for it.'

'She wasn't up for it.'

'Bullshit. You just don't want to admit that Harris arsehole got in there when you couldn't.'

'True, I wouldn't – if he had. But I'm not going back to Morphett's.'

'Yes you are. There's no way you can defeat Brent *and* your parents. You don't have it in you. Give in, and look on the bright side. You'll have a shot at Felicity, and even if that doesn't work out, you'll have me.'

'Nige, I didn't know you felt that way.'

'Fuck off. We'll hang out.'

'We already do. I'm not sure how much more hanging out with you I'm up for, anyway. I've dropped another sixty bucks on boozing tonight already.'

After finally staggering out of The Oaks, Nige and I found ourselves devouring fried eggs and bacon at Maisy's, the North Shore's only 24-hour café. It reminded me of Cold Chisel's 'Breakfast At Sweethearts': the coffee was hot, but the toast was Turkish instead of brown. All the while, Nige's campaign to get me back to Morphett's continued.

'Mate, if you're not working Saturday nights, we can do this every weekend. It'll be awesome. You might even pick up again. Maybe we can gatecrash a Year Ten formal or something? Or would that be too old for you?'

'When do you think you're going to get over that?'

'Never, mate. The amount of shit you've given me about

chicks over the years, I reckon I'll be cracking child-abuse gags for decades. Or until Emily's over the age of consent, whichever comes sooner.'

'You know Nige, I'm not sure I'm cut out for the corporate lifestyle. Can't I work a bit less hard, and not have to play so hard?'

'Soft. Mate, you can't fail me. You're gonna be a big part of my drinking team. And hey – you've already got a rugby problem.'

I glared at him.

'You know, like my T-shirt.'

I glared at him more.

'Oh c'mon, that's the best T-shirt ever.'

'And you wonder why I don't want to sign up for more of this.'

#29

★ WORKING CLASS MAN ★
JIMMY BARNES (1985)

Phil and I met for a drink a few days later — I figured I owed him that. Over a beer at the East Sydney Hotel, which is the best pub in town because it has no pokies, he seemed suitably chastened, and promised that in future he'd back his staff. If anything, he promised it too emphatically.

'We're a team at MobyDisc. It's us against the world, you know? No matter what, I have to back my people. Because, like I've always said, that's what we are — a people business.'

'That's what you've always said, yes.'

'Our clients aren't buying just our music, they're buying our people.'

'Sure.'

'People. Y'know . . . it's about *people*. Can I make myself any clearer?'

'Probably not Phil, thanks.'

'We've gotta be like the army. If one of us takes a bullet, we *all* take a bullet, you know?'

'Phil, I've got to tell you, I'm not taking a bullet for you.'

'You know what I mean, though. If you make a mistake, then I've made a mistake. That means it's *our* mistake. I have to own it as well.'

'OK, but I thought the main point here was that I didn't make a mistake.'

'Yeah yeah, I know – I just mean, if you did. It all comes down to one principle: "team". Like they say, there's no I in team. And there isn't a U, either. As in, "you". I thought of that one myself.'

'I see.'

'To put it another way – if I made a mistake, then you'd have to own it as well. Because it's a team thing.'

'Phil, you *did* make a mistake, in my opinion, and I'm actually *not* owning it at this point, remember?'

'Fine, I know. Yeah. OK.'

'But no hard feelings. It was just one of those things.'

'Good, good. So are you coming back?'

'I'm sorry mate, but at this point, I don't think that's a good idea.'

He looked so crestfallen, I felt like a real bastard.

'Not because I haven't forgiven you or anything, it's fine, really. Just because now that I've walked away for a bit, I think it's a good opportunity to think about some stuff, and try and work out what I want to do with myself.'

He'd never much liked my occasional suggestions that what I wanted to do with myself might have been something that didn't involve the Vengaboys.

'Ah, we have a good time, don't we, Paul?'

I'd been fairly honest with him in the conversation so far, but even I wasn't so cruel as to answer that question truthfully.

'Sure we do, Phil. And hey, DJing might well turn out to be my thing. There are great opportunities, I know that. I just need some time away for the moment.'

I was lying by that point, but as I always grudgingly admit, he's a nice guy.

'I'll let you know in a couple of weeks what I want to do, OK?'

'Sure mate, take your time. I just want you to know there'll be a place for you in the MobyFamily, OK? Remember when I told Tony you were my best man?'

'Yeah, I remember Saturday night in excruciating detail, actually.'

'Well, I meant it, OK?'

Shucks.

'Thanks boss, that means a lot. OK, I've gotta run. Say hi to the ladies for me, won't you?'

Finally the infamous moustache curled upwards with a grin. Ah, the ladies. Phil just loves the ladies.

'Aw, you bet, Paul. You *bet*.'

★ ★ ★

My chat with Phil left me free to do whatever I wanted, like the guy in the Soup Dragons song. In fact, he'd probably been free for decades, seeing as the Dragons only ever had one hit.

After leaving MobyDisc, I had ten completely empty days. Now, some people would have dealt with this challenge by getting up at a reasonable hour, reading the paper, going to the gym, and then buckling down and finally starting work on the music they'd always meant to find time to write. Whereas I – well, aimless internet surfing must have played a large part, and video games fit somewhere in the picture as well. But if I was to honestly describe how I spent those days, 'nothing' would have to be the best description.

Well, to be completely fair to myself, I did write one song. But it only had one chord, and the lyrics consisted purely of the phrase, 'Bored, bored, bored, God I'm bored, very bored' repeated over and over again. Its title? 'Boredom'. (I'm willing to bet you were going to guess 'Bored' but I surprised you with the abstract noun, right?) It wasn't the most sophisticated composition ever, although it still beat anything by Plastic Bertrand.

I did pick up my guitar a few times with the intention of writing something slightly more inspiring. But I had no motivation, and no idea how to get any. There was one single, solitary item in my calendar for the entire fortnight, in fact, and that was coffee with Brent. And by the time it came up, I was so bored I was bouncing off the walls. Bouncing balls off the walls, specifically: I spent a solid hour on the morning of our meeting lying on my bed and playing catch against myself with a squash ball. And believe me, it was even less entertaining than it sounds.

MobyDisc had been, I realised, the most solid thing in my life. And perhaps that's why, despite my principles, despite my protestations, despite my solemn promise to hang myself by the silk Armani necktie Nige gave me to wear alongside him in the corporate trenches, I agreed to go back to Morphett's.

They got me when I was vulnerable – I'd been pretty down after 'Fat Bottomed Girls' went pear-shaped. Everyone has their deal-breaker, and it turned out that mine was getting forcibly ejected from a harbour cruise that happened to be attended by a partner from Morphett Jackson. It was truly the perfect storm – in a plastic beer cup.

And the firm hadn't even brought out their big guns – I hadn't had to endure the plasticine platitudes of the infamous HR crew. It was just Brent and me, *mano a mano*. Or *mano a mouso*, as it turned out. The sales pitch session was brief, superficially friendly, but bang on point. The first part of the discussion was conducted with the air of an older mate taking a young bloke aside to give him a bit of advice. And Brent wanted me to feel that he *got me*, like he was on my side, like there was no agenda.

I spun a whole bunch of stuff about my ambitions and dreams so I wouldn't look like the lazy-arse I was. And I was so nervous he'd call me on the rubbish I was spouting that I can't remember precisely what my runaway mouth came up with. I avoided mentioning my own music, which felt too private, but I do recall telling him I wanted to be a Hollywood director – which led to an offer to make an in-house video which I immediately dreaded. I probably left Brent with the impression that I was planning to become a performance poet, a Baudrillard scholar at the Sorbonne, and a cage fighter. Simultaneously.

It wasn't very convincing, even to myself. When it came down to it, despite all my dreams of a creative lifestyle, the prospect of empty days and no income terrified me. Sure, I had a bit saved, but I'd squandered much of my MobyIncome on music gear and drinking with Nige. And, even though I'd told myself I didn't want it, the opportunity for structure appealed as well. Even though I hadn't much enjoyed it, my last stint working at Morphett's had made me feel professional and competent. And I wanted to prove to myself that I could still do it if I wanted to, just for a little while.

But what made it hardest to say no to was Brent's trump card – he knew all about the boat incident. It had been much discussed after my abrupt departure, and he thought it was hilarious. He also felt responsible, as he'd been chatting to me. So after he'd made me squirm for a bit while telling me about his conversation with an angry Tony, I couldn't help but agree that there really wasn't any good reason why I shouldn't come and work three days a week at Morphett's, just as long as I didn't have to work on the Toyota account. He was right, so I agreed. I thought I could scoff at those who couldn't escape the corporate chains. But forty minutes with Brent Fraser was all I needed to become a paralegal again.

* * *

Oh, how Nige laughed when he called me to gloat, a mere twenty minutes after I'd said yes – or, more accurately, been unable to say no. And oh, how gleefully he made a special trip down to Banking and Finance when I started the following week to welcome me back and introduce me to everyone as 'Paul, the prodigal solicitor, and an *awesome* DJ for children's parties.' At four that afternoon, he produced a special welcome-back-Paul chocolate cake 'from your pals at MJ', as he'd had them write in icing. And he took great pleasure in explaining that it wasn't actually cake I was eating, but humble lemon meringue pie.

Felicity was just a few doors down from my new office, promisingly and terrifyingly, and Nige made sure to bring her along to enjoy his grand gesture. My humiliation was complete when she told me that so I didn't get rusty, I really must play at the firm Christmas party in a month's time.

'You're definitely the man for the job – I reckon a lot of the partners would go wild for your Bryan Adams collection,' she said. 'I'm on the social committee, so consider yourself appointed.'

I was considering myself a lot of things. Hypocritical, for one. But I was also considering my proximity to Felicity. Perhaps my return to the grindstone would have more than one form of compensation.

#28

★ THE BITCH IS BACK ★
ELTON JOHN (1978)

I may have had reservations about my return to the law, but my parents certainly didn't. To celebrate, they took me out to dinner on the evening of my first day at a fancy Japanese joint down the road from the office. It was in honour of the belated fact that, as my mother put it while pinching my cheek in a manner she knew would infuriate me, their little boy was finally growing up. To be entirely accurate, she may have even said 'widdle boy'.

They were so pleased that they claimed to respect my decision to go part-time, to give myself a chance to 'get all that other stuff out of my system', as if my musical ambitions were an inconvenient adolescent phase to be grown out of, like acne. At long last, it seemed that their errant youngest son could be crossed off their lengthy list of Things To Worry About.

Or so I thought. About half an hour into dinner, just as a wooden boat laden with freshly-made sushi sailed its delectable way to our table, the assault continued on several new fronts.

'So, I don't imagine a lot of people who get early promotion to Senior Associate at Morphett's are living with their parents, Paul?' my father said, with his usual brusque air that concealed whether he was just trying to stir me or expressing an actual opinion. It was generally safest to assume both.

'You'd be surprised actually, Dad,' I said. 'Those kinds of people generally have no lives outside of work, you see. So I think you'd find more than a few of them haven't bothered getting their own place because they're too busy pulling those hundred-hour weeks.'

'Oh no,' my mother said. 'That would be terrible, Paulie. I don't think they should be giving you hours like that.'

Score one to Paulie. He may live at home, but he's mature enough to drive an Israeli security fence-sized wedge between his parents.

'I mean,' Mum continued, 'how would their partners cope? If you work that hard, you won't have any time to meet girls. I really think you should be focusing on that next – I'm sure having such a responsible job will make you much more attractive.'

Classic error – I'd celebrated my victory too early. My mother is a truly brilliant competitor, breaching my defence to effortlessly expose another vulnerable area of flesh.

'Hear, hear,' my father said. 'But you shouldn't always talk about girls, Helen. Paul might not like 'em. I mean, the jury's out because he hasn't brought anyone home to meet his parents for a long while. And if he does like the fellas, well, that's fine with us.'

Oh great. Only my father could turn a tolerant statement of approval for same-sex relationships into yet another way of giving me grief. Which in turn set off all my mother's progressive sensibilities.

'Oh *of course*, Paul!' she said. 'It doesn't matter to us who you choose to be with. You know that, don't you?'

'Yes, Mum.'

'I just don't want you to be lonely, that's all.'

At that point, spending eternity alone seemed a much better option than spending another minute in the company of my parents. But they were picking up the tab for dinner, so I caught myself and told them what I knew they'd want to hear.

'I have met some nice girls recently, now that you mention it. One of them works at Morphett's, actually.'

A potential daughter–in–law who also possessed a coveted swipe card to that august institution? My mother nearly fainted with delight.

'Good to hear, son. Knock 'em dead,' said my father, approving of the vague possibilty that I might be a chip off the ol' block after all.

'I won't say another word Paulie,' my mother added. I don't know why she bothers making those kinds of undertakings. All three of us knew perfectly well she would.

Still, with a proper job locked down, and the faint sound of wedding bells on the horizon, the elder Johnsons were pleased with their youngest son. Not that I care about parental approval, of course. But life's just that little bit easier when you have it.

#27

★ YOU'VE GOT A FRIEND ★
CAROLE KING (1978)

Not all in my social circle were applauding my return to the law with quite the same vigour, as I discovered the following night when I went to the opera with Zoë. Yeah, I said opera. Opera Australia offers discount youth tickets in the hope that they'll recruit the next generation of opera-goers by offering low, low prices when they're young, as opposed to the high, high prices that kick in when you turn thirty. It's exactly the same principle used by crack dealers when they give you the first couple of hits for free.

It provided a regular means of catching up with Zoë, which was great. Josh was only too happy to lose her for an evening with her ol' buddy Paul if it got him out of sitting through several hours of 'wankers in clown suits tossing off in Italian', as I believe he once termed the experience when Zoë dragged him along to *Rigoletto* because I couldn't make it.

And she loves the opera. I mean, to the point where she actually listens to Puccini on her iPod at work sometimes, geek that she is. Really, it's a tradition passed on from one bourgeois generation to the next: my parents took me when I was a kid, and coupled with a marginal interest in classical music cultivated by years of piano lessons, I've come to enjoy it.

So, six times a year Zo and I would front up to the Opera House in our swisher threads. We always met for dinner at Rossini's, a cheap Italian place down near the Quay, where we could watch the ferries coming and going over a few glasses of wine and pretend our lives were more glamorous than they actually were.

Although when you're down at Circular Quay taking in the imposing arc of the Harbour Bridge and the skewed, gleaming segments of the Opera House, you could be forgiven for thinking you're genuinely on the A-list. It's a seriously glamorous part of Sydney. So maybe the opera marketing people know their trade after all, and Zoë and I will still be doing it when we're old and grey?

Zoë and I were dining waterside on a perfect, balmy evening as the setting sun flooded the sky with a dazzling array of pinks and oranges. But right after I'd taken a few bites, and even before the inappropriately snooty waiter had brought our wine, my dining companion started hoeing into me even more violently than I had my lasagne.

'OK. What has Nigel done to you?'

'Nige?'

'Yes. I'm assuming that you didn't actually make the decision to go back to that bloody firm yourself. And note that I'm giving you some credit for mere spinelessness instead of stupidity, although I know you're infinitely capable of both.'

'Thanks for the benefit of the doubt.'

'Oh, and I hope you liked your crappy little email prank.'

I had enjoyed it, as a matter of fact, having pretty much anticipated this response. I'd chosen to break the news to her via an email from my Morphett's address, inviting her to share in my joy at the announcement with the subject line 'Wonderful News!'

It merited the terseness of her reply, which said merely 'Congratulations.'

'It's only three days a week,' I said. 'A temporary thing, just like the DJing, while I work out what I want to do with myself.'

'Jesus, Paul, you've had several years to work that out already. How much more time do you need, exactly? And how does starting a new job we both know you'll hate help you with that anyway? What is this, aversion therapy?'

I didn't have any answers, so she continued building up steam.

'We both know how these things work. Sure, it's three days *now*. But then you get so busy, and you stay back so late every day that you end up deciding to go full-time, just for a little while, just to get on top of things. And besides, why shouldn't you earn a decent wage while you're working so hard? Then, before you know it, you're thirty-five, you're burnt out, and you have no idea what happened to the past decade. The ambitions you once had are a smouldering wreck, and it's all too hard now because you've got young kids and don't dare risk your salary. So you'll start fantasising that maybe you'll finally get around to the music stuff when you've retired. Come on, smart guy, tell me how that's *not* going to happen to you.'

'Well, to have young kids, I'll actually have to sleep with someone. So I think that part of your vision is a touch unlikely.'

'Oh, I'm assuming you'll get Felicity, if you're willing to put in this much effort.'

I involuntarily smirked.

'God, I knew that was what this was really about. Dammit Paul, you could do so much better than some cookie-cutter law chick. You could *be* so much better.'

She shook her head while I tried to work out what to say. I'd expected a bit of banter about this, a bit of a laugh at my expense, like always. I'd hoped she'd just see it as another amusing phase in the ongoing situation comedy that was my life. Instead, she was behaving like I'd confirmed her worst suspicions. And, although I was flattered she thought I was wasting such brimming wells of potential, her reaction got to me.

'Look Zo, there's more to it than that,' I said, backpedalling. 'I really like the idea of regular hours in the same place instead of turning up to a succession of bizarre events to entertain people. And I like having the same people I can eat lunch with, and hang out with after work, and actually enjoy a bit of companionship with, instead of just seeing Phil once every couple of weeks. You've pointed out yourself that my social life's contracted because of the DJing. And I didn't quite realise this until I arrived back at MJ, but I've been pretty lonely.'

'Sure, I can understand that. But all those benefits you could get from any job. Why *this* one? And I won't accept getting to hang out with Nige as an answer – you already did more than enough of that before!'

'I guess because I needed a change. And sure, probably because it was an easy option.'

'It's your parents too, isn't it?'

'Well, I think they see it as a step in a more normal, stable direction,' I said. 'And to be honest, they've got a point.'

'I'm not so sure. You're still young – you still have time to try whatever it is you really want to be doing. While you're living at home, there's lots of time for mucking around with songs, or trying a slot on FBi – but you never even called my friend Angus, did you?'

Zoë was mates with one of the staff at Sydney's best-known community radio station, and had been trying to get me to try and get a volunteer on-air gig, sensibly pointing out that it would put my music knowledge to good use. Working in radio would have been a dream, but I strongly suspected that the FBi folk were the kinds of people who sat around drinking chai and namechecking art-rock bands in the hope that no one else had heard of them. I probably should have given it a go anyway, but I couldn't bring myself to.

Zoë has always pushed hard for what she wants and achieved it, so everything always seems so possible to her. Whereas I tend to see obstacles before I even get started, and give up. Even with MobyDisc, I'd only applied as a joke with Nige when we'd been walking past the uni employment office one time. I'd been astonished when Phil had hired me.

'They'd have despised me at FBi,' I asserted, a little sheepishly.

'You have no way of knowing that,' she snapped.

'Oh look, let's not go through this again.'

'But *you're* going through this again. It's all just talk with you, Paul. All this stuff about wanting to write music, when despite owning more CDs, and knowing more about it than anyone I've ever met, you've never produced anything. Tell me: if not now, then when?'

'You'll see, Zo,' I mumbled. 'It's a temporary thing, really.'

'Sure, I'll see,' she said. 'But not *hear*. Because I am not going to listen to you whingeing about Morphett's. Ever. Because you *chose* this. You signed up for it when you didn't have to. And the same goes for Felicity, for that matter. If it goes pear-shaped, all I'm prepared to do is sit back and smugly point out that I told you so.'

'OK, it's a deal,' I said. 'As long as I'm allowed to sit back and smugly point out how *happy* we are, and how much we're *in love* —'

'Of course,' she said abruptly. 'Look, if this really is what you want, and it really does make you happy, then great. It's just that I've listened to you complaining about that kind of life so much that I guess I thought you wouldn't do something like this.'

'Sure.'

'But perhaps this *is* what you want,' she shrugged, and then really stuck in the knife. 'Perhaps all those conversations about wanting to be a musician were just some kind of wistful fantasy? Like how I dream about what I'd do if I was UN Secretary-General? Sure, it's nice to dream, but if you aren't ever going to lift a finger towards making it happen, can we at least stop talking like it might?'

And she said it in such a casually dismissive manner, as if she'd already written me off, that I winced.

She grinned. 'A little too close to home, huh tiger? Sorry to get on your case Paul, but if I don't, no one will. Least of all you.'

I nodded slowly, and looked at Zoë as she sipped her white wine. She seemed to sense I needed a moment to think, and so she sat there in silence, a little smile curling up the edges of her mouth. Suddenly, I felt hugely grateful that she cared so much about what happened to me. And I realised just how bothered I'd be if she ever stopped believing in me.

I didn't know how to respond, so I was grateful when she let me off the hook.

'Now, about this opera,' she said, all cheerful again. 'I was reading up on *The Magic Flute* on the web today, and it's amazing how much Mozart got from Freemasonry. All the weird shit they do, with the trials and everything, is quite close to actual Masonic initiation rites. Can you believe it? I'd always thought they were just some strange supernatural mumbo-jumbo that he'd dreamed up –'

Those Masons really didn't know what they were doing with that whole excluding women thing. If I was starting a secret society, I'd definitely make Zoë a member.

#26

★ **LOVE IN THE FIRST DEGREE** ★
BANANARAMA (1987)

As paralegals go, I proved reasonably competent. I can read quickly, so it didn't take me too long to review the lengthy contracts that came across my desk and pick out the problem clauses among the thousands of meaningless words of lawyerspeak. I didn't exactly enjoy it, but at least I was bored in a whole new way.

My colleagues all worked hard, chilled out with family or friends, and were invariably proficient at one – no less, but no more – hobby that was totally unrelated to work, like rock-climbing or playing the cello. All of which created a completely false impression of the firm's employees' lifestyles for their recruiting brochures. But my workmates were certainly intelligent, and pretty good company. I often found myself having lunch or coffee with some of the other young lawyers in my section, and was surprised by how much I enjoyed all the joking around.

A few weeks in, our Friday after-work drinks went so late that it might have counted as a proper night out if we hadn't been lugging around our laptops and talking incessantly about work. We were at Café Sydney, a swanky rooftop joint with great views of the harbour. It was the kind of place I wouldn't have been seen dead in – or without Nige in, anyway – a week earlier.

Felicity and I spent most of the night talking to each other. It was very natural, very easy. My nerves had been melted away by the beers, and the things I was saying might not have been funny if we were sober, and weren't even intended to be half the time. But I was glad to have her laughing – at my expense, hell, at anything as long as she was having a good time in my company. Zoë is usually a great judge of character, but I was certain she was wrong about Felicity.

She'd had some bad boyfriends, she told me, chewing her long dark hair pensively. So she was just extremely careful when it came to guys.

'So am I,' I told her. 'I don't want to lead them on, you know? Give them the wrong idea with my incredibly toned body.'

'Oh, so you're straight?' she said, grinning. 'Damn, lost the bet.'

'I can't help being devilishly attractive to both sexes.' She laughed. 'It's just one of the crosses you have to bear when the Lord Almighty makes you a hottie. Did you ever ask to be gorgeous?'

A flutter of eyelids to acknowledge the compliment. On a roll with the self-deprecating humour, I continued.

'I know I sure as hell didn't ask to look this good. So people like us can't be held responsible.'

'And who's holding you responsible?'

'Well, a lot of people seem to think that this awesome body was put on earth for the enjoyment of everyone, you know? But I'm forced to apologise, and tell them access to my hotness is strictly limited to a very exclusive group. Some people call it not getting any, but I call it being selective.'

'Oh, you're very selective, I saw that the night I met you.'

'Hey, Emily is a reigning president, I'll have you know. A respected leader of her people.'

She laughed. 'So where do you draw the line? What do people have to do to gain access to Paul?'

'Oh, the door policy's tough.'

'What about me? Would I get past the velvet rope?'

This was so unsubtle, it registered even on my rusty antennae.

'It's too early to say, but don't worry, you definitely haven't ruled yourself out yet.'

She grinned, flashing those flawless white teeth again.

'Even though I'm not an office-holder in any teenybopper fan clubs?'

'Well, that's why you haven't ruled yourself *in* yet, either.'

'So the jury's still deliberating?'

'Very much so, I'm afraid. Even if you'd once been, say, honorary secretary of the Bananarama fan club, we could have worked something out. But don't worry, you'll be formally notified when a determination's been made.'

'Gee, you know, that's such a pity because there I

was, about to invite you back to my place.' She giggled. 'Bummer, I'll just have to wait for the jury's verdict.'

Her words had a sarcastic tone, but her grin coated everything in lashings of ambiguity. There was no way she could actually be serious, was there? Years of experience told me she couldn't, that the world simply didn't work like that for me. So I responded accordingly.

'The jury doesn't react well to sarcasm, young Felicity.'

I figured that had to be a safe response – keeping it humorous.

'Ah,' she said. 'But *was* Felicity being sarcastic? Or was she offering a once-in-a-lifetime opportunity, never to be repeated because of her own extraordinarily high standards? I guess you'll never know now. And after Emily had given you such glowing reviews . . .'

'And thus do two extraordinary hotties pass like ships in the night on account of their overly rigorous quality control,' I said, mopping my brow theatrically. 'The tragedy doth exceed Shakespearian proportions.'

'Paul, you are so magnificently, gloriously full of it,' she said. 'I'm glad you've come back to the law. Those bullshitting capabilities were wasted on DJing.'

'Why thank you. To the extent that was a compliment.'

'I'm going to get a drink, do you want one?'

I nodded, and she took off to the bar, leaving me wondering whether we'd had a moment there.

When she came back, she did that thing where you get into another conversation on your way back to the person you were talking to, and then briefly hand over the drink, allowing you to avoid continuing your initial conversation without being rude. So, to minimise the impression that I'd just been barred, I took myself off to the bathroom.

Staring at myself in the mirror, I splashed water on my face and told myself it was OK. Felicity was cautious. If I was going to actually land her, it was going to be a long game. A one-night thing wasn't a sensible option with a workmate, if that was all it was going to be. But all the logic I could muster couldn't dispel the gnawing sense that flippancy had cost me my moment.

Still, at least we were flirting. Normally I'd be stammering and failing to successfully make even the most inane conversation, not trading innuendoes. Even the fact I'd spoken in complete sentences was, frankly, a little bit of a surprise. Besides, she probably wanted to punish me a little for the Emily thing, and prove she was considerably harder to get. I didn't doubt it.

Still, her barbecue was the following day. Wild passionate love until dawn may not have been on offer, but I did nevertheless have an invitation to her home.

#25

★ LIVE IT UP ★
MENTAL AS ANYTHING (1985)

Since I don't really have the raw material to justify it, I don't generally care much about my looks. But you wouldn't have deduced that from the positively metrosexual amount of time I spent looking in the mirror before Felicity's party. Was my post-adolescent skin still too pockmarked? Would she like my hair? Were there any stray globs of product in it? Did the brightness of my shirt come over as confident, or desperate? Should I put on some cologne? How much would be too much? I hadn't answered one single question to my satisfaction before it was time to get dressed.

There used to be a time when you could just rock up to a barbecue in an old T-shirt, shorts and thongs, but that time was university.

Now that we all have incomes, even the guys put a modicum of thought into their clothes. That modicum tends to extend only as far as what the chain jeans stores are selling. But as a rule, whatever the hot product was last summer, all the guys I know will be wearing this summer. Then it was T-shirts emblazoned with huge line-art graphics, coats of arms and stuff. And we were still doing that distressed denim thing, unfortunately, the most distressing part of which was invariably the price. I don't know which genius figured out they could charge extra for jeans once they'd been ripped and had white paint spilt all over them, but they were raking in the dough and getting to laugh at their customers at the same time. Nevertheless, I donned the same uniform that I knew everyone else would be wearing, and headed out the door.

Felicity has a really nice apartment in Darlinghurst. Or rather, her parents have a really nice investment apartment and let her live in it. Her dad is a QC and her mother runs a boutique that imports European designers and resells them to price-insensitive Eastern Suburbs housewives, so I could see how they'd been able to afford the sanctuary in the trendy Republic 2 block. There is a Republic 1, incidentally – it's next door. And for the money they charged, you'd think the developers might have included a fresh name.

Like many recent inner-city developments whose trendy marketing campaigns have revolved around the notion of creating a 'community', it has a barbecue area with rustic wooden tables, large stone pavers and lots of nicely manicured bamboo, leading onto an immaculate swimming pool. Felicity's own apartment opens out onto it, and her party was spread between the two spaces.

My parents have done well for themselves, but Felicity's are on an entirely different plane of wealth. Which is typical of the law firm partners whose ranks I assumed she'd join one day. Being quite a restricted social elite, most lawyers come from such wealthy backgrounds that they don't even need their massive incomes.

Being confronted with her blue-chip status made me feel that even having an interest in this girl was presumptuous. I just couldn't see myself as the boyfriend in this chic environment, getting to be the one who put his feet up on that white leather sofa, and took showers in her immaculate marble bathroom with its row of expensive-looking lotions and elegant floral display. And it wasn't just the flowers – everything was so impeccably arranged that you could have been mistaken for thinking this was the display apartment. And it was, in a way – but marketing Felicity.

'Make yourself at home,' she'd told me when she let me in, right after I planted a 'hello' peck on her cheek – a kiss that I was feeling might be the most I was ever going to get. But there was no way of feeling at home there, so I told myself to snap out of it, play it cool. Darn it, she had told me she just wanted to meet a nice guy; there hadn't been a caveat with regard to social status. And I was a nice guy, wasn't I? Well, compared to Harris.

I wandered around, nodding at my new colleagues but opting not to join their conversations. I was seeking out Nige's friendly face so I could crack open a beer and relax a little, steeling myself for the forthcoming ordeal of talking to people I didn't know and wouldn't like.

He was outside, leaning on the pool fence with his usual Morphett's crew. Displaying an unusual amount of sensitivity, he refrained from teasing me about Felicity. Sometimes telling Nige something embarrassing or intimate can be the rough equivalent of posting enormous billboards all over town. But he's learnt that I can be fragile when it comes to girls, and that was certainly how I was feeling.

I find the dating caper manageable early on, when I'm still at the indifferent phase. I can flirt and just laugh things off if I get shot down. And Nige never leaves that phase, not really: that's why he's so confident all the time. But when I start to care about the outcome, when the thought of seeing the girl with someone else begins to make me feel a little queasy, when my head keeps filling with idyllic images of some far-off blissful future, I become incapable of pushing for anything to happen. Felicity was starting to get to me, and that wasn't a welcome realisation.

Nige was entertaining his usual crowd with a lengthy story about a recent bucks' night. He was just at the point where the groom had been blindfolded and handcuffed naked to the top deck of the Manly ferry when everyone noticed Harris arriving in the mandatory pre-battered jeans and a pinstriped shirt with paint creatively spattered all over it by some designer I hadn't heard of. He'd made an even bigger effort than usual, no doubt on behalf of our delightful hostess. And yes, he'd brought Emily, who was looking lovely in a polka-dotted summer dress. So much so that I winced a little – what with her outfit, her ponytail, and her slender figure, she looked about fifteen.

I raised a sheepish hand in her direction, and she grinned and waved from across the party. While Nige was displaying a commendable level of restraint about Felicity, this was more than he could take.

'Oh look, that guy's brought his little daughter along,' he said. 'He'll be needing a babysitter, I'd say. Reckon you could help out, Paul?'

'Yeah, yeah, very funny.'

'I wouldn't trust her with Paul,' said Sean, one of Nige's MJ mates who'd been hearing the story all week. 'There's something about him that tells me he gets around in a dirty raincoat during school hours.'

'I wouldn't worry,' Nige said. 'He's already exposed himself to her, haven't you mate?'

They shut up thereafter, which would have been a blessed relief if it hadn't been because Emily was coming over with a big grin on her face. She gave me a demonstrative hug and kissed me, and I was astounded not to hear the others laughing. But then it occurred to me that there were two ways to view this. While the six-year age difference was sufficient to bag me about, many guys would have been delighted to be in my position.

'Your friends won't mind if I borrow you for a moment,' she said, grabbing my hand and leading me away from the group.

'They'll feel a profound sense of loss, but they'll get through it,' I said.

'You didn't call,' she said, sounding a little more hurt than I'd expected.

'Yeah, sorry about that.'

'It's OK, I wasn't entirely expecting you to.'

'Oh.'

'It's cool. But since we're evidently kind of in the same circle of friends now, it'd be good to know where I stand.'

'Right.'

'So?'

'So where do you stand?'

'Yes.'

'I don't know, where do you want to stand? Because –'

'Geez Paul, you really are bad at this, aren't you? I thought you were supposed to be the mature one.'

'No, not at all, I'm afraid. Look —'

'See, there are a couple of other boys who are interested in me —'

'Right, so you want to know if this is going anywhere?'

'Yeah, just because, you know, if you aren't interested, there are other —'

'It's been a crazy week, I started a new job and stuff. But I'll tell you what: let's go and get a drink sometime soon, and see how we get along.'

'How we get along when you aren't bullshitting about knowing Kylie Minogue, you mean?'

'Exactly.'

She smiled sunnily at me.

'I'd like that. And don't worry, I don't want to be serious or *exclusive* or anything, it's just that I wanted to see you again, you know?'

Exclusive? God, I was having enough trouble organising one girl let alone juggling a whole tribe of them. It occurred to me, and not for the first time, that *Sex and the City* really has an awful lot to answer for. But 'not exclusive' gave me all sorts of ways of backing out so I told her that worked for me.

'Good, I'm glad we've got that sorted out,' she said. 'Cos, you know, Harry keeps saying you were just using me for sex.'

'No, Em, god —'

'Well not *just* sex, I hope, anyway! Not that I necessarily mind if you were. I mean, it was fun, you know.'

'Yeah. Yeah, it was great.'

'Well, I'll let you get back to your friends, but let

me know when you're going, yeah?' And she shot me a somewhat evil grin. 'Maybe we could leave together?'

I smiled, the worry on my brow finally uncreasing.

'Yeah, perhaps we could! Seeing as I owe you a drink and all . . .'

By now we'd wandered around the side of the building, behind some shrubs. And when we were out of sight, Emily suddenly snaked her arm behind my head and kissed me hard. I was hesitant for a moment, and then reciprocated. She broke the clinch, and then whispered in my ear, 'There's plenty more where that came from, old man!'

I laughed, and squeezed her affectionately. I still wasn't sure this was what I should have been doing, especially given how my feelings for Felicity had been developing; but hey, Emily was both fun and keen, and I couldn't help myself.

She moved as if to kiss me again, and then stopped short. 'You know what? I think I'm going to make you work for the next one,' she said.

She giggled before quickly tripping back towards the party. Then, just before she rounded the corner, she turned back for a moment and blew me a kiss.

Right, so I had managed to secure a date, and the strong possibility of action, with the girl I'd been avoiding for weeks. At a party I'd come to in the hope of cracking onto the hostess. How had my personal life suddenly transformed from empty to overly complicated without even a brief interlude at comfortable?

★ ★ ★

My sense of things having spun a little beyond my control escalated when I chatted to Felicity shortly afterwards.

There had been about forty people when I'd arrived, and the number had swollen considerably since then, meaning I'd hardly been able to say a word to her. But she spotted me and walked over, smirking disconcertingly.

'You and Emily are back from your little walk, eh?'

'And there I was, trying to be surreptitious.'

'Nige tipped me off that you'd disappeared in the direction of the bushes.'

So much for young Nigel being supportive. Presumably he was still laughing about it with his mates.

'Yes, the young lady and I took a brief turn around your delightful garden,' I said, hoping that my Jane Austenesque phrasing would allow me to joke away my embarrassment. 'And I must say, your dahlias are looking really rather lovely.'

'Although not as lovely as Emily, eh? What's happening there?'

'Oh, you know —'

'You're continuing your passionate romance that transcends the boundaries of age and musical taste?'

'Look, she's a nice girl, and I don't want to break any hearts.'

'Oh, how decent of you.'

'Well, you know, the news that someone may not get to spend eternity in my arms can be devastating. It's only fair to break it to the ladies gently.'

'And how's that plan going?'

I didn't want to make her think I was unavailable, of course — but I didn't want to lie either.

'Despite her youth, Emily's quite a woman of the world,' I said. 'She informed me that she is currently juggling several paramours, and I understand there's an ex in the picture as well.'

'Oh. So you're just one of the many boys on her list then, Romeo?'

'Yes, and the others, I think, are literally boys.'

Feeling I'd rather nimbly pirouetted my way through that particular minefield, I thought I'd do a little ribbing of my own.

'Speaking of the delightful Barnes family, how's Harris?'

'Oh, he's OK. We had a good chat earlier.'

'Excellent. Who knows, maybe we'll be in-laws some day?'

'I wouldn't count on it, Paul. But it's wonderful to hear you and Emily might be, you know –' and crooked her index fingers together to indicate a union. 'So *sweet*.'

'Oh yeah, look, it wouldn't be at all premature for you to start thinking about what to wear to the wedding.'

'I'll give it some consideration,' she grinned. 'And while I do, why don't you sit here,' she said, pointing to an unoccupied bench, 'and I'll join you in a few moments? Would you like a drink?'

Certainly I would, I told her. And sat there beaming because she wanted to take a little time out from her own party just to talk to me. Way to give a guy confidence.

Which waned immediately when she didn't return. I was a little off on one side from the main group in what would have been a perfect spot fora quiet little chat – but without Felicity, I just looked like a wallflower.

After pretending I was texting someone for longer than it could possibly have taken to SMS everyone in my phone book, I put my mobile away and headed back into the breach. Maybe I would just leave with Emily. Yeah, that was a good plan. I told myself: Felicity, honey, you gotta board this train because otherwise it's a-leavin' without you.

And if she declined my offer, why then I'd show her once and for all.

Well, if she noticed.

#24

★ LOVE THE ONE YOU'RE WITH ★
STEPHEN STILLS (1970)

I wandered the party, my cheeks burning with embarrassment at being slighted. I kept getting stuck in conversations with people I barely knew, and didn't particularly care to. So I put in minimal effort, with autopilot conversations about what I was doing, and how MJ was good, and life was fine, and then excused myself as rapidly as possible. I made sure to steer clear of Nige, whose boisterous laughter echoed across the party like a warning beacon. I really didn't need him, on account of his lowered inhibitions, to provide me with some forthright public advice about Felicity.

I had promised myself I wouldn't seek her out again but I couldn't help readying myself in case she came over to resume the conversation, as she'd promised. And in my head the word 'promised' sounded as indignant as it would have from a five-year-old admonishing a parent for not reading a bedtime story. And I kept telling myself I didn't care who she talked to. Even though all the while, every movement she made caught my eye, no matter how animatedly I was talking to some bland pal of hers about the many-splendoured joys of corporate law.

When I'm attracted to a girl, that radar kicks in quite involuntarily. I can tell myself to switch it off but it never works. With a crush nearby, I become a regular little Navman.

Abruptly terminating a conversation with someone who had the enthralling distinction of working as a judge's associate, I made my way to the drinks table and grabbed one of the many glistening bottles of imported beer that Felicity's guests had brought as a form of yuppie tribute. What the hell, I thought, and flipped the unnecessarily elaborate top of a Grolsch. At least I was getting something from her tonight, even if it was just boutique drunk.

I'm what Nige caringly describes as a 'pissweak' drinker, so the beer quickly supplied the relaxation I was after, and then some. It soothed me, making me want to sit down for a moment and take stock. I wished I could stop thinking about Felicity when I knew it was foolish. But experience had taught me that I couldn't just reason my way out of an attraction, no matter how futile I knew it to be. So instead I opted for the Australian male's favourite cure-all. The second beer tasted even better than the first.

I had no idea what I wanted. Emily? Felicity? Both, since I was clearly fantasising? Hell, both at the same time? Ridiculous. The easier path or the more rewarding one?

Perhaps the easier path *was* the more rewarding one, and I was being too foolish to see it? Or was I only interested in either of them because they were there?

I couldn't make any sense of it, and the beers weren't helping – although they did give me, as Blur put it, a sense of enormous wellbeing. So I wasn't exactly in the appropriate frame of mind to fend off Emily when she came up and started chatting. Especially when she brought me a glass of punch, which tasted simultaneously delicious and lethal. I wondered idly what it had been spiked with – there was a hint of coconut, and also of Midori – but this didn't dissuade me from drinking it.

I went for a refill, then another. It tasted nice, and yes, that was about the most coherent thought I could muster. And then I was struck by the impression that it would also be nice to kiss Emily. So I did, and it was. It felt good, to the extent that it felt anything. And then I could see Nige, off in the distance, pointing at me. But I'd show him. It wasn't Felicity I was kissing, was it? I didn't need his lawyer friend, with her ever-present BlackBerry constantly buzzing with messages from people who weren't me.

Really, I could have laughed in his face. If I'd had my mouth free.

If anyone had any suspicions about my feelings for Felicity, I felt I'd proved them wrong once and for all when I once again bundled into the back of a cab with Emily. I didn't even bid Felicity farewell because – stop the presses folks – the P–Man (retd.) was gettin' action. And it wasn't an end–of–the–night, bottom–of–the barrel thing. It was happening right in front of everyone. So let them talk, it was about time I got a little infamy. For something other than the lameness of my DJing.

★ ★ ★

When we eventually came up for air in the back seat of the cab, Emily quickly checked her phone. I looked at my own to see if Felicity had texted, but she hadn't.

'Harry says I should ignore any noises of passion coming from his bedroom later,' she said. 'We might be too busy ourselves to notice, mightn't we sweetie?'

'Yeah, we just might.'

And I realised I should be too busy with what was in front of me to be thinking about Felicity at all. So I put her out of my mind as we flowed seamlessly from the taxi to the sofa in the living room, Emily making a brief, grinning detour past the CD player to flick on Kylie's *Greatest Hits*. 'I Should Be So Lucky,' the elder Minogue warbled over a stagnant bed of Stock Aitken Waterman synths. I laughed, and felt pretty darn lucky myself.

'Just a teaser for when we go to that concert,' she said. 'Don't think I'm releasing you from your promise, even though you've got Buckley's of delivering on the backstage pass.'

'Fine.'

And yes, everything was fine. We knew each other now, a little at least. And in particular, we knew we wanted to be there. I didn't know where this thing with Emily was going, sure, and usually, that question would have made me paralytically cautious. But this was going more smoothly than the Santana song.

Sex is a silly thing, almost a surreal thing really, with the clothes-fumbling, the bizarre incongruity of seeing someone you hardly know naked, and the temporary dropping of all pretence and subtlety as your desires are finally stripped of the social niceties that prevent men from simply dragging attractive women off to our caves. And Emily and I didn't stop joking around, didn't stop laughing – at each other, at the strangeness of the whole situation, at everything and nothing – until early the next morning.

Sex scenes in books are always strange. They're comical – deliberately or otherwise. When you're a teenager, you're desperate to read everything you can about sex, to give some shape to powerful desires you can barely control. But the words they use, like 'penetrating', 'thrusting' and 'engulfed', give the whole event this sombre air that really isn't right for it. The same words are used to talk about war, and that bears no relationship to what happens in a bedroom. They might be appropriate in a dungeon, perhaps, but my tastes are way more vanilla than that. So I won't describe in precise technical detail what Emily and I did that night – there's no way of writing about it without sounding like a parody of a Mills & Boon bodice-ripper. But believe me, there was nothing parodic about the experience at all.

#23

★ KOKOMO ★
THE BEACH BOYS (1989)

The following morning felt very different to the last occasion I'd woken in Emily's bedroom. This time, I stretched contented arms around my lover (that's right, *lover*), luxuriating in her presence, the morning sun, the intimacy of the moment. In that mood, I decided, I'd happily luxuriate in anything going, even the Kylie posters.

My mood only improved on discovering that Harris was not in. Even if that meant he was at Felicity's. Hey, it was all good. Why not share a little love around? I was in no position to begrudge my gal's brother a little action now, was I?

The two of us headed down to Well Connected again. Hand in hand, folks. And at that point, if my life had been a cheesy '80s movie, let's say *Cocktail*, it would have been the point to cue Bobby McFerrin's 'Don't Worry Be Happy' on the soundtrack. Even his whistling wouldn't have bothered me at that point. Well, less than usual.

And my life was starting to resemble *Cocktail*, as a matter of fact. I was stuck, as New Order would have put it, in a bizarre love triangle – and one set to a tacky soundtrack. There were some differences, sure: I had been flipping CDs rather than liquor bottles behind my back, and the Bryan I had to work with was Adams, not Brown. Still, I felt like I was in the 'Kokomo' scene, which is the high point until the end of the film when Tom Cruise finally opens his own bar and wins back Elizabeth Shue. And I thought Emily looked even better than her, dressed down in an oversized grey T-shirt with a fluoro pink print on it, chunky retro sunglasses and a tight black skirt. Like in the Beach Boys song, I was sitting in the sun with a girl and getting a 'tropical contact high'. Whatever that is.

We were chatting idly about music, arguing over the songs in the charts. I maintained that the only ones that were any good were those that had Snoop Dogg, Kanye West or Jay-Z guesting on them – which was, at a rough count, approximately half of them. She was accusing me of showing my age, and passionately defended the pop pap *du jour*, not quite realising that I didn't particularly care about the charts – it was all far too recent to have filtered down to the bottom of the barrel that constituted the MobyDisc playlist, anyway – and was just needling her for my own amusement.

I hadn't enjoyed just spending time with a girl like this since Mel. We'd done this sort of thing every weekend before she'd ended it, saying she found me too dependent and serious; that she'd thought she was signing up for a boyfriend, not a puppy. Most girls I know tend to criticise their boyfriends' lack of commitment and wish they could find someone who's serious about them. So I had applauded her willingness to challenge gender stereotypes, at least. But I'm digressing, and bitterly. Which is why I tend not to talk about Mel.

Emily mentioned that it was her parents' thirtieth wedding anniversary later that month, and she wanted advice on what to give them. I'd faced the parental anniversary question a few years back and told her I'd bought them a print from the first exhibition they'd ever seen together, back in the Cretaceous era. Toulouse-Lautrec, it had been. And apparently looking at a bunch of exotic dancers in various states of undress had really put them in the mood, because they'd spent that night together. Glossing over the detail, I assume, that Toulouse-Lautrec himself was not so much a great romantic hero as an old perve who sat drawing dancers undressing.

My siblings and I had heard the account of that first date far more times than we cared to, and my satisfaction at having found them a great present quickly dissipated when they took the opportunity to run us through the story yet again. I told Emily this cautionary tale, and she laughed.

'Fortunately I've no idea how my parents met,' she said. 'Probably on the putting green or something. They got boring very early in life, my folks.'

'You could get them knitted doilies for the heads of their clubs, perhaps. His 'n' hers.'

'Very funny. But funnier still is that that's actually a good idea – they'd really go for that. Mum loves all that knitted shit, and Dad – well, Dad would approve because they were practical. Your parents sound a fair bit cooler.'

'Oh, a touch perhaps. More likely they're a different kind of uncool.'

'Do you get on well with them?'

'Sure – they give me a lot of shit but they're really down to earth. Sometimes I forget they're related to me, and we can actually have a decent conversation.'

'Oh really? No way could you do that with my folks. Not unless it was about antique furniture or something. Yours sound great.'

'They're not so bad,' I conceded.

'But as we're talking about parents, I do have a favour to ask, actually.'

'Oh yes?' I said, intrigued by the sudden change in her demeanour as she stared downwards and her voice suddenly became demure. I hadn't seen her like this since Harris's teasing.

'You can say no to this, but is there any chance – any chance at all – you'd be willing to come along to my parents' anniversary party in a couple of weeks? I know it's a lot to ask –'

'Gee, Em, that's pretty full on.'

'I know, and I wish I didn't have to ask, but I hoped maybe you'd be cool with it. It doesn't mean anything, it's really just that I need to bring someone. Well, in fact, Harris might just – maybe – a little bit – have mentioned you to my parents.'

'He did, did he?'

'Yeah, we had lunch with them the other day and he kept joking about my new boyfriend, the respected music industry figure.'

'Great.'

'And he said you had your own record label and everything.'

'Jesus.'

'That you'd started with Bryan Adams.'

I had to laugh. He may have been evil, but at least he was funny.

'Softroque Records,' she said, spelling it out. 'As it's Canadian. And he said you were one of the word's leading writers of love ballads, and wrote all of Bryan's lyrics.'

'You know that clever rhyme of "true", "do", and "you" in "(Everything I Do) I Do It For You"? My work.'

She was giggling, but then stopped abruptly.

'The thing is, he told my parents he was concerned you were only interested in sleeping with me.'

My jaw dropped. That was incredibly harsh.

'He loves to do that – sound like he's being protective, while he just wants to get me in their bad books, you know? And, well, they are concerned.'

The awkward thing was that I couldn't exactly deny that the sex was high on the list of things I liked about this fledgling relationship.

'So I thought –'

'So you thought I might be willing to help convince your parents that what I have with you is almost as deep as a Bryan Adams single.'

'Yeah. Look, you don't have to come, really. I'm sure I can fix things up on my own.'

'It's OK, it shouldn't be too difficult to set them straight.'

She smiled.

'Especially when I have such silky lyrical gifts. I'll just tell them that I wrote "Everything I Do" with you in mind.'

'When I was, what, eight?'

'Oh yes, good point. But don't worry. As Bryan would say, "Can't Stop This Thing We Started."'

I smiled, but at the same time I hoped I wasn't just agreeing because I felt guilty and wanted to reassure Emily's parents I was a good person. Because I'd just signed up for an engagement that would probably top the list of my most painful social events ever. And all the others in the top ten, I'd at least been paid to attend.

#22

★ LOVEFOOL ★
THE CARDIGANS (1996)

Even the most leisurely of breakfasts comes to an end, and when we'd finished sunning ourselves in the courtyard, I took myself off home again. I was in such a good mood that I opted for drinking in the delights of Sydney on one of its trademark bright, bright, sunshiney days. So I caught a bus from the Inner West down George Street, which runs the length of the gleaming CBD, with its smart granite pavements and funky street furniture that was bought specially for the Olympics. Australians, of course, only beautify their cities for sporting events.

The street outside was swirling with shoppers packing out the pavements even though they'd recently been widened. And the city's main thoroughfare was so choked with traffic and people that despite the special red-asphalt bus lanes we weren't moving faster than walking pace. The bus could take as long as it liked, as far as I was concerned – I had plenty to think about. Even the prospect of more sardonic parental enquiries about where I'd spent the night couldn't dull my mood.

The bus crawled down the hill to Circular Quay, at the northern tip of the city. I'm not sure which town planner decided that when Sydney's major thoroughfares grandly swept their way down to the water, the most appropriate architectural structure to greet them would be a giant freeway that blocked the view of the water. We really don't deserve our harbour.

I wandered across to a ferry – it's a pleasure cruise, more than anything, but one that saves me time by avoiding the circuitous drive around to my place. I stretched out on the deck and gazed across the water, watching the thousands of glimmering bursts of light as the bright spring sunshine reflected off the gently undulating waves. Really, the view as you navigate between the Harbour Bridge and the Opera House is sensational, and for only a few bucks. Best of all, sitting up the front, I couldn't see Circular Quay anymore.

I thought about how nice it'd be to share this sight with someone. All morning I'd been telling myself that Emily was a great idea. But after a little time alone, the doubts were starting to creep back. After all, how serious a relationship could I have with a nineteen-year-old? Wasn't there a danger that I was only into her because she seemed to be into me? And how into me was she, really? Probably not all that much. She kept implying there were other guys in the picture, and aside from finding the interest from an older guy flattering, I probably wasn't what she was looking for either.

I find this whole process so frustrating. If I had my way, establishing a relationship would be like a negotiation, where you sit down with your potential partner and gradually hammer out an agreement. Plus, I got a high distinction in negotiation class at uni. But things don't work like that, certainly not in Australia anyway. Here, there's really only one socially acceptable way to get your girl, at least when you're my age. You go out in a common group of friends, and everyone has enough to drink that it all comes tumbling out. And if you stuff it up, or choose the wrong person, you've a ready-made excuse in the amount you drank. Everyone's done it, so no one has the right to judge it.

Seriously, I reckon everyone I know except Nige would be single if they were teetotallers. The free grog at my twenty-first played a crucial role in Zoë and Josh getting together, just as it had the night she'd kissed me. For some reason, they'd been able to make a go of it, and she and I hadn't — probably because he'd pursued her in the weeks afterwards and I'd run away. There was a lesson there somewhere.

The outriders are the Christians, who do these things by talking. It's hard to believe that theirs was once the mainstream morality in this country because really, no couple I know would have gotten anywhere near the altar without more than a sip of communion wine. But drink enough of the blood of Christ, and you'll be partaking of the body of someone else.

And that means you make foolish decisions about who to be with — and Emily was a case in point. There wasn't much between us beyond a shared interest in drinking, sleeping together and Kylie — and my interest in Kylie had been faked. Sure, it was better than the drought I'd been experiencing, but I knew she still wasn't a long-term option like Felicity might be. And the proof of it was that while she'd asked to introduce me to her parents because of Harris's comments, I wasn't planning to introduce her to mine.

At this point, the ferry abruptly slowed. I'm always amused by how ferries stop – some grizzled deckhand lassoes a rope around a bollard, and even though the driver tries to ease their way in, they always bang sharply into the jetty. Then an inevitably suntanned bloke slaps down a hunk of wood so you can walk across to the pier. It's the only non-piratical form of transport where you have to walk the plank.

When I'd hit terra firma and started the long trudge up the hill, I checked my phone to discover a message from Felicity.

'hey paul,' she started. Casual, nice. Although lower-case, which was *un peu prétentieux*.

'never did finish that chat.'

Yeah, well, whose fault was that?

'sounds like u got distracted!'

And how. Look out, ladies, this business operates on a first-in, best-dressed system. Although the 'dressed' part had become negotiable of late.

'next time say goodbye OK?'

Oh yes, sweet Felicity, I could have said farewell, and lesser men would have. But not this cowboy. Stop talking to Paul Johnson at your peril, lest he ride off into the sunset with another li'l lady on the back of his horse. Well, cab.

She signed her message with a little 'x'. And who could say what that little kiss symbol meant? Was it a chaste peck on the cheek between friends, or something full-blooded and passionate? Don't girls know how confusing this stuff is for us guys? We never use little kiss-symbols like that, except with Official Girlfriends. But girls litter them about like confetti at a wedding.

They're best ignored, and the same goes when a woman you like writes 'love' at the end of an email. Your heart may flutter for a moment, but I've learnt the hard way that it doesn't mean she *loves* you. And that when you immediately email back 'I love you too. Thank god one of us was finally brave enough to put it out there,' you can expect a phone call within about ten seconds.

Incidentally, that's why one former crush of mine still thinks my email was a devastatingly witty joke, and that I meant nothing by it. Fortunately, she called while I was still halfway through an online flower order. A dozen red roses arriving at her doorstep might have been a little harder to pass off as a playful quip.

So I resisted the conclusion that Felicity's little 'x' might actually have translated into the real thing if I'd stuck around at the party. And that's another reason why it had been so much easier with Emily. *She* didn't need to bother with the symbolism of lower-case letters in text messages when the good Lord had given her a tongue.

Crafting the perfect SMS reply can take a little time. But that's fine, because it gives the impression that you haven't gotten to it yet because of the other exciting things happening in your life, or that you can't yet be bothered replying. Ironically, it's the immediate response that hints at desperation, not the one you sweat over. So knowing I should take my time, I ambled up the hill towards my house, sorting through possible responses in my head.

There was the reverse-guilt option: 'As I remember it, you were the one who was otherwise occupied'; the conciliatory option: 'Sorry, you were deep in conversation and I didn't want to disturb you. Let's finish that chat soon!'; or perhaps the jokey one: 'I didn't say goodbye because I haven't left your place yet – I fell asleep in your bathtub.'

As I turned the corner into our street, I decided that above all the occasion called for a spot of arse-covering. I was feeling reluctant about Emily again so I didn't want to rule Felicity out. And as ever, alcohol provided the perfect excuse.

'Sorry, didn't mean to be rude,' I texted. 'Enjoyed your party a little too much! Love to chat when over massive hangover – maybe in a month or so?' I was particularly proud of this effort because it blamed my actions on the awesomeness of her party. It worked so well that it almost immediately earned me a text-message laugh.

'haha hope u feel better soon, see you at mj. x'

Chalk that up as another hard-won victory for 'Thumbs' Johnson, king of the smooth text message. So, what better way to celebrate than sending the traditional 'Thanks for a great night' message to Emily?

That's right. For those counting, such as myself, I was texting *two* babes in the space of five minutes. My Nokia's social life had never been so good. So, throwing caution to the wind, I decided to cap off the message to Emily with a little 'x' of my own. Yeah, I was in the zone.

#21

★ THE GAMBLER ★
KENNY ROGERS (1978)

Sunday evening, as a rule, was poker night. A rule not always observed, what with the regular intrusion of family and girlfriend commitments, but that particular Sunday we managed to get together. 'We' being the elite among that very broad group, the Friends of Nigel – three or four workmates and me.

Poker night was partly about playing Texas Hold 'Em, that wonderful variety immortalised by the World Poker Tour, late-night cable TV's cheapest program not presented by Benny Hinn. But I think the real reason Nige created the institution was to give himself one more night of drinking and holding court before he found himself back at the office on Monday morning.

Our venue, invariably, was his city apartment. Nige had bought in the CBD shortly after starting at Morphett's, and as with everything he touches, it had worked out perfectly. Now, the sleazy southern end of the city was moving upmarket. Well, slightly less downmarket anyway, with new shopping centres, supermarkets and the odd boutique. Even the spruikers at the Eros Theatre on Goulburn Street were polite these days when they invited you in for a peepshow.

As I arrived on the sixteenth floor and walked through his front door, I was reminded just how little he'd done to the place in the two years since he'd moved in. He was very house-proud, but you wouldn't have known it by looking around. Other than the massive TV that accounted for what little home time he had, Nige's place was more hotel room than *Home Beautiful*. The walls were bare white, with a framed *Pulp Fiction* poster his only concession to decorating. The sofa was a generic Ikea number, and while it made an excellent poker surface, the trendy glass dining table had never been used for anything more elaborate than beer and pizza. Nige's place was a triumph of uncompromising minimalism, achieved entirely through indifference.

I arrived at seven, clutching the requisite six-pack of boutique beer. I knew Nige too well to arrive without one. It was Coopers Pale Ale tonight – the Aussie beer that's upmarket, and priced accordingly, but definitely not wanky. Nige loves the stuff, since he views himself as quite the connoisseur but can't quite bring himself to buy boutique European or Asian.

'Johnson,' he said as he opened the door. 'Bearing the fine work of the Cooper family again, I see. Solid effort.'

I bowed.

'You can come in then.'

I always meant to find out if he'd actually bar me from entering if I turned up with Stella Artois. I wouldn't bet against it.

Will and JP, Nige's fellow stars in the glimmering insurance law galaxy, were already sitting around the table. They are nice, if slightly dull, guys – characteristic MJers. In such a high-pressure job, you can't be stuck working alongside someone you want to strangle two hours into an all-nighter. So they don't tend to hire pricks, and when they make a rare recruiting mistake, it doesn't take them long to rectify it with a handsome exit package.

Will, a skinny guy with freckles and thick red curls, is even more of a joker than Nige, but less of an alpha male about it. And JP – Jean-Philippe, to his parents – is a Belgian gym junkie whose bulging muscles perfectly match his close-cropped blond hair. They are both utter gentlemen, as straight-and-narrow as the pinstripes on their suits. I'd trust them with pretty much anything except organising a memorable night out.

But while Will and JP aren't the most fascinating guys ever, they certainly know how to take my money. The guys were serious about their poker, and they bet up big. Sure, there was plenty of joking around as the night progressed, but never about the game itself. These guys couldn't have been more professional if they'd been playing poker for a client.

I found it tricky to muster quite the same level of concentration. I like the exhilaration of winning a tight hand but I tend to stay in too long, just to keep myself interested. Pretty soon my mind starts wandering, and I stop thinking through the possibilities properly. My three-of-a-kind gets beaten by a flush I hadn't realised was possible, that kind of thing. So for me, poker night was a wonderful opportunity to drink beer, eat dial-a-pizza (not Pizza Hut when trendy Arthur's from Paddo delivered thin-crusted taste sensations to Nige's door for only twice as much money) and hand over my precious cash to guys who needed it less than I did.

Most of the early conversational fire was focused on JP, who had competed in a triathlon that morning and was in a bit of pain. Not nearly enough, I thought – just talking about all that swimming, running and riding made my underused muscles spasm in agony. Will mocked his machismo as only a truly skinny man can, asking him if he was in training for his next battle against Skeletor, and whether he'd thought of having the decorators in to spruce up Castle Greyskull a bit. Nige got in on the action-figure action as well, saying he always thought GI Joe was a closer parallel than He-Man, or perhaps GI JP, and asked whether he was going to go back and serve in the Belgian army, which history showed needed all the help it could get. I took a shot at him as well, describing him a 'gallant little Belgian'.

Not much was off-limits at these sessions, and the more personal or awkward the gag, the better. We'd have been mortified if anyone had been genuinely upset. But then half an hour later, we'd have joked about how upset they'd been.

The most popular angles for making fun of me were the eccentricity of my previous career choice, of course, along with my monk-like personal life. So I knew that after the Emily thing, I'd get a fairly hard time. Somewhat perversely, I'd been looking forward to it a little. Everyone likes a bit of attention, even of the mocking kind.

And mocking there was, although initially only for the low quality of my poker. I'm a terrible bluffer, and I was caught out on several occasions. Almost all card players have a 'tell' – a subconscious physical reaction that reveals they're nervous. Maybe they do something with their eyes, maybe they rub their earlobe; whatever it is, it's generally uncontrollable. The other guys always reckon my tic is extremely obvious, and that they always know when I'm bluffing. So my attempts to pretend I had a straight, and then a full house, were easily detected. And yet again I succeeded only in helping Nige pay off his mortgage just that little bit faster.

I worry that perhaps I have a 'tell' when it comes to girls as well, that there's some little idiosyncrasy that reveals when I'm interested in them – when I'm, as usual, trying to pretend I'm not. I asked Nige about it.

'Yeah mate, it's completely undetectable,' he said. 'Oh, except for your inability to make eye contact, your pronounced stammer, and that expression on your face that looks like someone's slowly feeding you to a school of piranhas. But otherwise dude, you're the goddamn Sphinx.'

So much for that theory, then. Not that Nige can talk. He has a hilariously bad habit of occasionally licking his lips when he's trying to chat up a woman – as if limbering them up for later action. And, to be fair, they generally get a bit of a workout, so perhaps he does need to keep them nice and moist?

I made the mistake once of assuming the same thing applied in poker, and that his lip-licking implied anticipation of a big win. So I called him on a hand when his tongue had been working particularly furiously, only to reveal that he was bluffing, knowing how often I'd laughed about the lip thing when we were out drinking. Nige being able to outsmart me is something I generally feel ought not to be possible, and yet it happens disconcertingly often.

That night was a case in point: I lost sixty dollars to him in about two hours – roughly forty dollars more than I'd promised myself I'd stake. Irritatingly, the general poker seriousness extends to not offering anything like credit. Even though Nige owed me a hundred bucks from our last night out, he declined my offer to let him pay me back in the chips that had all too recently been mine in any case. 'Got to keep a big stack when you've got one Paul, you know how it is,' he said. 'I'll pay you back when I cash in.' So I was forced to do the walk of shame down to the ATM.

When I got back with a fresh supply of hard-earned, easily lost banknotes, Nige exaggeratedly said, 'Shh fellas, he's back.' The poker had temporarily been forgotten, so I couldn't figure out whether the guys had been gossiping about me, or Nige had assumed – correctly, as it happened – that he'd get a rise out of me if he pretended they had been.

'Glad I could entertain you fellas,' I said, as sarcastically as I could manage.

'Yeah, thanks Jono,' Will said. 'Your escapades have been more interesting than usual lately. Keep it up.'

'Here's to Paul,' Nige said, raising one of my stubbies. 'Who's finally grown a backbone.'

'Well, a bone anyway,' JP said. 'I feel sorry for these young girls, Paul. I hope you're being gentle with them.'

'The thing I like about Paul's recent progress is that he's gone from too few ladies to too many,' Nige said.

'I didn't think you thought there could be too many,' I said, unsuccessfully trying to throw him off-track.

'Johnson goes home with the nineteen-year-old again,' Nige said. 'And amateur heartbreaker that he is, upsets

Felicity so much that she crazily pashes the nineteen-year-old's brother all over her nice leather sofa, just to get back at him.'

My jaw dropped, and I sat down heavily.

'Aw, give Felicity a break, Jono. Bit of a double standard isn't it mate?' Will asked, inadvertently expressing a somewhat feminist perspective. 'When you pick one, you don't get to bags another for later as well, you know. A classy chick like her isn't gonna wait around.'

'How do you know it was to get back at me, Nige?' I asked, my earlier, pleasant live-and-let-live attitude to the Harris/Felicity concept now very much forgotten.

'Oh, it might have been something she said,' he said coyly.

'Bullshit,' I ventured, but without much confidence.

'You tell me, Paul. She asked me where you'd gotten to because she'd been bailed up by an old mate halfway through a conversation with you that she wanted to finish and then lost you. You know how it is when you're hosting a party, she said.'

'Damn.'

'I tried to put her off the scent, mate, but then she marched back up an hour later, quite a bit more smashed than when I'd last seen her. And she waved her finger at me and said she'd heard you'd left with Emily, and she'd bloody well show you.'

'Yeah. Of course she couldn't, seeing you'd gone off with the bird in the hand already,' JP chipped in. 'But geez, she sure showed everyone else in the place.'

Cue raucous laughter from three gentlemen, and a feeling of despondency in the fourth, as he'd completely misjudged Felicity and made something of a dick of himself.

'Did Harris stay over?' I knew it was pretty hypocritical of me to ask, but when's that ever stopped a guy?

'Nah,' Nige said. 'He was so smashed that I think that little mate of his took him back to his place. He wouldn't have been any use to any woman that night. I actually felt sorry for the dipshit – he had such a good chance, but he blew it. Then Flea sobered up an hour or so later and kicked us out so she could start cleaning the place up. Christ, it was a mess by the end. She's probably still cleaning up.'

'So we went down the road to the Strand,' JP said, redundantly.

And to think I'd felt I'd gotten *lucky* at the party. We switched to scotch on the rocks, the iconic tipple of hardcore *pokeristes*, and that took everything up a few notches. The bets got bigger, the insults got harsher, and the laughs got considerably louder.

I didn't lose any more, thankfully, but nor did I get a cent back from Nige before eleven, when we regretfully pulled up stumps so we could make some kind of appearance at work the next day. I was the most regretful of all. I wasn't looking forward to seeing Felicity.

#20

★ LOVE IN AN ELEVATOR ★
AEROSMITH (1989)

I'm not a morning person at the best of times, and Monday definitely wasn't the best of times. My head was woolly, my eyes were sore, and standing upright was much more of a challenge than it should have been. I was still in agony even after I downed a double espresso at the handy café in the foyer of the Morphett's building. I slumped in a corner of the lift so as to avoid falling over completely, readying myself for the ear-popping journey up to my floor, when a power-dressed tornado surged into the lift, her sheer momentum stopping the doors from closing.

It was Felicity, moving far more quickly than she should have been after such a massive Saturday night. I wondered whether she'd devoted her Sunday to a super-detox yoga session, where some secret trick perfected by Tibetan monks had enabled her to align her chakras as neatly as everything in that apartment of hers.

I wasn't anything like ready to face her, but after she'd made such a dramatic entry, staring at the wall and pretending not to notice her arrival clearly wasn't going to work. So the best I could manage was a limp wave, which received a wan smile in return.

My heart lurched when she smiled at me, and I wished I'd been considerably less drunk, and considerably more brave, on Saturday night. I wanted to start repairing the damage with an apology. But there were five other people in the lift so there was no scope for chatting. Instead, our ascent was conducted in that particularly impersonal silence you get when you cram too many people into too small a space. But we were the only ones to get out at Level 35, and suddenly we found ourselves alone in the entrance foyer.

We simultaneously reached to swipe ourselves through the security door, and both shrank back and embarked upon the word 'sorry' at precisely the same moment. We broke concurrently into nervous laughter, and Flea put her hand endearingly on my wrist as she giggled, the tension of the moment unexpectedly broken.

'You don't need to apologise,' she said.

'Yeah I do,' I said. 'I should have said goodbye. That was rude.'

'It's OK, I don't think you were entirely yourself!'

'And I've no idea why *you're* apologising,' I said. 'Let's just leave it at that.'

'Just one of those crazy nights, I guess.'

'Just an excellent party. Thanks for having us, by the way.'

She laughed again and blushed. 'Um, I'm sure Nige has told you that it wasn't you I had!'

'Yes, well. I'm hardly in a position to comment on that sort of thing, am I?'

'I think I might not want to know what positions you've been in lately,' she said with a raised eyebrow, perfectly timed to reach the door of my office.

'Embarrassed, mainly. OK, I'll catch you later.'

'Yes, make sure you do that this time,' she said, and gave me a final grin as she walked down to her own office.

Morphett's had resisted the scourge of open-plan, and I was grateful for it. I liked not having to don headphones to block out the endless noise of other people's conversations. I could even play music in my little room – a liberty not taken by everyone with an office, but I was already earmarked as 'the DJ guy' so people viewed it as a part of my general eccentricity, and I was only too happy to encourage that.

I steered away from vocal music because it can be almost as distracting as a colleague yammering in your ear. But mundane law work always felt that much less onerous accompanied by some instrumental jazz or a string quartet, or some trendy electronic stuff. I shudder to use the term 'nu-jazz', but that's what they seem to call it when funkster producers like the Thievery Corporation electronically meld easy-listening keyboards with world music rhythms and instruments. It sounds better than my description, and it was relaxing enough to form a major part of my lawyering listening diet.

I was feeling particularly mellow so I put on Air's *Premiers*

Symptômes, recorded before they started singing over their music in vocoderised broken English. I knew it was a bit pretentious to listen to songs with names like 'Casanova 70' and 'Le soleil est près du moi' – a bit 'I'm too cool for this job' – but bugger it. If I was going to sit at my desk all morning and annotate a contract, the least I could do was provide myself with a vaguely tolerable working environment. I was sure the client wouldn't mind just as long as I didn't stuff up the work. And if I did, it certainly wouldn't have been Air's fault.

After I'd played five of the albums on my iPod, it was lunchtime, and Nige poked his head around the door to see if I was up for the excitement of a trip to the food court. I told him sure, but it'd have to be a quick one. I knew he would agree with any suggestion of haste to avoid seeming slack, even though he'd gladly have sat and chatted over one of his beloved prawn laksas for forty-five minutes, condemning himself to stay back that much later in the evening.

We went down to the retail mall that connected directly to the foyer of our building, the developers having correctly judged that their tenants would appreciate the time saving so much that we wouldn't be too fussy about the selection or the price. Laksa isn't a great meal to take upstairs to your desk for a virtuous display of keeping busy, so we ate in. Nige strapped on the provided paper bib and tucked in while I grabbed a nondescript toasted sandwich from the place next door.

My afternoon would be devoted to reviewing the fine print on the advertising for a new credit card, in the hope that I could save Brent some time by identifying the more obvious problems. And when we were sitting down, I found

I could quite comfortably defer getting back to my desk. I hadn't felt very sociable earlier, but after Nige and I got chatting, I rapidly forgot the awkwardness with Felicity. He's good like that.

We breezed through the usual work topics, and it wasn't long before the conversation got onto girls. I attempted to defer Nige's usual forthright advice by asking how he was doing lady-wise, a topic that always requires frequent updates given the mutual admiration society he's formed with pretty much the whole of womankind.

When last I'd enquired, which couldn't have been more than four days earlier, he'd been seeing Janet, a glamorous twenty-nine-year-old senior associate from a rival firm. She'd just come out of a long-term relationship and had received invaluable comfort from Nige shortly afterwards, facilitated by a particularly vigorous session of loading cocktails onto her gold Amex.

Janet had overlapped a little with his fling with Tammy, a nose-ring-toting, buzz-cut waitress at our favourite café on Bronte Beach, where we often made a pilgrimage for a swim and hearty breakfast during the warmer months. Now in all probability we could never go back there. I often wished his libido could take these future inconveniences into account – the list of venues we couldn't enter because of a previous Nige 'situation' was already too long. But today, instead of entertaining me with tales of playing catch-and-kiss with half of Sydney, he was strangely bashful.

'Oh, you know how it is.'

'No, I don't,' I said. 'Your personal life updates more frequently than the ASX.'

'Steady on, mate. That's a bit uncalled for,' he said, injured. 'The ASX is updated by the second.'

'Sorry, sorry. Your outlook only changes once or twice an hour, at most.'

'That's a bit of an exaggeration.'

He seemed piqued. What was with him?

'I'm kidding,' I said. 'And I'll say one thing for you: they're never All Ordinaries, you bastard.'

'Come on, mate. Sure, OK, I liked to keep myself a little busy when I was younger, I'll grant you that.'

Like, a whole week younger, I thought. But given his unusual tetchiness, I opted to let it slide.

'And things have changed now,' I said, my tone of voice not quite successfully suppressing the question mark.

'Well, you might have obtained a bit of insight into that already if you hadn't been so busy making an exhibition of yourself on Saturday night.'

'Oh really? What did I miss?'

Nige was still Nige, and he couldn't resist a big, toothy grin.

'Well, you might have noticed me sharing a quiet drink and some civilised conversation with a girl next to the pool. Her name's Laura, and I met her a few times over summer while she was clerking over at Ainsley Macintosh.'

'Oh, you can drop that whole gentlemanly pretence right now. You've been chasing students again!'

'She's in her final year at New South, and she's twenty-three. Which, by your standards, would make her too old for me.'

'Fair cop. But hey, this sounds promising. Did you pick her up, then?'

Nige suddenly glared at me.

'Jesus, Jono, I'm glad *you're* finally getting a little loving, but for your information, it's not necessary to jump in the

sack with everyone five minutes after you meet them.'
And he harrumphed a little, with surprisingly genuine
indignation.

We'd somehow waded into some bizarre role reversal,
but I figured that calling him on it wasn't going to help me
get any more information.

'So, are you seeing her again?'

'Matter of fact, I am. We're going out to dinner on
Thursday.'

'Nice. Where are you taking her?'

'I was thinking Beppi's. Somewhere a bit special. But
I'm a bit worried about it, to be honest. D'you think she'll
like it?'

Nige asking my advice on where to take a date?
Unprecedented. Usually his attitude would've been that
he'd go where he wanted, and if the girl didn't enjoy it, then
bugger it, it reflected badly on her. This Laura must be quite
something, I thought.

As the granddaddy of Italian restaurants in Sydney,
Beppi's is far nicer than Nige would usually bother springing
for on a first date. Sure, he's always happy to shout round
after round of drinks as an investment in moving his agenda
along, but Beppi's is well outside his usual price range for
a non-girlfriend. Plus, it hadn't just been mentioned in the
Good Living section of the paper – it's an old-school place,
the kind of joint whose patrons are on first-name terms
with the waiters. In a warm-hearted, unglamorous way, it's
genuinely romantic.

'Nige!' I said. 'You're really into this girl, aren't you?'

He winced a little and averted his eyes. Only it wasn't
wincing, I realised – it was Nige being bashful. I'd never
seen it before.

'Oh, you know, perhaps. I'm seeing where it goes.'

'Sure. And hey – good luck!'

'Anyway, enough of that,' he said in a tone that suggested any further discussion of the mysterious Laura would be unwelcome. And he hadn't even told me in overly specific detail how hot she was.

'What about your situation, then?' he continued brightly, only too happy to shift the spotlight onto me. 'Or should I say situations?'

I exhaled. 'Geez, I've no idea.'

'Tell me something I don't know.'

'Well, after so long with too few options, I don't really want to complain about having too many.'

'And yet I know you will –'

'Well, I could use your advice Nige.'

'Finally he says something sensible.'

'The one girl is up for it, and a lot of fun. But I can't see it turning into anything serious. Then the other one *could* be quite a big thing, if we got together, but I don't know whether we'll actually get there – or whether it'd be much good if we did. So neither situation's ideal.'

'Oh, and you'll only go for it if an ideal situation is handed to you on a platter?'

'Ah, come on. Look at you, flipping over this Laura.'

'Yeah, sure, but it's not like I was sitting and wringing my hands in the meantime, was it?'

I grinned my acknowledgement.

'I reckon it all depends on how much you like Felicity, buddy. If you want to go for her, you've got to forget Emily, at least for now. Because otherwise Harris will make sure she finds out every little thing you do with Felicity.'

'Or don't do, more likely. Anyway, I've no idea if she's even interested.'

'Well, you're never going to *completely* know with a girl like that. You've got to put yourself out there – you've got to make a move, an unambiguous move, and see if she bars you or not. I reckon you've got a decent shot, but Felicity's the kind of girl who'll encourage you just enough to know she's got you, and then drop you cold, just like that. I've seen her do it.'

'Geez. You're not exactly making a good sales pitch for her.'

'I'm just telling you how it is with some of these super-classy girls. She's not a bad person, not at all; it's just how she functions. Maybe it's an insecurity thing, maybe she has to trust a guy before she puts herself in a position where he might be able to hurt her. Some people are like that after shitty relationships.'

'True. And I haven't exactly been worshipping at her altar to date, have I? If anything, she'd be thinking my interest was pretty casual since I seem to be so easily dissuaded.'

'Exactly.'

'I've ruled out Emily, there's no future in that. And to be honest, Felicity might be too much hard work.'

'Totally, if you're not a hundred per cent keen. But she could be good for you, I've always thought that.'

'Always, eh?'

'OK, I'll admit it – starting from shortly after she barred me.'

'Finally he admits it!'

'But whether you can get yourself into a headspace where you can really go for her, that I don't know. You're going to have to work out what you want.'

'Yeah, and that's the thing I really can't do.'

'That's true. Easier to drink to a point where you don't have to decide, isn't it?'

'You're quite the sage today, Nige, aren't you?'

'I'm the Buddha of Level 37, buddy. And speaking of which —'

'Yeah, let's head up. Good to chat though mate, thanks.'

'Any time.'

'And this whole Laura thing — could be the start of something beautiful.'

'Don't want to jinx it Paulie. But yeah, it just might.'

When I got back to my office, I put my feet up on the desk and thought how rarely Nige and I had serious, intimate conversations. It was good to know that we could.

The great thing about talking to Nige is that in his world, any woman is possible. From his perspective, it was simply a question of who I wanted to go for. Sure, he'd concede there was a chance of getting knocked back, but no worries, there'd be another girl along next week.

Yet after I stopped talking to him, I could only see those same difficulties I'd been worrying about before. So I decided that my total lack of strategy had served me reasonably well so far, and that doing nothing was the prudent option. Not coincidentally, it was also by far the easiest one.

#19

★ COUNTRY HOUSE ★
BLUR (1995)

Over the next month, my life contracted into three basic states: working, sleeping and commuting. Zoë's theory that I'd end up doing extra days was almost immediately proven correct, and I'm sure she would have enjoyed gloating about it if I'd had time to meet her for coffee.

I was putting in thirteen-hour days, with dinner provided by the firm – the least they could do. Sometimes I'd even squeeze in a quick late-night beer with Nige before the client-funded cab home. But although I made it very clear to Brent that I didn't expect this pattern to continue and that I'd been serious about having other things I needed to do, the reality was that I didn't mind much, at least for the time being. It was a change. Sure, it wasn't anywhere near as good as a holiday, but I still enjoyed engaging the parts of my brain that had been atrophying. And to be honest, there was a lot of ego gratification in there as well. When I left to do something else, I wanted it to be through choice, not because I wasn't good enough to make it at a place like Morphett's. But what I liked most was that the work took up nearly all of the space in my head, leaving little room for wondering what to do with myself – or about Felicity.

I hadn't experienced any pressure at all since my final uni exams, and the sheer effort of having to do anything before midday was taking a lot out of me. One Friday, I pleaded exhaustion only an hour into after-work drinks, to Nige's disgust. And the following Saturday, I just stayed in and watched a few DVDs – something I'd previously done purely to kill time during weekdays, but which now seemed wonderful because I didn't have to leave the sofa. I saw a bit of Felicity, but only in a strictly work context, which I'm sure was a relief to both of us. We had a brief chat in the kitchen at one point, while we were both making ourselves strong cups of tea in the hope that the caffeine and sugar would somehow keep us awake, but it was just the politest of enquiries about how each other's work was progressing. Nige made the odd comment about me being chicken, but I was happy to let things with her drift back to normal.

My new lifestyle earned approving nods from my parents and sarcastic text messages about turning into a corporate zombie from Zo. But I told myself it was OK as long as I didn't normalise it, approaching the future comfortable that this was how it would always be, the way my colleagues did. The first month just flew by, and even though I was really starting to hit the wall, I couldn't mark the milestone with a weekend of relaxation. Quite the contrary, in fact. Because even though I hadn't had much contact with her beyond text messages apologising for working all the time, I was still committed to going to Emily's parents' wedding anniversary.

Things were really busy – the launch of our client's new credit card program was imminent, and they were still tinkering with the product to add extra ways of sucking punters into signing up for exorbitant interest rates. And that meant we were constantly revising our advice to make sure it was all legal. (Whether it was moral was an area in which we had no expertise.) So there was talk of working through the weekend to get the thing to the printers on the Monday.

On the Thursday before the event, I called Emily and slightly hinted at the possibility that I might have to work, creating a mini-explosion on the other end of the line. She informed me in no uncertain terms that pulling out at the last minute would be the worst possible scenario. At least from her perspective; from mine, it would have been absolutely ideal. It was a sit-down dinner, so if I pulled out she'd have a conspicuously empty seat next to her, and proof positive that I wasn't interested in meeting the obligations that her folks felt should derive from 'squiring our daughter around town'. Still, parental approval was obviously elusive for Emily, and I could relate to that. So I backtracked, saying that the odds of having to work on a Saturday night were probably very slim anyway, and that I'd try to explicitly clear it with my boss.

My enthusiasm waned even further when she warned me, a little sheepishly, that as far as her parents were concerned,

I was her boyfriend. She apologised, but said her father, being a pillar of their local church, simply couldn't relate to the idea of casual relationships. The entire point of the exercise was to convince them it was reasonably serious, so I guessed it made sense, just as long as the two of us were under no illusions. So I thanked her for the warning and said I wouldn't freak out if I heard the b-word.

I really wanted to pull out, but I knew I'd feel like a bastard if I landed Emily in a difficult situation with her parents. It'd only confirm what Harris had suggested. So, verily it did come to pass that I found myself, at the civilised hour of five on a Saturday afternoon, strolling down the primly manicured Wahroonga street that contained the Barnes residence, 'The Laurels'. I hadn't been to a house with a name before, but the whole suburb seemed to be suffering from the misapprehension that it was located in rural England, so the posh yet dull-sounding label fit right in.

Whereas most hosts would be content with merely writing 'RSVP' on an invitation, the lord and lady of The Laurels had deemed themselves above such plebeian abbreviations, instead instructing their invitees to '*Répondez, s'il vous plaît.*' Mon dieu.

The suburb likes to refer to itself, inaccurately, as the 'village' of Wahroonga, as if it's surrounded by rolling fields instead of other identical suburbs. Although, to be fair, there are plenty of rolling rugby fields, given the high concentration of posh private schools. It's God's own country, if you truly believe that the Almighty prefers his suburbs stuffed to the gills with wealthy conservatives.

I'd walked from the station, which took a good fifteen minutes, so I was sweating a little underneath my suit by the time I arrived at the ostentatiously ornate gates. Given my apprehension about the evening, I'd have been sweating even in the middle of winter.

The Laurels was one of your classic North Shore battleaxes, a term that refers equally to the shape of the blocks and their typical inhabitants. It's ever so much more refined to be a couple of hundred metres back from the nasty roadway, don't you know, and it gives one the desired illusion of being in the country – an effect that's also generally attempted via quaint, designer-rustic décor. Unfortunately there's only so much a knitted toilet-roll doily can do to make a suburban home seem rural, and I wish someone would clarify that point with the entire North Shore.

Reaching the end of the driveway, I rapped on the wrought-iron knocker and the door was immediately opened by a severe-looking dinner-suited man who I placed in his mid-fifties.

'Mr Barnes?' I ventured.

The hint of a smile crossed his lips before being swiftly suppressed.

'Not quite, sir,' he said. 'I'm handling security for the evening.'

'Really? I'm surprised.'

'Well, given our host's position, it's regrettably necessary.'

'I'm sorry, I'm a friend of Emily's and I'm not really all that familiar with what her folks do.'

I had gathered Emily's dad was a big-shot lawyer of some kind, but we'd never really gotten into all that much conversational detail on that – or, in fact, anything much.

'Well, *Justice* Barnes is a member of the Family Court bench.'

'Oh, I see.'

Suddenly his presence made sense. No judges have higher security than Family Court ones. People flip out if they lose their kids even more reliably than if they lose their liberty.

'That's *Mr* Justice Barnes. Whereas Mrs Barnes, QC, is a Crown prosecutor.'

I made appropriately impressed noises. I'd realised the Barneses would be putting me on trial that evening, but I hadn't realised quite how much capacity they had to do so.

'So, your name,' he said, by now bored with our little chat.

I almost pulled out my driver's licence, so great was his air of authority. But it appeared not to be necessary, and his slow perusal of his clipboard eventually produced a match, so he waved me in.

'Carry on then, eh, old thing?' I said, deciding in that instant that I'd probably enjoy my evening significantly more if I treated the entire event as a kind of surreal Regency house party.

'Thanks, sir,' he said, the words by now dripping with contempt.

I hadn't taken Family Law at uni, preferring to fuel my depression about the state of the human race with the non-stop gigglefest that was the Human Rights and the Holocaust elective. So I didn't precisely know the powers of a Family Court judge. I was fairly sure he wasn't allowed to have me shot on sight by GI Jeeves, but locking me up in his basement for a couple of days might well have been perfectly well within his rights. I hoped I wouldn't have to find out.

Quietly humming David Bowie's 'Under Pressure' before abandoning it in disgust after remembering it had been sampled in 'Ice Ice Baby', I opened a large set of double doors and tried to make an unobtrusive entrance. I failed.

#18

★ FATHER AND SON ★
CAT STEPHENS (1970)

'Hey,' Harris yelled as I entered the room. 'Look who just rode in on his wheels of steel. MC Paul is in da house!' And he sauntered towards me, making an odd clicking sound that I suspected was an attempt at beatboxing.

The room was enormous, and decorated as if someone had seen the Oval Office set from *The West Wing* and decided it wasn't quite formal enough. I desperately looked around the room to try and locate Emily, but among the thirty-odd guests I couldn't spot anyone else who wasn't at least twenty years older than me and pompous-looking.

'Yo DJ,' Harris said, and clasped a hand to his ear, stretched out a finger and made a high-pitched 'wigga wigga wigga' noise. The chatter and clinking of champagne glasses abruptly stopped at this odd behaviour, the unsuccessful attempt to evoke scratching lost on everyone except me.

'Harris,' I said. 'It's been too long.'

'Tell ya what, buddy. I'd actually be happy to hear you on the decks for once, if the alternative is this racket.'

It wasn't much of a compliment, given the sprightly baroque woodwind tones that were wafting in from the patio.

'Emily's outside,' he said. 'It's a tough crowd tonight. There's, like, one table of our friends, and the rest are fogeys.'

'Oh well,' I said. 'It'll give us a chance to finally get to know each other.'

He laughed uproariously and clapped me on the back.

'Not as well as you've gotten to know my sister though, I hope.'

'Yeah, I think we can agree on that.'

We started making our way outside, which took a while because everyone kept stopping to make small talk with the young man of the house. He never failed to introduce me as 'Emily's friend' in a manner that was loaded with considerably more innuendo than the situation required. He didn't give actual nudges and winks, but he might as well have.

We'd just chalked up our fifth awkward conversation – or entertaining conversation, if you were Harris – when a small man with square glasses strode purposefully through the patio door through which I'd been hoping to escape.

'Dad!' Harris exclaimed. 'Allow me to introduce Paul.'

'Ah, Paul,' he said, shaking my hand more forcefully than was necessary. 'Thanks for coming. I've heard so much about you.'

'Pleasure to meet you, judge,' I said.

This was the point where many parents might have invited me to call them by their first name. He did not.

'Judge, eh?' he said. 'Most people I meet call me Mister Justice or Your Honour or something like that.'

'Paul's quite the man of the world, aren't you?' Harris interjected.

'Oh, you aren't the first judge I've met,' I said.

'Really?' Barnes Senior said, frowning a little. 'In a courtroom situation?'

'A few times,' I said, thinking of the compulsory courtwatch sessions I'd endured at law school. The frown deepened.

'Crimes against humanity, wasn't it?' Harris said, grinning. Which made the penny drop.

'I suppose I shouldn't be too surprised,' his father said. 'People in your line of work often find themselves in a little trouble. I've had a few musicians in my courtroom. So passionate over custody issues, you know — artistic temperaments and so on. Nothing too serious, I hope?'

I smiled, realising that I was in a stronger position in this odd little world than I'd anticipated.

'No — I was in Justice Emsley's Roman Law class,' I said, casually namedropping one of the more senior Supreme Court judges. 'He still likes to teach it as a hobby, and he ran us through the appropriate etiquette in our first class.'

'Ah, Miles,' he said. 'Lovely fellow. I hadn't realised you had a legal background. Harris, why didn't you mention it?'

Harris grinned a little and said, 'I didn't realise it myself, Dad.'

'Sydney University?' he asked.

'Is there anywhere else?' I replied, knowing that in his day there probably hadn't been.

He laughed and clapped me on the back.

'They tell me there are a few new places these days, but I've never believed them. So you gave the law away for the life of a musician then, Paul? How very bohemian of you.'

'Not exactly, judge. The music stuff's only a hobby, really. I'm at Morphett's.'

'Really!' he said. 'A fine firm. A few of my colleagues on the bench did articles there, as a matter of fact. I met William Morphett himself once, you know, when I was a young man.'

'Really?' I said politely.

'There's a funny story about a tray of *vol-au-vent*, but I'll bore you with the details later,' he said, smiling for the first time. 'I might take a few moments of your time after dinner, as a matter of fact. I've given up hope on Harris here, but I'm still trying to convince Emily to consider graduate law. I really think it'd suit her.'

I fervently disagreed, but I was hardly going to jeopardise my get-out-of-jail-free card by saying so.

'Happy to,' I said.

'And make sure you have a word to my wife, won't you? She'll be very pleased to hear you're at such a fine firm.'

As opposed to being an aimless reprobate, I assumed. The cachet of the law really did come in useful with parents. And playing my Morphett's trump card in front of Harris almost made my job worthwhile.

I always felt a little dirty after I'd indulged in legal namedropping, but under the circumstances I felt it was perfectly justified. Harris had started the social snobbery contest, so I was only too happy to outplay him.

I took my leave of the Barnes boys and made my way out the back, pleased to overhear Harris being scolded by his father for giving him 'quite the wrong impression'.

Out on the patio, in the words of GANGgajang, the source of the baroque music was revealed as a young, black-clad trio of serious-looking musicians – an oboe, a clarinet and a flute. Evidently the power lawyer couple were fans of wind.

Emily spotted me almost instantly and waved me down to the grass where she was standing with yet another group of older people. She was dressed in an simple but classy black dress and pearls – more elegantly than I'd have thought she'd attempt before I'd seen The Laurels. Her hair was primped and pinned to within an inch of its life. She seemed every inch the young mistress, a fan of showjumping and croquet rather than grungy cafés and jumping around on dancefloors to Kylie.

Observing the contrast reminded me of 'Common People' – the Pulp original, of course, not the ghastly William Shatner cover. Her terrace bedroom featured cockroaches climbing up the wall as well, and Emily's dad could have stopped it all even more effectively than the girl's dad does in the song – with a court order.

Emily spared me another raft of introductions and took me off to one side. She looked really lovely, and for a moment I wondered whether I should change my stance on not pursuing her.

'You made it! I honestly thought you'd pike.'

'Not a chance,' I said.

'You probably just came in case I gave you a tour of my bedroom later though, right?' She grinned mischievously, and I blushed.

'To be honest, I hadn't thought of it.'

'Yeah, *sure* you hadn't. I've got to warn you though, it's pretty girly.'

'As long as it's mainly Kylie posters, I'll feel right at home.'

'Not even – I brought all that stuff down to my place. It's got, like, dolls and stuff.'

I really didn't need an environment that made Emily seem even younger.

'Oh, by the way – Harris already introduced me to your dad,' I told her. Her face suddenly turned ashen.

'Oh god, I wanted to be there for that, in the hope he'd be slightly less of a jerk about it.'

'I'm not sure that would have prevented him. Still, as you can see, your dad didn't kick me out or anything.'

'I'm relieved! How'd it go?'

'Surprisingly well actually, seeing as I work at a law firm these days.'

'God, yeah, that's right! I didn't take in a whole lot of what you said at Flea's party, so I didn't really put two and two together about your new job.'

'Well, I was doing all I could to distract you. But yeah, I've got to say, your dad and I got along reasonably well. Put it this way – he wants me to try and convince you to study law.'

'Geez, Paul, there's such a thing as making too good an impression!'

I laughed. 'Under the circumstances, I'll take it.'

'Thanks so much for coming, I know it's a big ask,' she said. 'But that night Harry and I came up here for dinner, it just got a little out of hand, you know? They were encouraging us to bring our "special friends" to their big do. So Harris totally went to town, and I figured the best way to shut my brother up was to tell him I'd bloody well bring you then. To show them I'm not just, you know, easy.'

'Yeah sure, Em. And I don't think you are. My theory is that you're extremely hard-to-get, but I just happen to be extraordinarily attractive.'

'Whatever works for you! But I'm not bothered either way, to be honest. I don't really have any hang-ups about all that stuff. But my parents – you know.' She waved her arm to encompass the surroundings – a picture that said a thousand words, and hundreds of thousands of dollars.

'I know, Em. It's cool. I'm kind of flattered you asked me.'

'And don't freak out too much, OK? I'm not expecting that we're somehow committed or anything, even though we were kidding around about it and that. We're on the same page there, aren't we?'

'Sure, and it's a fun page to be on.'

She smiled. 'The funny thing though, is that because I brought a date, Harry felt he had to as well. So Felicity's coming.'

I didn't think that was a funny thing at all.

'Really? I didn't know they were still, uh – involved.'

'I don't want to say anything bad about her, I think she's cool,' she said, issuing the standard disclaimer that means you're about to really sink the boot in. 'But once she found out who my parents are, I don't think it was the toughest sell in the world.'

'Hey, why do you think I'm here?' I asked, grinning.

'Come on. You, a legal arse-kisser? I can't see it. There's no way out of it, you're here for *me*.'

She laughed cheekily at me. 'Although you know, marrying into this family would be an excellent career move.'

'Yeah,' I said, laughing myself. 'I wonder if Felicity has thought of that?'

But inside I shuddered slightly. No doubt she had.

#17

★ THE JOKER ★
STEVE MILLER BAND (1973)

Harris's date didn't arrive until we were sitting down to dinner in a marquee at the bottom of the garden. Her entrance was even more conspicuous than mine, taking place just as the local priest was finishing leading us in grace. Felicity's arrival came as a welcome distraction from my guilt about how far some of Emily's and my recent activities had deviated from the standard Sunday School curriculum. She was wearing a dark blue dress dotted with peach flowers – pitch-perfect for the refinement of the surroundings, and yet displaying enough of a hint of cleavage to attract wandering male eyes. It was a bolder option than Emily's, and it reaped the rewards.

She was momentarily taken aback to see me,

but then smiled in my direction as she joined us at the lone youth table. Her seat was directly opposite mine, but since it was a round table, she wasn't within comfortable speaking distance unless we half-shouted – and neither of us were game to do that.

The table was split largely along gender lines. I remembered some of Harris's noxious male friends from that first night I'd met him, and his crew was dressed in penguin suits that were already well on the way to dishevelled, along with one token girlfriend who was parked next to Felicity. But at least Harris's crew boasted two women – I was the odd man out among Emily's friends, who were all her age.

It's easy to feel trapped at a formal dinner when you aren't enjoying the conversation, and I wished they'd just opted for drinks where you can shift around or even disappear for long stretches. I'd always enjoyed talking to Emily, but with a gaggle of four friends around her, the conversation revolved almost entirely around fashion, celebrities and who liked who at uni. I had nothing to contribute on any of those topics so I valiantly tried to strike up a conversation with Harris's buddy Leon, a sallow creature who had clearly earned his place in the group only because he was Harris's biggest fan.

He was friendly enough, but tended to talk exclusively about his little gang's exploits. Like how totally, like, drunk they'd gotten last weekend and how awesomely funny Harry'd been, awesome, and how many times he'd nearly gotten into a fight with a bouncer, and *just* managed to talk his way out of it, shit man, it was just an awesome night. I had trouble figuring out whether he wanted to be Harris or be with him, and I suspect Leon did too.

I spent an hour picking at the roast chicken and bouncing between the two unattractive conversational alternatives.

Occasionally I'd glance towards Felicity, and one of us would faintly roll our eyes upwards. The speeches came as an unusually welcome interlude.

A succession of old friends told us that Emily's parents had a wonderful life together, did wonderful things on a wonderfully regularly basis and were wonderfully in love. The only humour came from gentle jibes at the wonderful couple for just being *too* wonderful, bless them.

Then the MC announced that we were to be treated to 'a perspective from the next generation', and Harris stood up. Emily looked nervous.

'I really hope he doesn't mention me,' she said, turning to me. 'And I really, *really* hope he doesn't mention *us*.'

I hadn't even considered the possibility. So I did, and she was right – it wasn't pleasant.

'You've all heard about Mum and Dad's many achievements,' he said. 'Their amazing careers, their happy life together. It all sounds perfect, doesn't it? *Too* perfect. Well, what you don't know, and what it's time you *did* know, is that they have a dark side.'

Emily visibly winced. 'Harry has this dream of being a stand-up comedian,' she whispered to me. 'I really hope he isn't intending to start his career now.'

But he was. Oh, so many jokes, and oh, so many of them ill-advised. Like the one about how he couldn't believe that his father, as a Family Court judge, didn't pick up more chicks.

'Think about it,' he quipped, with an air that suggested he didn't care whether anyone else found this gear funny because he sure as hell did. 'The parties – they come and see him in his chambers when they're at their most vulnerable, right? They come looking for guidance, for resolution – in many ways, for love. Dad could have started three or four families by now, I reckon. And he probably should have – just think how much useful real-life experience he'd have brought to the bench then! Gotta tell ya, the man's a saint.'

Emily's father went very red in the face, and I think it would be fair to say that everyone except Harris noticed. He ploughed on, magnificently oblivious.

'And then Mum, the Crown prosecutor. I tell you what, if she's half as tough in court as she was on us kids, then I feel sorry for the poor suckers in her courtroom.' Polite titters at that, which marked his first positive reaction. He didn't manage to build on it.

'Seriously, if you take a close look at my arse, you can still clearly see the wooden spoon mark. Felicity over there will tell you all about it, won't you babe?'

She turned bright red and cupped her head in her hands. When she looked up, her expression was livid, and I was sure that if there had been a wooden spoon handy, she'd gladly have gotten stuck into Harris's posterior then and there.

'Honestly, given how much Mum used to get into hitting us as children, I'm surprised she doesn't ask her judges to sentence the crims to a good hard thrashing. Which she'd be happy to deliver to the guilty parties herself, maybe dressed in leather dominatrix gear. You'd like that, wouldn't you Mum?'

Mrs Barnes didn't look any more pleased than her husband had, especially when he started to snigger.

'I don't know what he's talking about,' Emily whispered. 'She never hit us.'

'Shh,' I replied. 'I don't want to miss a moment of this.'

But I would've been well advised to, given what came next.

'I know I've suffered a great deal at her hands, so it's no wonder I'm attracted to hard-arse lawyers like Felicity. I think it's called Stockholm Syndrome. And yes, the little lady over there has asked to borrow Mum's wooden spoon. The upside though folks, is that she looks great in a leather catsuit. Miaow!'

I couldn't help laughing out loud at how extravagantly bad that joke was, earning me my own laser-beam stare from Felicity.

'But I haven't suffered the most, oh no,' he said. 'The biggest victim of my parents' cruel regime has definitely been Emily over there.'

His target blushed and gripped the table, bracing herself.

'She's been so brutalised that she's had trouble forming normal relationships with the opposite sex, I'm afraid to say. So it's no wonder she was an easy victim for an older sexual predator. And on that note everyone, say a big hello to her new boyfriend Paul!'

Emily seemed on the verge of tears but I decided the best course of action was to play along. So I got up and took a bow, earning a laugh or two.

'Ladies and gentlemen, give it up for Harris Barnes!' I said, and started applauding. 'He'll be here all week,' I continued. 'Because he'll be locked in his room.'

He tried to go on, and I cut him off again.

'Mrs Barnes, I understand you've never *actually* hit your son. Might be time to give it a try, eh?' I sat down, and earned a smattering of my own applause.

The room's disapproval clear, Harris tried to reel it back in.

'Like Paul was suggesting, of course, none of what I just said is true. Well, except the stuff about him.' He laughed, alone.

'Keep going, Harry,' I shouted. 'You're nailing it.' Which got another laugh. He glared briefly at me, and then resumed.

'See, I just thought it was time someone making a speech tonight said something *bad* about my parents. And the stuff I said was all ridiculous, of course, because you *can't* say anything bad about them. They're just amazing people. An inspiration to so many of us, and they've set a yardstick Emily and I will never live up to –'

'Speak for yourself!' she heckled, now emboldened.

'So, Mum, Dad, congrats on the anniversary. Best wishes for thirty more fantastic years together. And seriously, any-time you guys want to start being a whole lot less amazing, your kids'll thank you.'

This time he got a bit of applause, and beamed, evidently thinking he'd hit it out of the park.

'Bloody hell, I should've agreed to make a speech,' Emily said, loudly enough for the adjacent tables to hear. 'Harry's was a shocker.'

Harris embraced his parents with an air that seemed a touch forced, and then waltzed back to the table, high-fiving his homies as he strolled to his seat. But when he reached Felicity, she suddenly stood up and slapped him hard on the face. He recoiled in shock, and sat down heavily while Felicity grabbed her handbag and hotfooted it for the exit, leaving a stream of surprised oldies in her wake. She could move surprisingly quickly in those heels.

I turned to Emily and muttered that I'd better follow her. She nodded, so I headed for the door as well.

She was stamping fiercely down the driveway, her spiked heels affording considerably reduced traction on the uneven bricks. As I ran towards her, she stumbled as she caught her heel in the gap between some pavers, swore and clutched her ankle. I lent her a steadying arm.

'Thanks Paul,' she said. 'I'm leaving.'

'Yeah, I gathered that. Can I help you hobble?'

'Yes. Fuck, it hurts in these stupid shoes. I think my pride hurts more, mind you.'

'I take it you weren't a huge fan of the speech, then?'

'He is such a prick.' Ah, that was good to hear. '*Prick*.'

'I'm not gonna argue with you, Flea. It was pretty nice of you to even come, to be honest.'

She turned to face me. 'You were funny in there Paul. I wish I could have laughed it off so easily.'

'Oh, I was pretty embarrassed too. I hadn't expected our activities to be announced over the PA.'

'Well, you shouldn't stay either then,' she said, smiling. 'Come and get a drink with me to take our minds off this crazy family.'

I frowned. 'I'd love to get out of here, believe me. But I'm not sure that would be fair to Em.'

'Well, it's up to you, but I reckon you've done more than enough. She's got her posse here, and if you really *want* to, you can hook up with her later in the city – she said she was going out afterwards. And people are going to start leaving shortly anyway, I reckon.'

'OK, you've twisted my arm,' I said, pretending I'd been in any doubt. 'Give me a couple of minutes, though – I'd better go and say my goodbyes.'

'All right, I'll just go sit in the car. Don't take too long though. I'm desperate to be out of this stupid suburb.'

'The preferred term is "village".'

'Huh?'

'Don't worry.'

We'd almost reached her car by now, and her ankle had

just about recovered, so she sent me back into the house. I regretted giving up her arm – I'd enjoyed the physical contact. But perhaps there'd be scope for more of that later.

#16

★ ESCAPE ★
ENRIQUE IGLESIAS (2001)

I sprinted back to the house and quickly found Emily. People had started leaving their tables and mingling, so it was easy to grab her for a moment.

'Hey Em, I think I'm going to take off. Felicity's driving, and it's an expensive cab fare, so I figure I should grab a lift . . .'

'OK, but that's not why you're leaving really, is it? Be honest.'

I tensed a little at this.

'It's my brother, isn't it?'

And I relaxed again.

'Yeah, and I don't know many people here, either. But if you want to meet up later, text me or something.'

'Sure. You've done your dash. And Mum

just came over to check I was OK, and she thought you were funny. So hey – both parents are onside!'

'Good to hear.'

'Probably more onside than you'd be comfortable with, actually,' she said, grinning. 'Mum told me she thought you were quite a catch.'

'Little does she know.'

'You are,' she said, and kissed me quickly on the cheek. 'You're just about the sweetest dirty old man I know.'

'By tonight's standards, I'll take that as the highest of compliments.'

'I think my parents would appreciate it if you said goodbye. If you don't mind.'

'Sure, Em.'

I kissed her farewell again, just for good measure, and then strode off in search of her parents. One would suffice, so I searched the room for her father. But Emily's mother found me instead.

'Paul, I believe?'

'Mrs Barnes. Pleasure to meet you.'

'The pleasure's very much mine, actually. I did enjoy your suggestion for my reprobate son.'

'Oh, it was all a bit of fun.'

'I'm not entirely sure you're right,' she said, frowning. 'He and I are going to be having quite a long chat in the near future, although I hope I won't have to resort to violence. No, that was a mean thing he did to Emily, and as for me and my husband – well, it wasn't in the best of taste. But I won't go into that.'

I laughed, a little nervously.

'Thanks for coming, it meant a lot to Emily. She's rather

fond of you, you know.' And she fixed me with a stern prosecutorial eye. 'I do hope it's mutual.'

'Of course it is,' I said, only slightly stammering. 'She's great.'

'Harris's poor attempts at humour aside, she is young, Paul,' she said. 'And a bit vulnerable just now, so I hope you'll bear that in mind. She's had some shocking boyfriends, to be frank. You're the only evidence we've yet seen that she might be growing out of the rugger-buggers.'

'Believe me, I've no intention of hurting Emily, if that's what you mean,' I said, wondering whether leaving with Felicity would make me a hypocrite almost instantly.

'Sorry to give you the third degree, but grilling Emily's boys is something of a hobby of mine.'

'No problem,' I said.

'All right, well, I've bullied you enough,' she said. 'Which was a little unfair of me after the treatment you've already had from some members of this family, I know. But I'm quite protective of my daughter. Or "interfering", as she calls it.'

'I couldn't possibly comment,' I said, grinning. 'Actually, I wanted to thank you for having me. I'm afraid I've got to leave.'

'You work with Felicity, I understand,' she said. 'I'm concerned about my son's crassness. I hope she'll be OK about it all.'

'Yes. I'm going to get a lift with her, actually. I have to say, she's a little upset.'

'I'm glad she'll have a friendly face in the car,' she said. 'Well, I won't detain you any longer.'

'Thanks again. I'm sure she'll be fine.'

'You might mention to her that I'll be having stern words with my son about some of his – humour choices,' she said.

'Sure, I'll pass that on.'

'Paul, I do hope we'll see you again,' she said. 'I might have Emily invite you to dine with us sometime, if that's amenable. Without our son, I think.'

I wasn't eager to spend too much more time in a world where grabbing a bite was described as "to dine", but I appreciated the gesture.

'It's very kind of you to offer,' I said, politely yet non-committally; after all, she wasn't the only lawyer in the conversation.

Released from the dock, I bolted for the door, fending off Leon's attempts to engage me in a little chat about how 'fucken funny Harry's speech was, eh?'

'One word,' I replied. 'Awesome.' I knew that for him, it was the highest of praise.

As I passed my security-guard buddy, I couldn't resist bidding him farewell in a Wodehousian style that befitted the surroundings.

'There's a fiver on the dresser, Jeeves. Collar the lot, eh? Pip pip.'

He snorted derisively and started to say something, but I was already out the door and breathing a sigh of relief. Harris could publicly humiliate me anytime if it got me an early mark from a dinner like that.

But my getaway wasn't quite as clean as I'd hoped. I was halfway down the driveway when I heard someone bellowing my name. I didn't need to turn around to recognise the abrasive sound as Harris's voice.

'Where the fuck do you think you're going?' he enquired somewhat impolitely. Nevertheless, I felt I'd navigated the treacherous Barnes shoals fairly successfully so far, and I was disinclined to buy into any confrontation. So I retained my Bertie Wooster cheer in replying.

'Home, old thing.'

'I bet you think you did pretty well in there, hey? You fucking cocksucker.'

His tone wasn't quite as gentlemanly as I might have liked.

'Look mate, no hard feelings, OK? I was only trying to stick up for Emily.'

'Oh, aren't you the fucking hero. You fucking smartarse, trying to turn the rest of my family against me in our own fucking home. Who the fuck do you think you are?'

The lack of variety in his vocabulary was no doubt thanks to the well-stocked bar his parents had provided, and I began to suspect it wasn't going to be easy to defuse the situation.

'Hey, just a second. You're the one who made that speech. If your family's pissed off with you, it's got bugger all to do with me.'

'Bullshit,' he spat. 'From the second you walked in there you were trying to make me look bad in front of my dad with that "oh-I'm-a-lawyer-now" crap. I'll tell my parents what a fucking worm you really are. You won't get within a hundred metres of Emily when I've finished.'

By this point, he was literally shouting in my face and more than a little spittle had made its way onto my cheek. Being several inches taller, and now angry, I pushed him away.

'Do your fucking worst,' I replied, making a late entry to the swearing competition. 'Emily only invited me because you teased her in the first place, you stupid prick. I don't give a toss who your family is, and if I never see any of you again, I'll be delighted.' And I resumed my march down the driveway.

'I'll tell Emily you said that,' he replied smugly, feeling he'd scored a major point. I kept walking. 'Forget about getting any more action with my sister.'

And it was then, probably because I was annoyed with myself for taking his bait, that I made a significant tactical error and turned back to face him.

'Whatever, buddy,' I said. 'Oh, and in case you hadn't realised, I'm leaving with Felicity. It seems she prefers my company to yours all of a sudden.'

I'd been well on the way to making a smooth exit but this piece of information enraged him, and he charged down the driveway after me.

At this point, I was angry enough to stand and fight. Breaking his nose, I was thinking, would be a good option. But then I figured there'd be minimal upside for me, and perhaps the prospect of an assault charge from the couple who, as annoyed with him as they were, were nevertheless his parents. And there was also the fact that despite my height advantage, his build was considerably bigger than mine. So I sprinted down the driveway myself. He abandoned the pursuit after thirty seconds or so, and stood his ground shouting more obscenities from what had already been revealed as a fairly limited repertoire.

My tactical retreat had succeeded, and without involving any of the other Barneses. So, whistling The Clash's 'I Fought The Law', I wandered back to take Felicity up on that lift.

#15

★ WALKING ON SUNSHINE ★
KATRINA AND THE WAVES (1985)

The car ride was a pleasure, and not just because we were escaping from Wahroonga. Felicity and I had never talked so easily. Hanging shit on Harris definitely helped to forge a sense of camaraderie.

Felicity kept clarifying, 'just for the record', that she had never had the pleasure of viewing Harris's posterior, let alone paddling it with a wooden spoon. For my own entertainment I refused to accept it, insisting I approved.

'You don't need to defend yourself to me,' I said. 'I've got no right to pass judgement when it comes to Barnes liaisons.'

'But nothing happened. At least, nothing that involved bare arses. OK?'

'I am a man of the world. And I don't care

what you guys did. Catsuit or no catsuit, it's all the same to me.'

'How many times do I have to tell you, there was no catsuit!'

'Really, I'm cool with the catsuit. In fact, if you *don't* own a catsuit, I'll be disappointed.'

'He made the whole thing up!'

'OK, OK, I'll believe you –'

'Thank *god*!'

'If you just say "Miaow" for me. Just once.'

'Jesus, Paul, would you stop it!' she laughed, and punched me in the arm.

'I'm not the one keeping this topic going! It makes no difference to me.'

'Well, it makes a *lot* of difference to me. And it'll make a lot of difference when I go into work on Monday and everyone keeps saying "Miaow".'

'And making little cat ears, like this.' I wedged my index fingers behind my ears and waggled them.

'Yes! So please, can we put a lid on this? I don't want you to tell anyone about it.'

'Geez, don't get your whiskers in a tangle.'

'You know what it's like at MJ,' she said, pushing the buzzer that raised the gate of her building's ritzy underground carpark. 'It's harder for women.'

'Yeah, it's harder for women, fair enough. The sexist prick quotient is high in there. But has it ever occurred to you that maybe if you were a little bit relaxed about the possibility that, in the privacy of your own home, catsuits might occasionally come into play, your reputation would be all the more enhanced?'

She pulled into her car space with a screech, unbuckled and turned to face me, perplexed.

'I don't get what you mean.'

'At the moment, the word at MJ is that you're unattainable. Well, other than to Harris.'

'Would you quit that?' she said, and punched me again, this time crossing the line between 'endearingly cute' and 'likely to leave a bruise'.

'Listen, I'm actually trying to say something here. The guys at work, they're dorks at heart. You're one of the hottest girls in there –'

'Really?'

'Don't bat your eyelids at me. You must've noticed how men flip over you.'

'*Really*?' she cooed, batting them all the harder, and then couldn't sustain it and burst out laughing.

'So because they can't get you, because no one there can, they gossip about you as a way of trying to drag you down. And you're so defensive about the whole thing that it works. You should be a bit more Angelina Jolie about it, use your awesome sexual power or something. Have them thinking that sure, you're probably a total tigress, but they haven't got Buckley's of finding out.'

'Hang on,' she said, with a grin that bordered on evil. 'Is this genuinely helpful advice, or is this some tricky Paul Johnson pretending-to-be-a-nice-guy way of getting me to invite you in for a drink so I can *practise* being a bit less unattainable?'

'Um,' I said, my attempt at suaveness abandoning me as soon as she called me on it. 'A little from column A, a little from column B?'

'Ah, let's not kid ourselves,' she said. 'We're already in

my building. Of course you're coming up – it'd be rude otherwise, right? For a *drink*, anyway.'

'Fair enough,' I said. 'And you're already working the tigress thing, you know. Bringing a poor young innocent thing like me into your dark underground lair.'

'Oh really?' she said. 'I could do anything to you and no one would be any the wiser, would they?'

'Uh, well, people saw us leave together,' I said, feigning panic. 'A Crown prosecutor, even.'

She leaned over, grabbed my chin with her hand and pulled my face towards hers. Wow.

'Well, I'd better watch myself then, hadn't I?' she whispered seductively, and then pushed my face away as she dissolved into laughter.

'I don't think I'm the black widow type, babe,' she continued.

'Of course you aren't. That dominatrix thing of Harris's was way off. At least I hope it was since I'm currently in what may well turn out to be your dungeon.'

'Perhaps you'll find youself in a position to correct him,' she said, and got out of the car, laughing at me some more. 'Or perhaps you *won't* be, but will correct him anyway. That'd be a very boy thing to do.'

'Nah,' I said as I got out myself. 'He wouldn't buy it. Harry knows that little old me wouldn't have a shot with you while there's a quality catch like him in the picture.' And I laughed heartily myself. 'That's why you barred me at the Strand, remember?'

We were in the elevator now and she leaned back against the mirrored wall, looking a touch sheepish.

'I didn't think you were interested,' she said.

'No, you didn't think I was interes*ting*,' I said. 'And I

don't blame you. I was shy, I had nothing that night.'

'For me, anyway!'

'That's true. Others were – well, I'm not sure if it was more or less discerning, really.'

'Yeah, that's the thing though. The guys who initially come over as all attractive and confident are sometimes that way for a reason,' she said. 'In Harris's case, I've recently discovered, there's a fine line between "cocky" and "cock".'

'Oh, you've learned to appreciate the nervous ones, have you?' I laughed. 'To give the wallflowers a chance? Very decent of you.'

'Some of them,' she said. 'Sometimes you find a wallflower grows on you.'

'On you, eh?' I said.

'Maybe.'

We continued in this cheesily flirty vein for some time. I settled into the embrace of her sumptuous, spotless sofa while she opened a bottle of champagne and loaded some smooth jazz compilation into an expensive-looking hi-fi. Sure, there was altogether too much soprano sax in the mix for my taste, to the verge of sounding like one of Kenny G's infamous *Songs In The Key Of G*, but I decided not to comment on it. I have learned *some* things in my years on this planet.

It seemed I'd learned more than I thought. We didn't stop joking the whole time, even when my arm gradually snaked around her and she leaned in and put her head on my shoulder. I started stroking her hair, and I knew then that finally, I'd kiss her.

And I wasn't nervous at all, like I had been when I'd first talked to her. I was just – myself. I was talking as easily as if I was chatting to Nige. No, that's a totally inappropriate analogy. Truth be told, it occurred to me that the situation was a bit more like being with Zoë.

And I wished Zoë hadn't popped into my head. After not thinking about her all night, I suddenly found myself wondering how on earth I'd explain this new liaison to her. She'd always been dead against Felicity, but that wasn't the issue. She'd advise me to clear the air with Emily first, especially since her brother had been so keen on Felicity. Even though I didn't feel we were serious about each other, it'd be a little thoughtless to start something with another girl on the night I'd been presented to her parents as her boyfriend. Even though technically it wasn't, it still felt a little like two-timing.

And so I gently disentangled myself from Felicity and her sofa, and said I needed to go to the bathroom. Which gave me a moment to think. I'd spent my life judging men who play games with women, saying I'd never do that, when the truth was that I'd simply never had the opportunity to be that guy. I wasn't sure how Emily would react – probably with indifference. But until I knew, I should play it safe, especially given her parents. And if Harris found out I'd been with Felicity, he'd definitely tell them and make Emily's situation awkward all over again. My resolve only firmed when I pulled out my phone and found that Emily had texted me, asking what I was doing. Like I'd asked her to.

I couldn't go on with this – rightly or wrongly, I'd feel too guilty. So I went back out, my awkwardness returning with a vengeance, and said I ought to go.

'Why?' she asked, surprised.

'Look Flea, I really like you, OK? But I need to sort things out with Emily.'

'Um,' she said. 'I thought that was pretty casual.'

'It is, between us,' I said. 'But her parents think we're going out, and her mum invited me to dinner, so it's not the best form to be here with you right now.'

'Do you have feelings for her?'

'No, it's never been anything serious. But I don't want to do something with another girl right when I should probably still be out with her. She'd think I was a jerk, and I don't want that to happen.'

'Yeah, that makes sense, I guess. Forgive me if I don't extend the same consideration to her brother, what with him embarrassing me in front of half the Sydney law world.'

'God, of course not. The jerk in *that* scenario is one hundred per cent Harris. But let me make sure things are tied off with Emily and then – well, I'd like to see you again. You know, for dinner or whatever.'

'I'm going to interpret this as you being a nice guy rather than not interested. Is that on the level? Because if you're not, you know, now'd be a good time to say so.'

'Interested. Really. Just – not tonight.'

'Well, the MJ party's on in two weeks,' she said. 'Is that enough time for your scruples?'

'Yeah, good idea,' I said, and kissed her goodbye. Platonically.

#14

★ TIME AFTER TIME ★
CYNDI LAUPER (1984)

It wasn't easy to drag myself away, and as I stepped out onto the footpath, I felt virtuous but deflated. At a quarter past ten on Saturday night, a time that always reminds me of a Cure song, Darlinghurst brimmed with potential. Muffled music hinted at awesome house parties lurking behind the door of every second terrace, if only I had an invitation and a six-pack of VB stubbies to chuck in the scungy, ice-filled bath.

Oh, and if only I wasn't in a suit.

It was too early to call an end to the best night of the week but I didn't have a whole lot of options. I rang Emily who said that she and her friends had gone to the Greengate pub just down the road from her parents' place, if I wanted to tag along, but acknowledged

I probably wouldn't. I told her I was already on the other side of the Bridge and would probably hook up with Nige. But his phone was off, and experience showed that I wouldn't want to know why.

So I tried Zoë. It turned out Josh was out drinking with 'the boys' and she was curled up on the sofa, reading a novel. I told her she had to come out, and it'd be great if she could spruce herself up because I was in a suit. She said she would join me, but in her trackies to draw attention to how ridiculous I was for dressing like a toff on a Saturday night. And that was certainly how I felt as I sat and waited at Bill & Toni's, with its pinball machines, menagerie of indie band posters and artworks that some local paintslinger had long since abandoned all hope of selling.

I almost didn't notice her when she walked in half an hour later, wearing a smart black dress and makeup.

'Paolo,' she said.

'Dude,' I replied. Which always seemed a wonderfully inappropriate word to call Zo, which was why I regularly did. 'I'm not Marco. I'm not going to offer you a free coffee just because you pull out a little bit of *la lingua Italiana*.'

'No, you're going to offer me a free coffee because, against my better judgement, I've hauled my arse out to come and meet you,' she said. '*And* a scoop of tiramisu gelato.'

'OK, fair enough,' I said. 'Since you dressed up and everything.'

'Oh, I have an ulterior motive, actually,' she said. 'You know how I'm always on at you about going out for cocktails and you always blow me off? Well, guess what?'

'Um, I'm going to need to ring and raise the limit on my credit card?'

'Correct. Since one of us is on a fat corporate salary and is already working the five days a week that the other one of us so wisely predicted. That other one, incidentally, is slaving away on a part-time university wage.'

'Socialist.'

'Enough with the compliments. I believe I requested tiramisu?' And she clapped her hands twice.

I shook my head. 'And to think Josh opted for male company.'

'I'm surprised you didn't meet up with them, actually. He wound up in that pub near your place that Nige likes – what's it called, The Oaks?'

I shook my head and slumped my shoulders in ironic disappointment before heading to the counter.

★ ★ ★

For someone who retains a certain fondness for the word 'socialist', Zoë sure knows her expensive cocktail bars. She directed the cab to Darling Harbour and sashayed easily past a snooty doorman, and we found ourselves in a bar called the Loft. The place has a Moroccan theme, and she ordered us some blended fig concoction that I knew would taste delicious right up until I signed off on the bar tab. We settled into a pair of plush leather armchairs on a beautiful balcony overlooking the water. Reflected in the gentle undulations of the inky harbour, even the casino lights opposite were pretty.

Before long, she was signalling to the waiter for a second round of daiquiris. We were flying, and we'd only been there for half an hour.

'I don't expect you to buy all the drinks, by the way,' she said. 'I was kidding.'

'No you weren't,' I said.

'OK, so I wasn't. But give me credit for feeling slightly guilty about it now.'

'I know it's penance. That's quite all right.'

'I'm glad you see it that way. Perhaps you could convince Josh of the same principle? He's neglected me in favour of work for far longer than you have. And let's face it, he's got a much bigger bank balance as well.'

'I'll do no such thing. He dotes on you more than enough as it is.'

'Of course he does. I deserve it,' she said, and curled up on her chair, contentedly tucking her legs underneath her. 'Let's do something else out of the ordinary, shall we? Since we're already drinking somewhere *I* like for once.'

'That's fine,' I said. 'Can I get my credit card back from behind the bar? Because I'm worried they'll break it.'

'No, no. Nothing like that. In fact, I insist you keep it there: we'll need it for more of those banana-fig thingies. No, I was thinking of *me* asking *you* for relationship advice for a change.'

'Happy to, but you know my experience of these things is pretty much theoretical, don't you?'

'That never stopped you before, babe. You're a guy, and that's all that's required at this point. Tell me: how would you react if I asked you to marry me?'

Boy, the cocktails were more potent than I'd realised. Presumably she hadn't meant that sentence to come out quite so ambiguously.

'I'd definitely suggest we tried dating first.'

She collapsed into her armchair giggling. And I sat and watched until she rejoined me.

'Oh, you're so sensible Paulie. That's great. But I just meant – as a guy.'

'Do you mean as a generic guy, how would I feel about being proposed to by you? Or are you asking about how Josh'd react?'

'Well yeah, he is kind of the leading candidate, what with us living together and everything. But don't worry babe, you're totally in the top ten.'

'Cheers.'

'Well, more like the top twenty. But you're definitely on the list.'

'Are you asking me how'd he feel about the *idea* of marrying you, or how'd he react if you asked?'

'Oh god, they've made you such a lawyer already, what with all this clarifying the question stuff. The latter. I don't see why it always has to be the guy who pops the question.'

'Speaking as a representative of the class "wussy men", I'm a big fan of the woman proposing thing. But Josh – well, I've got to be honest with you, I think he's an old-school kind of guy.'

She frowned a little. 'I guess you're right. And I think it's sweet that he's like that. But I dunno, I've just been thinking it might be time. I mean, we've been together for ages and I can't imagine things any other way. You know? I guess I'm just *there*.'

'That's great,' I said, trying to smooth away my slight feeling of shock. 'And I've no doubt he is as well. He probably just wants to plan some whole horse-and-carriage, release-a-hundred-white-doves kind of moment. You know, to make it perfect.'

'But do you think he's *thinking* about it, at least?'

My friendship with Josh was more cordial than close, and I'd never really talked to him about Zoë. But surely he wouldn't be foolish enough to think he could find someone better – no one in their right mind would let her get away. The question I had, to be honest, was whether Josh was good enough for Zoë. And that was an issue I definitely couldn't raise. So I opted for a non-committal response.

'I'm sure it's crossed his mind after so long together, Zo. But I assume you've talked about it?'

'Oh, we've touched on it here and there, and we both want to marry someone, sometime. Like, you know, in the next five years. But you know how easily guys get freaked out if you start getting into all that before they've had time to get used to the idea.'

As we talked more about the idea of marriage, our conversation predicated on the easy assumption of their togetherness, the casual assuredness about her future that was Zoë's dividend from the years she'd invested in Josh, I realised I had no way of relating to what she was talking about. Even though she'd asked me for advice, I had no right to give it. I kept waiting for the penny to drop, and for Zoë to say, 'Hang on a sec, I've just realised – you don't have a clue what you're talking about, do you?' To which I'd have no alternative but to laugh embarrassedly and say, 'No, no I don't.'

But hey, I'm good with the theoretical, at least. And even though I was making it up as I went along, I think I gave her helpful advice about how to wrangle Josh, about taking it slowly, about subtly pushing him towards it in a way that made him think it was his idea.

Zoë ran me through her beautifully ordered plans for her beautifully ordered future with Josh. What age to have children, how many to have, where they'd live. She'd mapped it all out, the plan would work, and she knew it. And Josh would take the kids to soccer practice, and grumble good-naturedly as he paid the bills that would scarcely make a dent in his broker's salary, and Zoë would expertly juggle her career and the children nipping at her ankles. She'd never spilled all this stuff before, and I was initially surprised at the conventionality of her aspirations. But then I came to realise it was just that she knew what would make her happy – conventional or otherwise. And all the while, in the back of my mind I couldn't help contrasting her plans with the blankness of my own romantic future.

Zoë and I sometimes lose track of time when we talk. Two-and-a-half hours passed without us even noticing, and I'm sure we could have kept going for several more. But she was yawning, and I'd had my fill of hearing about her perfect future with Josh. Plus, the whole thing still felt a bit too date-like for me to be completely comfortable, even though we'd spent the entire night talking about her boyfriend. So I liberated my credit card from behind the bar in return for a sizeable ransom. And as Zoë dozed contentedly beside me in the back of the cab, I called her intended husband and got no reply. I did get onto Nige though, but he was scarcely comprehensible, and not just because of the noise of the pub. 'Josh who?' he kept asking. 'Where?' And then he'd piss himself laughing.

After a few rounds of this, I decided that my sleepy cargo would be better off at home than meeting up with whatever mess I'd heard on the other end of the line. So I told the cabbie to wait while I helped her through the door with one arm and fished for keys in her handbag with the other. I deposited her gently on the sofa just inside the door of her terrace, and made a hasty retreat before the meter inflicted too much more damage on my credit card.

'Paul,' she said, lifting her head as I backed out the door. 'That really meant a lot, you know? I'm glad we did this.'

'Me too,' I said. 'Good night.'

'Don't get so busy that it's another month before we talk again, OK?'

'OK.'

'Do ya promise?'

I laughed. 'Sure, why not.'

'Cross your heart and hope to die?'

It was all sounding a touch primary school, but she'd had enough cocktails that she was within her rights to regress.

'Scout's honour, Zo. The cab's waiting, I'd better go.'

I mulled it over during the drive home. Of course it made perfect sense, it was the inevitable next step along her path, but it was just all a bit more concrete than I'd been expecting. And it only reminded me once more that I needed someone with whom I could plan my own cosy future. It wouldn't be Emily, but things had gone very well with Felicity that night – better than I'd have hoped. And I reached the disconcerting realisation that now, my performance at the Morphett's Christmas party actually mattered.

#13

★ I WANT YOU BACK ★
JACKSON 5 (1969)

Emily and I met for a coffee late the following week so I could explain that I didn't want even our casual arrangement to continue. I'd been expecting her to be a little disappointed now that her parents were onside, so I was a bit taken aback when she beat me to the punch. It turned out she'd run into her rugby-playing ex-boyfriend down at the pub after leaving her parents' party. And they'd been messaging each other on Facebook since that night. He seemed interested again, so they were going to hook up that weekend.

'My parents don't like him much,' she told me. 'But I do, so they'd better get used to it. Right now I'm the favourite child, so I may as well take advantage!'

She was excited about it and thought I'd understand, because even though it'd been nice, we didn't exactly have *heaps* in common. Well, at that moment we had more in common than she realised. But there was no need to tell her about my interest in Felicity, particularly when her brother would want to know about it. So I cut short her attempt to let me down gently by saying I'd also been thinking it probably wasn't a goer in the long term. We both breathed a sigh of relief and left it at that, vowing to keep in touch but knowing from experience that we probably wouldn't, and that that was fine.

Encouraged by how easy it had been to smooth things over with Emily, I decided to try and resolve a more difficult relationship – Phil. After a prolonged campaign of calling on his part, I really couldn't blow my old boss off any longer, so I caught up with him a few days later.

The P-Man wanted to meet for coffee, which came as a surprise. He wasn't exactly a latte sipper, our Philip – in fact, in the years I'd known him, we'd never had a drink together that wasn't beer. But he'd been insistent not only on a coffee, but on having it at a trendy café in Surry Hills, one of those former workers' suburbs whose little terrace houses have been usurped by the beautiful people. These days it's wall-to-wall designer homeware stores, art galleries and cafés whose signs are exclusively printed in lower case. Like bills – note the ultra-trendy lack of apostrophe – which is run by one of Sydney's most prominent celebrity chefs.

bills surry hills (it seems even more ostentatious to leave it uncapitalised at the start of a sentence, I reckon) is best known for its scrambled eggs. Which are very nice, but I'm not quite sure why they merited giving bill his own TV show. I mean, I boil a pretty mean egg myself, with toast cut up into soldiers and everything, but no one's sent a camera crew round to record my opinion on the correct use of polenta.

I sat at the communal table that was the place's trademark, reading the latest edition of *wallpaper** magazine, which rather overtrumped bill with its pretentious asterisk. No doubt bill wishes he'd thought of it first. I mean, thought of it first*.

When Phil came bowling over, I realised the man had made some changes. Not only was his trademark Peter Sterling-circa-1983 mullet gone but, to my astonishment, the moustache had vanished as well. It was as if he'd walked into the chic wood-lined space stark naked. He was also wearing notably trendier clothes: a well-tailored white shirt, shiny new trainers, and new-looking jeans. This creature bore only minimal resemblance to the Phil I'd known and mocked for so many years – for one thing, he belonged in this café. Fortunately, he hadn't discarded his affability the way he had his polyester wardrobe.

'You're an imposter,' I said. 'I'll give you whatever you want, just don't harm Phil.'

'Ha, you like the threads?'

'Mate, you're looking a million dollars. What's the story? Don't tell me you're paying my replacement even less than you paid me?'

'Nah, I just made a few changes. Or rather, Ange took me shopping. Did I tell you about Ange?'

'Believe me, I would definitely have remembered someone who wanted to remake your wardrobe. Who is this mysterious woman of taste?'

'Met her at a gig a month or two ago. She's in marketing – brand imaging, that sort of thing.'

'Brand imaging? I don't even know what that is.'

'You're looking at it, son. And that's what I want to talk to you about today.'

'Sure – but I'm not done with Ange yet. Tell me more. What gig was it?'

'A team-building night at Rockdale Bowls for one of her clients. We got talking, and something just clicked. I really make her laugh, she says.'

I could relate to that, and yet I'd managed to avoid sleeping with Phil. Clearly a lucky escape.

'It was amazing. That very night she invited me back to her apartment. She lives around here – in fact, she's the one who first took me to this joint. I've been staying mainly at hers, and it looks like we might even move in together. She's a bloody awesome bird, mate. Not quite sure what she sees in the old Philster, but hey, I'm not complaining!'

'Gee Phil, that warms the cockles of my heart,' I said – and what's more, I meant it. I'd never seen him this happy. Phil was talking like he couldn't believe his luck. And to be honest, neither could I.

'It's gettin' serious,' he said, with an appropriately sombre tone. 'I think she's the one.'

I leaned over the designer salt and pepper shakers and clapped him heartily on the back.

'Congrats, and I mean that. From one P-Man to another.'

After that, he wanted to know about my personal life, of course, and I tried not to be too annoyed at his well-intended but somewhat patronising suggestions, seeing as how he'd had his shit together for all of about five minutes. Still, I couldn't talk when it came to patronising Phil – I was just shocked to find it coming from the other direction.

His wisdom dispensed with, Phil got down to business.

'Ange hasn't just been remaking me, you know Paul. We've also been doing a lot of thinking about the business.'

This was promising. If she'd managed to make Phil look cool, turning the raggle-taggle MobyDisc mob into the funkiest DJ posse on the eastern seaboard would be a cinch.

'And we think that while MobyDisc has worked well so far, there's a whole other opportunity set that we might be able to capture.'

'Opportunity set'? This woman had made profound changes indeed.

'So Paul, I want to introduce you to our new concept – mDisc.'

And he pulled out a black sheet of paper with a stylised white line-drawing of a 1980s boombox and the word 'mDisc' in a slick, graffiti-style font. He'd dropped the 'Moby'? His finest comedic hour? This was almost too much change for me to handle.

'We figure that with a different brand, and most importantly a different playlist, we can go for some of the corporate event market. You know, soul, funk – a bit of rare groove. Maybe throw some electronica and hip hop into the mix. Take things more upmarket. And most importantly – no retro.'

Rare groove? Electronica? I hadn't realised he even knew those words.

'Wow Phil, it sounds exciting. But of course you'll still keep the MobyDisc brand, right?'

'Oh yeah. I'm not going to throw away fifteen years like that. And it suits me perfectly well, it's what I do, and Ange really values that. So I'm looking for someone to head up this new division. It's got to have a younger feel, something I can't deliver myself. And I thought of you. I want you to be my partner in this. You could select the playlist, develop the whole presentation style, train up some new guys, the whole thing.'

'Wow,' I said. This was a much more impressive pitch than I'd been expecting.

'And I'd offer you fifty per cent of the new business. I'll front up for all the equipment and the upside, we'd split down the middle. I want you with me on this mate. It'll be like old times, but with new music.'

Remarkable. It seems you can teach an old dog – or dawg, as I sometimes called him when we were doing that whole faux-rappers thing – new tricks. So what could I say, other than that I'd think about it, and it seemed like an excellent idea? And I meant it. Which was, like the name of that INXS song, rather a new sensation.

#12

I figured I should think carefully before I got back to Phil. Sure, compared to staying on the thirty-fifth floor until they carted away my suit-clad corpse, his offer was attractive. But Phil hadn't quite been offering the commitment-free casual work that my previous stint in the MobyGulag had involved. The mDisc plan would make me a partner in the business, and leave me owing a heap of responsibility to Phil. I wouldn't be able to simply walk away when I finally decided to start the next phase of my life. If I took up his offer, it would *become* the rest of my life, or at least a sizeable chunk of it.

And then, as I was mulling it over, Morphett's threw the decision into sharper relief.

Brent invited me into his office for a chat late one afternoon after I'd been at MJ just over three months, all but the first few weeks of which had been practically full-time. I was reassured to see that he had loosened his tie, indicating that I was going to be graced with his relatively friendly façade.

'So Paul,' he said. 'Three months, eh?'

'It's flown by.'

'Are you happy with how it's gone?'

A thorny question. Had I performed well, or not? And then there was the question of how I felt about being so thoroughly enveloped by the corporate cocoon. I decided to play it non-committally.

'I feel I've settled in quite well, and made a — reasonable contribution to all our projects.'

'We've been very happy with how you've performed — and it was in line with our expectations based on your previous time with us.'

'Glad to hear it.' And I was. If you're going to bust your gut doing something, you want recognition. And of course I wanted to feel that while I could take or leave the law, it would certainly rather take than leave me.

'But we've been very busy, and I know that as a result you've been working more than we'd discussed. Have you been OK with that?'

'Well, it wasn't what I was expecting. But I know that these things ebb and flow, often without much warning.'

'That's true, and we usually do a little better with our part-time employees. The new mothers in particular. It is OK to push back and say no sometimes, and I hope that's been clear.'

Well, it's not quite that easy, I thought to myself, when you haven't a baby-shaped pretext. It's not hard to get a reputation as a shirker.

'But it's raised a few issues internally, and that's what we need to discuss.'

'Oh.'

'First, I've got HR breathing down my neck because we haven't kept our deal with you.'

'Really? They're concerned about my hours?' I was touched.

'Well, yes. But not *just* because of your wellbeing, as it happens. It's raised a few resourcing questions.' And immediately I was un-touched again.

'In essence Paul, we've been paying you casual rates for what's been full-time work – even including overtime, which as you know isn't available to our salaried employees.'

This was true, and it always seemed unfair. Law firms bill for time – obsessively so, down to each tenth of an hour. If you put in fourteen billable hours in a day instead of the regulation seven, the firm gets to bill the client double, but you only get paid your standard rate. So the partners, who profit-share, have all the incentive in the world to push your billable hours as high as possible.

'Is it that much of an issue, Brent? I mean, you bill me out at much more an hour than you pay me.'

'Sure, but it's creating a little resentment. You aren't admitted, so you're technically a paralegal, and you've been taking home almost as much as our junior solicitors – in some weeks more.'

And as far as I was concerned, I'd bloody well earned it. But this was so typical of big firms, where everyone obsesses over whether anyone else is getting a better deal. I could just imagine some of the ambitious young lawyers on our floor sitting down with a scowl and a calculator to make the comparison.

'Yes, I can see how that might put a nose or two out of joint.'

'Then there's the fact that you've done great work for me Paul, and I'd really like to keep you on a more permanent basis.' Aw, shucks.

'So we'd like to offer you a full-time graduate solicitor position, starting immediately. We'll pay you while you do College of Law and get yourself admitted. You're doing real legal work so you really should be qualified. We see it as a win–win, because you'll end up with a higher rate, especially with the bonus component, and we'll be treating everyone consistently.'

A win–win unless, of course, I didn't want to tie myself quite so tightly to MJ.

Why was everyone wanting commitment all of a sudden? Couldn't they see that was the last thing I was capable of? Well, probably they could, which was why they were trying to force my hand.

Still, would being a graduate solicitor be so bad? Perhaps I should stop thinking I was above it. They were offering me a great job at a top firm, one a lot of people would want. And yet I couldn't help wincing a little as I thought about signing away my hopes of spending part of my week doing something for myself – something with music. Something that would enable me to have the life I really wanted. Sure, I hadn't had time to actually *do* any of that stuff yet, but that was only temporary. Wasn't it?

I told him I appreciated the offer but that I'd need to give it some careful thought before getting back to him. He laughed and said I couldn't put off deciding about my career forever.

I knew he was right. But I could try.

#11

★ DREAMER ★
SUPERTRAMP (1974)

I had told Brent I needed to consult my family, and I did – but not because I had any doubt what they'd say. Both parents were very much in favour of the Morphett's, or as my father put it, 'growing up' option.

'We know you've had a lovely time with all the music, dear,' my mother said as we chatted over Weet-Bix. 'And we understand it's cool, and that that's important to you.' Proving, by equating a business run by Phil with coolness, that she actually didn't understand at all.

'You can't sleep in all day forever, kiddo,' my dad said. 'It isn't good for you.'

I was tempted to ask them whether they thought it was good for their beloved Rolling Stones, whom they'd made a pilgrimage to see the year before, to sleep in all day until the age of ninety. Instead I pointed out that mDisc was a new business proposition so I'd actually be a partner. But they didn't buy it.

'I thought you hated working for Phil,' my mother said innocently but with a slight grin on her face. 'At least that's what you're always saying.'

'You should be grateful to Morphett's for giving you a way out,' my father added.

So that was two votes cast against a return to DJing. My next focus group session was with Nige over lunch, and I was hardly surprised that he felt the same way about the desirability of Morphett's. And not just, he hastened to add, because he'd get a recruiting bonus if I signed on the dotted line.

'They always pay it to the person who's done most to recruit you. You don't mind, do you? Because if I don't take it, it'll go to waste,' he said. 'I'll shout you a big night out with the cash, I promise. It'll be huge.'

There are times when Nige, for all his bluster and bravado, still seems like the kid in my primary school who wanted to invite everyone in the class to his birthday party. I don't think he's really capable of viewing things from my perspective, and giving me advice based on my own interests, but I don't resent him for it – it's just the way he is. If he is into something, everyone else has to be, or he'll start to worry. And I was flattered that he was so keen for me to come and work with him. As far as I was concerned, it was incomparably more bearable working at Morphett's with him there, and I liked that he felt the same way about my company.

Among my regular brains trust then, that left Zoë to consult. I knew what she'd say as well, but at least she'd articulate it in a way that would help me reach my own decision. We met for beef pho in a mid-city arcade.

As I laid out the options for her, she looked increasingly unimpressed. When I'd finished, she just shrugged her shoulders.

'Am I allowed to vote for neither option?' she asked.

'I'm not doing this on the basis of votes.'

'Why not? It'd work a whole lot better than leaving you to make the decision for yourself.'

'If we were voting, Morphett's would already have won 3-1.'

'Oh, come on. For one thing, Nige is recused from voting, he's got a financial interest.'

Law grads.

'Dammit, I'm awarding myself the casting vote, OK?' she continued, rather undemocratically. 'This is crazy stuff Paulie. Are you or are you not miserable working at Morphett's?'

'I wouldn't go so far as to –'

'Yes you are. I can tell. There's some weird masochism thing going on here, where you tell yourself you don't mind the work as a way of punishing yourself for not having gotten your shit together.'

I sighed. 'Let's say I don't love it. But it's a good job, and we don't get to follow our dreams forever.'

'What bullshit, Johnson. Name one step, *one* little step, you've taken towards your so-called dreams?'

'I can't.'

'Look, you're *free*. You're the least committed guy I know. You aren't even paying rent anywhere, for god's sake. You could get up tomorrow and move to an ashram on the steppes of the Himalayas and no one would blink.'

'I couldn't do that.'

'Why the hell not? Honestly, you could do *anything*. There's nothing tying you down at all.'

'Felicity would miss me,' I said, unsuccessfully trying to suppress my grin. Which ratcheted up Zoë's rant beyond what I'd previously believed to be the maximum.

'Oh Jesus, don't get me started on that subject. You aren't still pursuing that stuck-up little pants-suited poodle, surely? God, you are, aren't you? And that's what this whole Morphett's ridiculousness is all about. You're about to make the stupidest decision of your life so you can take a lick at that stick of human fairy-floss, am I right? I'm right.'

As I slurped my rice noodles, I could feel my cheeks turning almost as pink as the slices of beef in my bowl. Because it *had* occurred to me that cementing my place at Morphett's wouldn't exactly hinder my mission with Felicity.

'This is bullshit Paul,' she said, slamming down her chopsticks and glaring at me. 'The others won't call you on it, but *I* will. You'd hate to be a grad at Morphett's, and you'd *hate* to be with Felicity, and if I'm wrong about that, then best of luck – but you really aren't the person I thought you were.'

I sat there silently for a moment.

'I'm sorry to be so adamant, but I guess after so many years of hearing you talk, I'm playing your own words back at you. But like I said before, if this is what you want, *actually* what you want, then go for it. Just don't let them flatter you into it. Because if you go into a place like that without motivation, without sufficient passion to put in those hours and climb that ladder, it's not going to work. You'll be unhappy and you won't do well at it. That's all I'm saying.'

I nodded. That, undoubtedly, was good advice. But I wondered to myself why, if this was how she felt about these kinds of jobs, she hadn't taken this approach with Josh. The thought led me to purse my lips ever so slightly, and because I always seem to be an open book to Zoë in these kinds conversations, she was all over it.

'See, Josh is a good example, actually. He's really into the stockbroking thing. He loves the adrenaline of the market and he's hugely motivated. Sure, it may not be a world whose values I share, but I know it's hugely fulfilling for him so I respect it – and I think it's good for him. It makes him happy. But I know full well that if you did his job, it'd make you miserable – and of course the same goes for me.'

'Yeah, I see what you mean,' I said.

She softened her tone a little, realising I was feeling scalded.

'But I think you're asking the wrong questions,' she said gently. 'What you need to ask yourself, babe, is where you actually want to be. It's time you made a call. If you want to do music stuff, then now's the time to take a risk. It's only going to get harder as you get older, you know. When you have a mortgage, kids and all that, do you think it's going to be *easier* to put the rest of your life on hold and go touring around the country?'

I shook my head slowly.

'And, while I hate to twist the knife, I have to say this: can you see someone like Felicity agreeing to support you while you took leave to do that?'

'No,' I said huskily. I felt like an idiot. And worse, a hypocrite.

'OK,' I continued. 'So let's say I want to spend maybe three days a week on the music stuff, and maybe even go to a producing course or something. I found one where they teach you advanced-level Pro Tools, the recording software I've got. It sounds amazing. Isn't Morphett's quite a good match for that, if they really will cap my hours?'

'Maybe,' she said. 'But it's a question of focus. They'll get their thirty hours out of you, and then on the other days you'll probably just take it easy, won't you? If you want to do something creative, shouldn't it be the main thing you do? Otherwise – no offense – I think you'll spend more of your day getting RSI from your PlayStation. I hate to bring this up, but your plans to write a screenplay didn't exactly go anywhere, did they?'

I blushed a little. One night a few years ago when I'd had far too much to drink, I'd pitched Zo my million-dollar screenplay idea. It was part – or even mostly – a joke, but I had actually started writing it, just for the hell of it. Artistic credibility could wait, I'd said, my aim was for something super-trashy that could earn me as many bucks as possible. And my idea had been a Japanese-American cheerleader who was also a ninja. Her name was Yumi, and she was really popular on campus because she did all these ninja backflips in her cheer routines. Then her father would have been killed by a rival from Japan, and she'd have to leave UCLA and return to Japan to avenge him.

At the time Zoë had commented that she thought it was not so much a screenplay idea as a crude conjunction of two sexual fantasies; that she hated absolutely everything about it but that I should definitely write it because it would appeal to a hundred million other sexually frustrated overgrown adolescents like me and make a fortune. So supportive.

As she'd probably calculated, the reference to my masterpiece-in-waiting cheered me up enormously.

'I don't think you ever entirely comprehended the breadth of my vision there, Zo. You do realise that Yumi is both a cheerleader and a ninja?'

'Yeah.'

'Combined?'

'I ascertained as much when you gave it the title *Cheerleader Ninja*.'

'Zo, c'mon. Could you at least pretend to respect the idea by remembering its proper title? *Ninja Cheerleader* is so much catchier. Hey, I could write the soundtrack album for it, and get known as a musician that way.'

'Charlie Chaplin used to write his own movie scores,' she said. 'And you're an even bigger clown than he was.'

'Exactly.'

'And he liked the young girls too, didn't he? The resemblance is remarkable.'

'Marrying my cousin – now there's something to aspire to. But anyway, to get back to the subject: you really don't think Morphett's could fit in with the creative stuff?'

'Oh look, it potentially *could*. But to be frank – perhaps for someone more self-disciplined than you? Besides, really, there are easier ways to make the same money. DJing worked quite well with that, and at least it was actually to do with music.'

'So maybe I should try this business with Phil?'

'Well, it definitely beats the law thing. That is, like I was saying, if you actually believe in it.'

'And Phil could buy me out when I move to NYC to focus on my music career.'

'Sure, or you could buy him out with the profits from *Ninja Cheerleader*.'

'I don't think you understand just how amazing the movie could be, Zo. If you like both cheerleaders and ninjas, and the prospect of a girl who fuses both things in one sounds like an awesome idea –'

'Then you should probably be lobotomised.'

'Ah, you're just jealous because you have neither of Yumi's awesome skills. Whereas if I wrote *Activist Opera Singer*, you'd think it was awesome.'

She laughed, and asked for the bill. So, we had one vote for the Phil option – and from Zoë, of all people. She's had very little time for the man since his crude attempt to pick her up one night. The historical record differs on the point, but some scholars claim that while in an advanced state of intoxication, he asked Zo if she was interested in 'taking a moustache ride'. As you can imagine, Nige and I have had considerable difficulty letting that phrase go.

My shiny corporate tower was just beyond Zoë's ramshackle law school building, which retains some level of studenty charm despite boasting what must be the crappiest edifice in the entire CBD. The technical term for the architecture style is 'Brutalist', and that's being complimentary. Still, I'd always had a soft spot for the place where I'd earned a degree despite skipping most of my classes to play ping-pong.

We gave each other the obligatory quick peck on the cheek and she disappeared into her academic ivory tower. Well, pebblecrete tower, to be precise. My pace slowed as I strolled back towards another afternoon of intense contract reviewing.

As a further dawdling tactic, I grabbed a coffee from the foyer of our building and sat on one of the elegant benches to think about what Zoë had said. What I was doing was by no means bad. But I'd be settling, compromising, before I'd even seriously tried anything more creative. And to sign up for a decade or so with my nose at this particular grindstone would constitute an admission of defeat – of acknowledging I didn't have what it takes before I'd even found out.

Perhaps if I was genuinely supposed to make it as a musician, though, I'd have already done something? I'd have put up some quirky song on MySpace, like Lily Allen, and the word would have spread like wildfire until the record companies tracked me down to offer me multimillion-dollar advances. Now I was already too old to be the hot young thing.

It needed more thought, but I didn't have any more time for that. The contracts upstairs wouldn't review themselves. But I did make one decision as I wandered towards the lifts. I was going to hit Phil up for the gear I needed to play the Morphett's Christmas party, and give this whole upmarket mDisc concept a proper go with a crowd I thought would appreciate it. I'd put time into compiling a seriously excellent playlist, and then I'd dazzle them. So much so that if I wanted to leave and try the DJing business, Brent himself would understand why. Hell, even Felicity might.

#10

★ EYE OF THE TIGER ★
SURVIVOR (1982)

Phil, bless him, was enthusiastic about me borrowing the gear for an mDisc trial run. As he saw it, we were mates, despite the fact that I'd only ever hung out with him in a work context, and since I'd stopped working for him I'd seen him a grand total of twice. So the practical side of my big performance was easily sorted.

I couldn't say the same for the rest of the party planning though, after a quick coffee meeting with Felicity. While normally I'd have relished the one-on-one time, her level of stress made the experience less pleasurable than I'd hoped. It was the first time she'd put her hand up to help organise a 'firm-wide event', and she was even going to be up on stage introducing the managing partner for his Christmas thanks. She was going to make an impression on virtually everyone at the firm, and she wanted to make sure it was a good one. Subsequent to the meeting, in each of three frenetic phone calls to needlessly check some minor detail, she'd been at pains to stress that I would be playing a big part in that.

I started to wonder whether I mightn't be better off spending a carefree night drinking at Nige's table. But I couldn't say no to Felicity, especially as she'd pushed for me to get the gig despite the reservations of the other committee members who just wanted to hire a professional.

'I said, "Paul *is* a professional. Or was",' she'd told me. 'So don't let me down, OK?'

'I wouldn't dream of it,' I'd said. 'I've never been more prepared.'

And I hadn't. I spent an entire weekend finalising my selections, and even borrowed some proper decks so I could, for the first time in my DJing career, play stuff off vinyl. Yeah, that's right – I was kickin' it old school. Sure, most people wouldn't have noticed the difference, but I would, and that was reason enough to get it right.

The event itself mightn't have mattered much to me, but Felicity did – and so did the mDisc concept. I'd always maintained that it was possible to play music that people enjoyed because it was good instead of because it amused them to recall that, in some strange bygone era, the world had embraced Billy Ray Cyrus's 'Achy Breaky Heart'.

I'd put together a great selection. James Brown featured prominently – not the overexposed 'Sex Machine' and 'I Feel Good' but groovier tracks like 'Funky President', 'Funky Drummer' and Funky everything else. I had a bit of George Clinton, Sly and the Family Stone, and some Sharon

Jones. Hip hop was well-represented too – both the soulful end of the spectrum, meaning early De La Soul, A Tribe Called Quest, and stuff with more of a beat, like RUN-DMC and Public Enemy. Then, when I wanted to get a bit more electronic, I'd lined up Duran Duran, Depeche Mode and a bit of Chemical Brothers and The Prodigy in case things got raucous. I threw in some iconic rock for people to jump around to, as well – The Clash, some Stones and Bowie. Stuff that I figured everyone from partners to the most fresh-faced paralegals would enjoy. I'd even set aside a little Chet Baker and Coltrane for late in the night, if the mood fit. I was locked and loaded.

The selection, I felt, would finally show my true musical colours. I was aiming for eclectic credibility – kind of like a Tarantino soundtrack without the dialogue inserts. Recognisable but not clichéd. And as I set up on the night, meticulously organising my audio arsenal so I could switch moods at a moment's notice, I was confident. Like Felicity, I was going to make an impression all right. Come Monday morning, the entire firm would know that I had one hell of a good record collection. And before I triumphantly departed for greener pastures, I'd gladly accede to the managing partner's request for a mix CD.

The party was in the function space at the Museum of Contemporary Art, a beautiful Art Deco pile down by the harbour. The high ceilings and green marble floor gave it a refined, New Yorkish ambience I thought would work perfectly with my selections. It was the classiest venue I'd ever played at. Then again, most of my previous venues have pokies.

During the first few hours, as the room gradually filled with women in a huge variety of elaborate ballgowns and men in identical tuxedos, I stuck to the funk/soul stuff. Marvin Gaye, Al Green, that kind of thing. And I got a whole heap of compliments, particularly from some of the thirty-something lawyers who shimmied over to congratulate me on my taste. Even Felicity stopped by to give me a big grin and a thumbs up. Then she whispered in my ear that she hoped she was still seeing me later. I just smiled.

The caterers brought everyone their smoked salmon entrées and poached chicken mains. I swallowed mine quickly while I spun some jazz LPs, enjoying the unfamiliar feel of the vinyl in my hands. Julie London, Stan Getz and Nina Simone all got a workout over dinner as I went into background-music mode. Then, as the mains were cleared away, I faded out so they could start the presentations. We were scheduled for an hour of them, what with the platitudes from senior management, a few 'funny' corporate videos and a renowned performance by the MorphTones, the firm's very own *a cappella* group of private school refugees who'd never quite managed to leave the cloisters of their adolescence behind.

I figured the friendly neighbourhood disc-spinner could take a break, so I wandered over to Nige's table and sat down for what I assumed would be a session of sarcastic comments about whatever was happening onstage. But first, he couldn't resist commenting on my new musical repertoire.

'Dude, you've changed,' he said, poking me in the chest. 'What's all this refined shit? Where was Tina Turner? Olivia Newton-John? ABBA? You've forgotten your fans.'

'You know these people, it's too highbrow a crowd,' I told him. 'Felicity wanted me to keep things classy.'

He scoffed at me. 'Bollocks. At the rate people have been putting away the grog, they'll be wanting to jump around to

"Eye Of The Tiger" in no time.'

'No, I've got it all worked out,' I said. 'They'll jump around all right, but there's no way I'm playing "Eye Of The Tiger". In fact, the whole of Survivor's recording career is off-limits for tonight, I'm afraid.'

'*Was* there any more of Survivor's recording career?'

'I don't think so – their name did turn out fairly ironically.'

'I know you're the expert, but really – are you sure they'll be into stuff that isn't quite so retro?'

'Trust me.'

'I've heard the wanky music you play in your car, Jono. There's no way I trust you.'

Before I could reply, the corporate video started and suddenly Nige appeared on the screen in a dinner suit, parodying the classic 007 opening sequence.

'Oh shit,' he said. 'Go easy on me mate. It wasn't my idea.'

He'd mentioned something a few weeks earlier about being dragooned into helping with some video, but was very sketchy on the details. I was evidently about to see why.

'The name's Bond,' the onscreen Nige said. 'Claims Bond, 007 per cent. Solicitor Agent.'

And he rapidly pulled something out of a holster and held it out. The camera crash-zoomed in to show him brandishing a piece of paper marked 'SUBPOENA'.

'Was that *Claims* Bond?' I asked.

'It gets worse,' he mumbled.

And so it did, with elaborate titles showing Bond surrounded by a number of suit-wearing Morphett's women against a lava-lamp-style background. They were brandishing pens like revolvers and signing pieces of paper in what I imagine they thought were seductive poses. But whatever limp raunchiness they achieved evaporated when they overlayed the title: *Courtsino Royale*.

It continued in a similar vein for about ten unhilarious minutes, as Nige battled the evil forces of MECTRE – an awkward pun using the initials of a rival firm, Minter Ellison. Our firm's managing partner even made a cameo as 'M', which no doubt he was now regretting. Unlike much of the audience, I loved every minute of it, albeit ironically. There were several moments when I was the only person in the room laughing, like when the head of IT, who did a shocking job of impersonating 'Q', warned Bond about the addictive properties of CrackBerries. But what I enjoyed most of all was the absolute certainty that I'd be calling my good buddy Claims until at least the following Christmas.

The rest of the presentations were dull, although Nige and I managed to make them considerably more bearable by whispering to each other. 'M' himself got up to give his Christmas message, which annoyed me almost as much as the Queen's does. I kept thinking that a heartfelt thanks was the least our managing partner could do, since he had a hell of a lot more goodies under his tree than the rest of us and I didn't remember seeing him working back late to earn them.

And it occurred to me that if I didn't have much time for the boss, if I didn't aspire to be in that chair someday, then Morphett's really wasn't the place for me.

After dessert, formal dinners always become considerably more informal. Everyone's sucked down more than enough liquor to have stripped away their self-consciousness, so if you choose the right tracks you'll get a large proportion of the guests up and dancing, and if you keep the energy up, they'll stay there. I swore to myself that I'd keep the dancefloor literally jumping until the last guest was reluctantly ushered out into the night.

But as the waiters circulated with tea and coffee, getting the punters moving proved harder than I'd hoped. Aretha Franklin didn't do the trick, and nor did a great piece of electropop from the last Goldfrapp album. They even stayed in their seats for Herbie Hancock, and I'd been certain that with this kind of crowd, 'Watermelon Man' would be a surefire winner.

I was starting to worry. And so was Felicity, who came over to talk to me. Her frown was not exactly the response I'd been looking for.

'Uh, Paul,' she said, a little nervously. 'Personally I think this track is *super* cool, whatever it is — and the music's been excellent tonight. But people keep asking me when you're going to start playing stuff they can dance to, you know? And I thought the schedule said that after dessert —'

'It did. Sorry, I don't know why they aren't dancing. I figured this'd be perfect for the MJ crowd . . .'

'Sure. I don't want to tell you how to do your job, I know you're really experienced, but —'

'You want to tell me how to do my job.'

'Um, a little bit. Look, I can't quite believe it, but you know how when we first met, you'd been playing Bryan Adams and stuff?'

'You want Bryan Adams? Really?'

'No. Not him specifically — but just, you know — something that's a bit more accessible? Something fun?'

'OK, I'll see what I can do.'

And, though the idea made me wince, I knew she was right. I'd made a massive miscalculation. These people may have been high-paid lawyers by day, and for a classy dinner party, my choices would have been ideal. But after drinking themselves silly on the firm's tab, they didn't want to be impressed by my taste in music. They wanted stuff they could sing along with. But I didn't have any of the regular MobyDisc CDs. I hadn't even brought any CD players, since I'd been relying on vinyl and the contents of my iPod.

Fortunately, I had a few albums on the MP3 player that might serve. I quickly dialled up Justin Timberlake's 'Rock Your Body', and crossfaded from the vinyl to the iPod. When JT's first few chords rang out across the room, people cheered, and Felicity boogied over in excitement to give me an enthusiastic thumbs up.

She and Nige were right. This was no place for my careful selections, it was a MobyDisc gig like any other. And I was woefully underprepared. I flipped through the rest of my iPod and began to despair. I had very little that was suitable. What good were the loungey likes of Stereolab here? If I was having an elegant cocktail party at my bachelor pad – in the event I ever actually got one – then they'd have been perfect. But this event was a million miles removed from that, and I had been foolish not to realise it.

I felt humbled. And then shuddered as I realised just how humble I was going to need to be. I was going to have to make a mayday call – to Phil.

#9

★ YOU CAN'T STOP THE MUSIC ★
VILLAGE PEOPLE (1980)

I frantically whizzed around the scroll wheel on my iPod, trying to choose a few more tracks that might work on the dancefloor so I could duck outside. Kanye West's 'Gold Digger' would work, and I thanked my Lucky Star that I had Madonna's *Immaculate Collection*. I locked in Gnarls Barkley's 'Crazy' and Joy Division's 'Love Will Tear Us Apart' as well. And then, with about ten minutes' breathing space, I stepped onto the balcony to call Phil, desperately hoping for once that he had his phone on. Fortunately he answered almost immediately.

'Paulie!' he shouted over background noise so raucous that my heart immediately sank because I could tell he was mid-gig and unable to come down and bail me out. 'Ringing to tell me the new music's knocking the lawyers dead, hey?'

'Not exactly. I've got a problem.'

'Gear playing up, is it?'

'No – look, I got it wrong. Turns out the lawyers want to have a good time jumping around to Madonna. And I don't have the right stuff.'

'Geez, who knew? I thought your tunes'd go down a treat.'

'Yeah, well, they aren't – and it's kind of a bad night to find that out. I'm in big trouble here, P-Man. I've only got what's on my iPod, and that's not much. I need your library.'

'Heh heh. The ol' MobyDisc collection comes through in the end, eh?'

'I've never needed the Spice Girls more. Where are you?'

'Jeez, I'm miles away – Hornsby Ex-Services Club.'

'God, what'll I do?'

'Yeah, plus I can't send anyone else out because all the team's got gigs tonight. Um, look – give me five to think about it, orright?'

'I'm dying here boss,' I said, temporarily forgetting that we didn't have that relationship anymore. In fact, I'd sighted my current boss not two minutes earlier, obeying Justin Timberlake's command to rock his body. Brent was having fun for now, but I didn't want to think about what I'd do if Phil couldn't come through.

I'd become blasé about the years of experience that had been distilled into the MobyDisc playlist, and my ability to choose songs that kept people happy. If they're not managed well, a crowd of moderately-to-highly intoxicated people can be a very tough proposition – even if under usual circumstances they're respectable lawyers. Put on a track they're not into, and they'll heckle or boo. Worse still, they can vote with their feet – and there are few more dispiriting sights than an empty dancefloor. There's nothing worse for a DJ than toiling away, trying to keep your expression free of the embarrassment you feel because you're playing music to nobody. And I was well on the way to rendering the dancefloor emptier than a Ricky Martin lyric.

I stared intently at the phone, willing it to ring. In the room, Cee-Lo was just about done professing his craziness as the Gnarls Barkley track wound up. I was running out of time. But then, as Ian Curtis started his slightly tuneless warbling, my trusty Nokia lurched to life.

'Private number', the screen told me. I was perplexed. It was unlike the P-Man to be private about anything, least of all his phone number, which he chucked around gigs like confetti in the hope of getting more clients. Still, I answered.

'Hi, is that Paul?' a female voice asked. 'It's Angela here.'

She elongated and rounded the vowels, making a faintly aristocratic name seem all the posher. My mental Rolodex was producing a grand total of zero Angelas, so I asked her if we'd met, to which she laughed melodiously.

'No,' she replied. 'Although I must say I've heard a lot about you.'

Given the pleasantness of her voice and the alluring tone of her laugh, I was hoping the things she'd heard were very good indeed. And then she explained she was Phil's 'partner'.

I'd gathered from our discussion that there was a whole

chalk–cheese dynamic happening between my old boss and his new girlfriend, but speaking to her, it seemed like chalk and imported Camembert. Although that analogy would have made Phil not the cheesy one in the relationship, which seemed improbable.

'I understand you're in a spot of bother,' she said, using a tone she might have used to discuss a showjumping misadventure. 'I've got a key to Phil's place, so if you can meet me there I'll let you in.'

'You aren't too busy? I'd hate to put you out,' I said. Which was a barefaced lie – I'd have been delighted to inconvenience her if it meant my night wasn't a disaster.

She laughed. 'Sadly, evenings without my man around tend to be quieter.'

'Yeah, I've noticed that myself.'

It had just gone nine o'clock and the party was going until one. I estimated it'd take around forty minutes to get to Phil's and back, so it was a little risky. But not going would be far riskier. By ten, everyone would have drunk so much that they'd be desperate for music I simply couldn't provide. So I decided to go for it, and told her I'd meet her in a quarter of an hour.

Now I needed to find someone who could hold the fort until I returned, and I didn't have a lot of options. If the evening's musical entertainment was going to collapse in a screaming heap, I didn't want Felicity to be trapped in the wreckage. Whereas Nige wouldn't care: if his reputation could withstand that 007 parody, it could certainly cope with a bit of DJing.

My friend was delighted to 'take the decks for a spin', as he put it.

'I'm gonna rock the house,' he informed me.

'Not exactly. What you're gonna do is stand there and look like you're having a good time while my iPod plays music I've already chosen.'

'Come on mate. Have a little faith, eh?'

'Look, if it was a slightly different crowd, I'd be happy for you to play both of Hunters & Collectors' greatest hits in succession. But you need to trust me on this.'

'Yeah, because *you* understand the vibe so well that you've got to run off and get more CDs!'

I conceded the point, but still, I wasn't going to let him pick the songs. I dredged the depths of my iPod as thoroughly as I could, and put together a quick playlist that I thought might just get us there. Prince's 'Kiss', The Beatles' 'Twist and Shout', and I figured I could get away with James Brown's 'Sex Machine', some Duran Duran and 'Song 2' by Blur. After a few frenzied minutes of scrolling, I'd queued up twenty songs, enough for about an hour, and ran for the door just as Nige was putting on the headphones and pretending to be in control.

I reached my car after around forty-five seconds of sprinting, but Felicity had taken only forty to call.

'What the hell is Nige doing?' she hissed.

'I have to rush off and get some more music,' I said. 'Trust me.'

'I've *already* trusted you,' she said. 'And you've given me Nige.'

'That's true, but don't worry – I've programmed in the tracks,' I said. 'I even locked the iPod so he couldn't change anything. He's just a figurehead so people won't worry that no one's choosing the music.'

'OK, I guess,' she said. 'When will you be back?'

'Aw, you're missing me already –'

Felicity hung up, evidently not appreciating the flirting. But if I could just get the rest of the music right, she'd come around. Or rather I'd be coming round, to her place. I pulled away from the kerb and fanged it to Phil's.

#8

★ KHE SANH ★
COLD CHISEL (1978)

Chez Phil is a little bungalow in Willoughby, a quiet, middle-class suburb further up the North Shore from where I live. Most people seem to choose to live in Willoughby because it's easy to get to, boasting its own exit only a short distance up the freeway from the Harbour Bridge. A feature I, conversely, appreciate because it makes it easier to escape from. But I was very grateful that Phil valued proximity over personality in his choice of suburbs.

The chief operations centre of the MobyDisc empire – MDHQ, as I like to call it – is a garage at the back of Phil's house. Angela and I rendezvoused at its door. She's in her late thirties, with shoulder-length brown hair in a somewhat severe cut, and I could tell she'd be even more at home in a suit than she was in the jeans and rugby jersey she'd thrown on to come and meet me.

We hit it off immediately, quickly discovering a common interest – jokes about Phil.

'Here's the key to the Batcave then,' she said, handing over the padlock key so I could pull up the roller-door, which I did with an air of great ironic drama.

Phil's garage was full of crates of CDs, and an extensive collection of decks, speakers, mixing desks, thick black cables and other paraphernalia, only around half of which was actually functional. I knew my way around the shed, but to the untrained eye, it looked utterly chaotic.

'I've been offering to come in and reorganise the place for Phil,' she said. 'But he keeps saying he wouldn't know where anything was.'

'It is organised – it's just that the system is secret men's business,' I said. 'You should feel flattered you're even allowed in here.'

'Believe me, I'm very grateful.'

'I'm the one who should be grateful, Angela. It's so nice of you to rescue me like this.'

I grabbed a crate of CDs, knowing that whichever box I took, the contents would be the same carefully selected MobyDisc compilations that were Phil's standard issue.

'Not at all,' she said. 'He thinks the world of you, you know.'

I smiled. 'He's a pretty great guy. And by the way, the mDisc idea is really interesting, but I think I may have discovered a few problems with it tonight!'

'Maybe the three of us should get together for dinner sometime and talk about it?'

'That'd be great,' I said.

As I was pulling the garage door down, Felicity rang, and she was far from happy.

'Paul!' she shouted. 'What the hell were you thinking?'

'What?'

'The song you programmed – it's appalling. Some song about a guy who likes big bottoms or something.'

My skin turned cold. Surely the 'Fat Bottomed Girls' debacle hadn't been repeated?

'What, by Queen? I didn't program that.'

'No – it's a rap song. A highly *offensive* rap song. I swear the managing partner just looked daggers at me.'

And then I realised what had happened. Nige had figured out that he could just plug in his own iPod. And having had a few drinks, he couldn't resist playing Sir Mix-A-Lot's ode to the posterior of the African-American woman – 'Baby's Got Back'. To say the least, this was a problem.

'Look, it's not my fault. Nige must have programmed it in.'

'Paul, there is no *way* this is not your fault. Get back here already.'

So I decided – in the interest of haste, of course – that it was my turn to hang up.

Angela was grinning at me. 'Sounds like you'd better run.'

'Yeah, just a little bit,' I said. 'Let's do that dinner soon though.'

'Absolutely,' she said. 'Ciao for now!'

Angela really had been very kind to me. So not only did I decide to let that phrase pass without a sarcastic comment, I even said, 'Yeah, ciao for now!' back.

I climbed into my car and rushed back to the city as quickly as my sedate Volvo could manage, knowing that every three minutes I took meant another song from Nige's playlist. And although I had only a passing familiarity with the contents of his iPod, the fact he'd paid to see Bon Jovi in concert didn't bode at all well.

Rushing down the freeway to the city, my mind played through the various scenarios. Perhaps Nige had simply emptied the dancefloor. And it'd be conspicuously empty, too – some kind of avant-garde arty tumbleweed would probably be rolling past.

But no, Nige was too popular for that. That Sir Mix-A-Lot track would have seen him surrounded by his mates, raucously rapping along with those few lyrics they remembered. The women would be sitting with their legs crossed and arms folded, talking about how awful the music was. And in the centre would be Felicity, furiously explaining how I'd let her down.

Or perhaps he'd followed up 'Baby Got Back' with something even more explicit, like NWA's 'Fuck Tha Police', perhaps? In which case some curmudgeonly partner would have pulled the plug completely, leaving a silent, sullen room. But no matter which particular disaster scenario Nige had wreaked, I couldn't get back there quickly enough.

★ ★ ★

I heard the singing well before I reached the building. The words were indistinct, the melody non-existent – but although musicologists might have disagreed, it was clearly singing. Had the PA been switched off and were the lawyers performing some kind of protest song? Had the whole of Morphett's suddenly grown a conscience about their overinflated salaries, and started singing the 'Internationale'? I began sprinting.

But I need not have worried. Nige, bless him, had pulled out the most reliable song in any Aussie's DJ's arsenal: 'Khe Sanh'. No matter where you go in this country, there is only one way dancefloors react to Cold Chisel's song about that screwed-up Vietnam vet. All dancing will stop, and everyone will link arms in a kind of rugby scrum. And everyone will sing along because everyone knows the words. Then, towards the end, when Barnesy starts singing about the last plane outta Sydney, they'll jump up and down. And when the song finishes, you always get a massive cheer.

It occurred to me that while Nige might not have much musical taste, at least in my somewhat snobbish opinion, his favourites coincide almost exactly with those of your average lawyer.

I went over to the DJ booth, where he was clearly having the time of his life, and high-fived him.

'Jono!' he shouted. 'Mate, this is easy. They love it!'

'Awesome. What've you been playing?'

'Oh, a bit of everything. Powderfinger, some Oils, a bit of Pearl Jam, and of course my man, JBJ.'

By which he meant Jon Bon Jovi. All stuff I would never have chosen. But I could concede it would have done a much better job of keeping the crowd happy than Miles Davis.

'Of course. Feel like a break, then?'

'Yeah, I'm gonna have a bit of a boogie. But hey, maybe I can come back and help you out later?'

I smiled and said, 'Of course.'

He made his way to the middle of the dancefloor, attracting cheers from everyone around him. So I pulled out

Phil's *Movie Themes #3* disc, faded in the James Bond theme and grabbed the microphone.

'Ladies and gentlemen, give it up for Claims Bond!'

He got a huge cheer. Nige may not have the skills to save the world from a moon-based laser, or even a corporate video from sucking. But he'd definitely saved my arse.

I still had three hours to fill, but with the MobyDisc selection, I'd get there easily. Nige had done a good job with the rock stuff, but it was time I served up a little somethin' for the ladies. So I kicked in Blondie's 'Girls Just Wanna Have Fun' and we were off. Several secretaries screamed in delight when they heard the intro, and grabbed nearby boys, dragging them onto the floor.

I fired off Madonna's 'Hung Up' followed by Young MC's 'Bust A Move'. Numbers swelled further, and now there were as many women as men dancing. Next I tried Michael Jackson's 'Beat It', and as an Eddie Van Halen solo rang out around the art museum for perhaps the first time, I felt I was redeeming myself. Wanting to keep things at least a little contemporary, I threw in a bit of The Killers before taking things back to the '70s with the Jackson 5's 'ABC'. And I did actually like all of these songs, I realised. Perhaps I could keep the retro enthusiasts happy without spinning any of the standard MobyDisc selections that would make me want to throw myself into the harbour?

I even threw a mash-up into the mix, something I'd never done before. I had a 2 Many DJs disc on my iPod, so I tried their combination of Destiny's Child's 'Independent Women Part 2' and AC/DC's 'Back In Black'. Putting Beyoncé's vocal over Angus Young's iconic riff worked surprisingly well. They were loving it, and to my surprise, so was I.

There must have been 150 people spilling off the dancefloor by this stage. And suddenly I noticed that Felicity was in the middle of the throng, spinning crazily around with Nige as she finally let go of all that tension. Apparently Sir Mix-A-Lot had been forgiven. She hadn't touched any grog earlier because she'd wanted to stay in control to deal with potential emergencies, but from the way she was dancing with just about everyone in her orbit, she could well have accounted for a couple of the firm's specially labelled bottles of Domaine Chandon all by herself.

Clearly, the night was going to go down as a success for her and her team, and after something of a false start, I was doing my bit. I only hoped she wouldn't be too worn out by all the dancing.

★ ★ ★

At 1.30, half an hour after the last guest had tottered off to one of The Rocks' many beautiful pubs full of ugly people, Felicity and I finished packing up. She'd signed off with the venue, and I'd cased up the last of my gear and lugged it to the safety of the carpark. We strolled across the lawn in front of the museum and wandered down to the waterside railing. It was really hot for November, and we breathed a sigh of relief as we looked out at the Opera House across the water, having survived the night's festivities intact.

In front of us, the dregs of several harbour cruises were slowly being disgorged onto the jetties. It wasn't long since I'd spent a few nights a month on boats like that. At the Morphett's party, I'd entertained a far classier crowd. But the two groups weren't so different, really. Just people who wanted to dance to a song they loved, and maybe get a bit of a grope or a pash on the dancefloor. Maybe there'd been a little less of the vomiting at the law firm party, but I'd still noticed plenty of people rushing queasily to the bathroom. As professional as they were during the week, everyone's the same with a good song and alcohol.

I subtly snaked an arm around Felicity's waist as we stood there. She nestled into me, resting her head on my shoulder, and I smiled. There was no need to say anything, we were content just to watch the harbour moving in front of us. I'd made our colleagues happy with my DJing, and there was nothing to be ashamed of. It may not have the parent-pleasing prestige of law, but they are both customer service industries where skilled technicians do their client's bidding, and are well compensated for it. And there's no denying that most of MJ's lawyers spin just as much shit as a MobyDisc jockey.

No iPod's shuffle mode could read a room and adapt like I had in there tonight. I'd nearly screwed up with my foolish attempt to garner credibility, but I'd pulled out of the tailspin, and without playing a single song I disliked. It was a victory, and the greatest part of my spoils was snuggling next to me.

'So, what next?' I asked.

She turned to face me, her face betraying a sheepish grin.

'Um, the others are over the road at the Orient and I got a text saying it was going off. Do you mind if we drop in there for a bit?'

'Of course not. It's your night, you should enjoy it!'

'You're still invited back to my place. That is, if you're still interested.'

'Oh, I'm interested.'

'You were great tonight Paul. I freaked out, but everyone loved it after you came back. I owe you, seriously.'

'Yeah, keep thinking that.'

We wandered up the hill, still arm in arm. Felicity was talking about how complimentary the managing partner had been, and how she really thought she'd helped her career, and how she was going to organise the Christmas in July party next, and perhaps even the Melbourne Cup Day, and how she'd gotten lots of compliments on her dress, and everyone wanted to know where she'd bought it, and there was no way she'd tell them. I just kept walking happily beside her.

All the while, I was pondering mDisc. Sure, Phil could change the brand-name and tart up the logo to try and get more of an upmarket crowd if he wanted. But if I'd been able to nail the MJ party, using just the standard MobyDisc selection, then it would work anywhere. So I resolved to tell him I'd come back, but that becoming a partner was too much of a responsibility. Sure, I'd help him train people, and he could pay me more for that if he wanted. But even though I'd always looked on it with contempt, I'd succeeded only in proving that what he was doing already worked.

My resolve to return to getting easy money from my DJing skills was only bolstered by Felicity's compliments. But as the booming sound system from the pub indicated we'd neared our destination, I couldn't help wondering whether she'd accept me regularly filling dancefloors instead of Morphett Jackson timesheets.

#7

★ ETERNAL FLAME ★
THE BANGLES (1989)

As soon as we got inside the door, Felicity screamed excitedly and ran to embrace her girlfriends, who immediately made her drink a glass of celebratory champers. She wasn't going to want to leave for ages, which would have been fine if I'd been able to drink as well. But no – I was stuck in the designated driver's nightmare: a pub filled exclusively with drunk people. The cabbies were going to make some serious coin out of these people tonight. Much of it through cleaning surcharges.

I wandered over towards the bar. I wouldn't be leaving for an hour or two, so I could afford one beer. Not knowing anyone in the immediate throng around the beer taps, I pulled out my mobile while I waited for an opening.

I marvelled at the background image Nige had provided, which was one of those terribly ironic Photoshopped images of David Hasselhoff, substituting the former *Baywatch* star's cheesy grin for the mysterious knowing smile of the Mona Lisa. The wit responsible had called it the *Mona Hoffa*.

I was wondering whether I should change it for something slightly less crapola when I noticed a little yellow envelope just above Hasselhoff's thick curls. It was a text message from Zoë.

'Josh's been screwing some little skank from work,' it read. 'Just thought you'd better know your taste in friends sucks.'

I rang immediately, but it went straight to voicemail. So I left a disjointed, garbled message expressing my sympathy, calling Josh an arsehole, expressing my sympathy again, and telling her to call me.

And then, wanting desperately to do something but knowing I couldn't, I stood there, temporarily oblivious to the rest of the room while I tried to get my head around what I'd just read. The news left me shocked, and furious with Josh. What on earth had he been thinking? That someone as smart as Zoë wouldn't find out? God, at least she hadn't followed through on our little chat and proposed to the guy. The blissful future she'd outlined to me was in absolute devastation. And so, I figured, must she be.

A few minutes later, when I'd finally fought my way to the front of the bar, the phone beeped again. I hastily opened the message.

'Not really up to talking now. I'll call you later or maybe in the morning. Thanks though.'

'Anytime,' I texted back. 'I'll be up for a few hours yet.'

Sure, he's good-looking and charming, so he must have had no shortage of opportunities, but Josh had never seemed like the kind of guy to play around. He is a placid character, an economics grad who'd gone straight to work for a big stockbroking firm. He's the kind of guy who likes to tick off his boxes – nice job, nice girlfriend, nice car, holidays. I wondered what on earth had happened.

Sometimes though, when a guy's been with one woman for a while, he can come to take it for granted and think he can get anyone, and that it'll always be as good. He can forget that a successful relationship's about the chemistry between two people, and fancy that he's just become hugely attractive to the whole of womankind.

When my schooner finally arrived, I decided to go and tell Nige, and see if he had any idea what might've been going through Josh's head. I dragged him away from his friends, and he came a little reluctantly, nursing his own fresh beer from one of several jugs.

He'd had plenty to drink by then so I wasn't too surprised when his first response was simply to gape a lot, punctuated by several 'fucks'. Though we'd all been at law school together, Nige and Zoë had never been close whereas like me, he'd known Josh since schooldays. But Nige obviously felt genuinely bad for her, and I was glad to see it.

'I've always thought Josh was a little bit full of himself, you know,' Nige said. 'And you know what? Maybe his bit on the side was at the pub with us the other night. There was some little redhead from his work who I hadn't met before.'

'Once, I'd have defended him. But this – I don't know how to take it. I guess I'd better hear his side of the story before rushing to judgement.'

'Oh come on. I'm not nuts about Zoë the way you are, but even I can tell he doesn't treat her well. It's always about what *he* wants, you know?'

An unexpectedly subtle analysis from Nige. I'd built them up as the perfect couple, but sure, in hindsight, it had sometimes seemed a little one-sided.

'And really, why some little naïve leftie like her would want to date a big bad broker was always beyond me.'

I didn't like the characterisation, but I took his point.

'And vice versa,' he continued. 'Geez, can you imagine taking someone like her to a firm event like this? She'd turn up her nose at the whole thing.'

I acknowledged that I couldn't. But unlike Nige, I didn't think that reflected poorly on Zoë.

'I don't know what to do. I'll have to meet up with her for a chat later –'

'You don't know what to *do*? Are you kidding me? Buddy, this is the best news you've ever had.'

'Huh?'

'Oh, come on, don't pretend you don't know what I'm talking about. You've been wanting her for years.'

'You're kidding me.'

'C'mon, we've been mates too long for me not to notice. I've never called you on it because I figured you'd be embarrassed about it. But geez – whenever you mention her, you get this silly little smile on your face. Jono, you've been holding a candle for that girl since first year.'

'Bullshit. She's just a really good friend.'

'Forget the candle. You've been holding a big fucking *lighthouse* for that chick. Now's your chance. You've gotta get in there before someone else does.'

'Seriously, fuck off,' I said, and shoved him in the chest.

He laughed, implying that I'd just proven him right. I tried another tactic.

'Look, I'm just upset that she's been stuffed around by someone I introduced her to, OK? I wouldn't want any of my friends hurt like that. You included.'

'You've never reacted like this when *I've* been dumped.'

'That's because you've never cared enough about anyone to get hurt –'

'Bollocks, it's because you don't want to sleep with me. Which comes as a relief, believe me. Come on, you *luuurve* her buddy, even if you can't admit it to yourself. So for once don't screw this up by denying it. Get in there. Tonight.'

'That's just typical of you, Nige. Even if I did have feelings for her, and I'm not admitting for one second that I do, the last thing I'd do is take advantage of her when she's vulnerable.'

'Mate, it'd be for her own good. She's perfect for you. Time for your two bleeding hearts to bleed as one.'

'Seriously Nige, bugger off. I'm telling you –'

'OK, OK. Keep on denying it. But when you two inevitably get together, I'm gonna insist on your firstborn being called Nigel.'

'Fat fucking chance!'

I stormed off, and he just laughed and rejoined the others.

God, why the hell had I gone to him for helpful advice in a crisis? Nige has no idea how to be a good friend to a girl. When he spots a wounded gazelle, he just thinks he's got a better chance. And Zoë? What if she thought I was planning to make a move when I was only trying to cheer her up?

No – when I'd gotten dumped, she was the one I'd called, and I was damned if Nige's innuendo was going to stop me from reciprocating. I hated the idea of her lying all alone in her terrace, surrounded by the familiar artefacts of something that had just been destroyed, like the charred remains of household mementos after a bushfire. But for the time being, there was nothing I could do for her.

#6

★ GO YOUR OWN WAY ★
FLEETWOOD MAC (1976)

Thinking more about it, I decided Nige had just been winding me up. Trying to lighten the situation, really. He'd never understood my relationship with Zo, and he'd kidded me about her for years. I'd laughed along, because with her and Josh an item, that kind of speculation seemed preposterous.

But if I'd wanted to prove to Nige that I had feelings for Zoë, I couldn't have found a better way than storming off in a huff like that. I needed to relax and make him realise I was only showing friendly concern, and nothing more. So I went back over to where he was drinking with JP and Will.

'Sorry about that mate,' I said. 'I guess I'm just a bit shocked.'

'Yeah, I could tell. I'm surprised you haven't heroically rushed off to rescue her already.'

'Nah, it's all right. I can catch up with her later.'

'Are you going to challenge Josh to a duel?' JP butted in. Aw crap, I thought to myself. Now everyone knew.

'Nah, he's just going to sneakily edge in there while she's vulnerable,' Will said. 'This is when SNAG wusses like Paulie come good.'

'All those heart-to-hearts are finally going to pay off for our boy here,' Nige said. 'Bloody slow way to pick up though.'

'Never fear, young Zoë,' JP said, doing a decent job of channelling Colin Firth in *Pride and Prejudice*. 'I shall defend thine honour, or perish in the attempt.'

'The one I feel sorry for is Felicity,' Will said. 'First Paul bars her for the kid, then he bars her for his best mate. Shocker.'

'I bet you feel sorry for her,' Nige said. 'But I don't think you'll be comforting her in the same way Paulie's going to be comforting Zoë.'

It was news to me that Will was after Felicity. But I figured she offered a great avenue for nipping all of this shit in the bud, and I took it eagerly.

'Talk it up boys,' I said with sarcastic innocence. 'That's right, Zoë's the one. There's nothing between me and Felicity at all. Nothing. Just keep thinking that, would you? That'd be perfect.'

They liked that, and whooped in unison.

'You devil,' JP said. 'You've been keeping it very quiet.'

'Yeah,' I replied. 'Because there's nothing. Nada. It's all just speculation.'

'Buddy, make yourself clear,' Will said. 'I don't want to cut a mate's grass if you're into her, but otherwise I'm totally going for her tonight.'

'OK guys, look – it's a possibility. But sure, go for your life Will, I've got no claim on her. No Claims Bond, even.'

Nige chortled. 'Let the lady choose, eh? Bad plan – she'll probably choose that Harris prick again.'

'I don't think so somehow,' I said, and launched into the story of his speech at the garden-party, delighted to be talking about anything other than Zoë.

Half an hour later, I figured it was time to check up on Felicity, who was still downstairs with a bunch of what women of her social set like to call 'girlfriends'. The champagne had been flowing steadily, and Felicity indiscreetly screamed 'Paulie!' when she caught sight of me. She told her group she'd be back in just a sec because she had some important musical questions to consult me on, and then giggled all too transparently.

Well, if she wanted to talk music, I was only too happy to oblige. I figured I should float the idea of my departure from Morphett's. If it was a deal-breaker, it'd be good to know before things progressed between us.

'Isn't this the best night ever? Are you having as wonderful a time as I am?'

'Not quite as wonderful – I'm driving.'

'Oh, you're no fun,' she said, poking me proprietorially on the nose and grinning. 'No fun at all.'

'Actually Flea, I do want to ask you something, since you liked my playing tonight.'

'Oh I *did*, Paulie! You were so great, all the girls are so jealous of me!'

Obviously discretion wasn't our watchword anymore.

'So, what would you say if I told you I'd been thinking of leaving Morphett's and going back to DJing?'

'Whoa,' she said. 'Like, whoa. That's serious. Serious, Paulie.'

She shook her head, a little confused by all that seriousness. And it occurred to me that this might not be the time.

'But what about *us*?' she pouted. 'We wouldn't be on the same floor.'

'I'd have thought it'd be easier, away from all the office gossip and stuff.'

'Your DJing was awesome, Paulie. But I dunno, doing it for a job – isn't it a bit – meh?'

'Meh?'

'Yeah, you know, meh.' She giggled. '*Meh*. No offence.'

'We'd probably better talk about this later,' I said. 'And let's put a raincheck on tonight – you should stay out with your friends and celebrate and I'd better go, I'm tired.'

'Oh, you don't have to go just because I said it was meh. It's not that bad, lots of things are meh. Like Harris!'

'Yeah, OK. You know what? I am gonna go. I'm sober.'

She giggled. 'I'm not!'

I laughed, and she gave me a peck on the cheek while simultaneously saying 'mwah', and I went to rejoin my friends, delayed by a few congratulatory high-fives from smashed colleagues who'd enjoyed themselves on the dancefloor. As I climbed the stairs, I checked my phone and noticed two missed calls. One was from voicemail, and the other was from Zoë. I swore, and sat on a step to retrieve the message.

'Paul, it's me,' said a voice almost too husky to recognise as hers. 'Can you come over? No worries if you're busy – but I can't sleep, and I'd rather not be alone. Plus, you know Josh, so maybe you can offer some insight into what the hell he was doing. Anyway, call me.'

It was far too noisy to ring her from the pub, so I just texted to say I was on my way. It wasn't a hard decision: the idea of a quiet chat to Zoë appealed to me far more than going back to Felicity's place. The realisation came as something of a surprise, but there was no denying it. I went up to bid Nige and the boys a quick farewell.

Nige and the boys weren't surprised in the least, and when I told them I was going, they guessed my destination and whooped accordingly. I weathered it.

'Tuck her in good and tightly, Jono,' JP said.

'I will,' I said. 'Before heading home myself.'

'Jokes aside mate, good on you for going over there,' Nige said. 'Seriously though – don't keep her up half the night talking shit about Josh. Just get her mind off it, maybe watch a bit of TV, give her a few drinks and get her to sleep.'

Was this Nige being concerned for Zoë and giving sensible advice?

'And seriously,' he added, 'there's nothing like sex for distracting a woman. You'd be doing her a favour.'

It had seemed too good to last.

'Hate to ask man, but what about Felicity?' Will ventured.

'Downstairs drinking champagne, buddy. Do with that information what you will.'

He grinned and gave me a thumbs up.

'I wonder if she'd be interested in a fresh bottle?'

'More than she'd be interested in you, mate,' Nige said.

'Maybe you boys should go down and join them?' I suggested. Nige gave the plan his blessing, announcing that nothing would entertain him more than watching Felicity shoot Will down, and they followed me downstairs to meet up with the girls. I waved a general goodbye, and walked out into the fresh air.

I hurried back to my car, thinking back on my earlier conversation with Nige. Was everyone else going to assume that I'd make a move on Zoë now that she was single? Would *she* be thinking the same thing? And then I considered a trickier question. If she really was available, why on earth wouldn't I?

#5

★ YOU'RE THE ONE THAT I WANT ★
JOHN TRAVOLTA
AND OLIVIA NEWTON-JOHN (1978)

I pulled up near Zoë's house and rested my head on the steering wheel for a moment, trying to get my head straight before I went in. My feelings about my friend had always been, to say the least, complex. I'd been instantly attracted to her when I met her, but we'd become such good friends, and it would have been silly to sacrifice all that because it occasionally occurred to me that, in an alternative reality, being with her would be pretty darn great.

The Jurassic 5 track 'Thin Line' puts it perfectly. It's a great song, even though Nelly Furtado appears on it. It's about how even though friendship and attraction inevitably overlap, you respect the line because you know it's the right thing to do, and crossing it would destroy everything. Without these somewhat arbitrary boundaries, friendships with the opposite sex would often be impossible. There'll be times when you wonder 'what if', but it's not so much a question of what you feel as what you do about it.

I'd considered my occasional feelings towards Zoë as symptomatic of my singleness. When I'd been with Mel, I'd only thought of Zoë as a friend, and that had been fine. After it ended and there was no one else in my life – well, it was hard to avoid sometimes wondering what it would be like with Zo. But I'd known it wasn't going to happen, and especially when she'd outlined her marriage plan, the need to find someone for myself had seemed urgent. In hindsight, that was probably why I'd so badly wanted Felicity – and at times even Emily – to work out.

But they couldn't compete, and it sometimes seemed an impossible yardstick for anyone to match, given the depth of our friendship. Because Zoë just *got* me. She laid out things I was embarrassed about in myself with devastating clarity, and then she made me feel better about them. All the subtleties, all the complexities of our relationship, our companionship, equated to one simple thing: everything was better when I was with her. *I* was better when I was with her.

Previously, Zoë's relationship with Josh had set limits on our relationship – and without them, it might never have blossomed in the first place. I'd known where I stood, and I was happy enough with it. But if she was single now – well, that was a lot trickier. Still, even if I wanted to try for something, it was definitely too soon. She'd called on me to help her through this, and that had to be my only priority.

When I knocked, Zoë came out clutching a bag.

'We're going to your place. I'm damned if I'm staying here, surrounded by his stuff. I don't want to be some freaky bunny boiler, but there's a genuine danger I'll torch that signed Gordon premiership jersey. Which he apparently cares about more than me.'

And she burst into tears. So I put my arms around her and let her sniffle on my shoulder for a moment. This was getting sketchy already.

'I can't face telling my mum yet, so I can't go home,' she said, finally coming up for air. 'She'll be so hurt, and so angry on my behalf. All men are bastards, you know – it'll be like Dad all over again, and I don't want to deal with that whole justifiable anger thing –'

'OK, I'll put my own justifiable anger on hold then as well –'

'You know what I mean? God, I *know* how bad it is, I *know* he's a complete fuckwit, but tonight I just want to forget about it.'

'Absolutely.'

'So I figure we'll watch some silly TV, maybe make some cocktails or whatever, and then I'll pass out in a drunken stupor on your sofa.'

'Sounds like an excellent plan.'

We got into the car and started towards my place. She sat silently for a minute or so, and I wasn't sure what to say. Before long, she thought of another proviso.

'By the way, I reserve the right to behave badly, and cry, and say terrible things I don't really mean, OK?'

'Understood.'

'And you just have to sit there and put up with it, and not think any worse of me for it – because he was *your* friend. I think that's fair.'

'Absolutely. *Was* my friend is about right, incidentally.'

A corny effort at gallantry that only set her off a little more. It's not every day I reduce a woman to tears using merely grammar. Fortunately, I had half a packet of tissues in the car.

My parents were up at the Hunter Valley, fantasising about retiring to a place that was even more middle-class than where they currently live. So Zoë and I stayed up undisturbed until dawn, watching trashy DVDs. She voted for *Dumb and Dumber*, *Grease* – with which she told me I had to sing along, since I knew the words from DJing – and *Deuce Bigalow: Male Gigolo*. Just the thing to take her mind off it all, if not lobotomise her entirely.

The fridge was well-stocked with comfort food, so I put together a delightful selection of microwave pizza, popcorn and ice-cream. And Zoë insisted on drinking quite a lot of vodka and lemonade, vodka and lime, vodka and tonic, and ultimately just vodka and vodka.

Here and there she burst into tears, and even threw a cushion at the screen during a particularly tender moment in *Grease*. We decided to skip the ending.

'We should have watched a horror movie,' she said. 'I'm in the mood to see people die horrible, violent deaths. Especially people who look like a certain someone, who will remain nameless. Let's just say a certain dickfaced someone.'

'I think comedies are probably best for tonight. But sure, we can get going with some kind of chainsaw massacre tomorrow.'

She fell asleep on the couch a few minutes into *Deuce Bigalow*. My brother had bought the DVD, and almost worn it out, but honestly, that movie could put a truckie on amphetamines to sleep.

I gently pulled off her shoes and brought out a spare doona to drape over her. I'd drunk more vodka myself than was wise, considering how tired I was. So I staggered towards my own adjoining bedroom.

I plugged in my mobile to charge and noticed two more text messages. I opened one from Emily first – it merely said, 'Felicity? WTF?'

Harris had done his worst, as threatened, but there was nothing much to tell. Emily probably wouldn't be bothered once I explained, and if she was – well, I had other problems on my plate now.

Then there was one from Josh that had been sent at around 3.30 am, presumably either because he was wracked with guilt, or with his new lover. I wouldn't have been willing to bet which.

'Dunno if you've heard but me + Zo are done,' he'd written. 'Sorry to land u in it but she might like a call 2moro.'

I almost replied, 'It's cool, she's with me, I'm taking care of it,' to try and make him jealous. But I thought better of it. We'd had enough disruption for one night.

★ ★ ★

I had only just drifted off when I was awakened by a sniffly someone climbing onto my bed.

'I don't want to be alone. I woke up and just cried,' she said. 'Do you mind?'

I should have said it was a bad idea. But if I'd told her not to get in, it might have suggested there was some good reason why she shouldn't, that we weren't just friends. Then there was the fact that I really wanted her to. So I pulled back the cover.

My commitment to platonic supportiveness became a little harder to maintain once she'd wrapped my arm comfortingly around her waist. After a few moments, she flipped over to look at me. Her eyes were still red but she was smiling, and that had to be a good thing.

'You're a great guy, Paul. The best friend a poor, lonely cheated-on girl could have.'

'Thanks, but you should go to sleep.'

'I'll be able to now. I just know it.'

And she flipped over again, this time snuggling more closely. I lay there apprehensively for five minutes, not moving an inch. Her breathing became more regular as she slowly drifted off to sleep. I was going to get out of jail here, I thought, but some small part of me was disappointed. And then she suddenly turned and kissed me on the cheek.

'What are you doing?'

'Oh, a little goodnight kiss. Just to say thanks.'

She kissed me again on my cheek, my ear, my neck. And then moved her lips slowly towards mine. My heart was thumping so hard in my chest that I was terrified she could hear it. Mustering all the self-control I could, I pulled myself away and sat up.

'Zo, is this a good idea?'

'Definitely not. But what if we just did it anyway?'

'I don't want to feel like I'm taking advantage of you.'

'That's sweet, but I don't hear you saying you don't *want* me to kiss you.'

'I don't think you should kiss me, OK?' Oh, that was hard to say. 'It's not a good idea.'

'Look, I know I'm vulnerable, and drunk, and my head's not right —'

'Exactly. I'm supposed to be helping you through this, not —'

'But don't you think that gives us the perfect excuse? If it's such a bad mistake, we can just tell ourselves we got carried away. Don't worry, I won't hold it against you —'

'Hmm,' I said, my voice now a little husky with sheer nerves. 'I still don't think it's a good idea.'

'Objection noted,' she said. 'But denied.'

God, I thought. Law nerdiness even at a time like this. Ah, who was I kidding? Her legalistic pillow talk was the hottest thing I'd ever heard.

And it got hotter still as she moved her body slowly over mine, discovering in the process incontrovertible evidence that I wasn't as uninterested in the idea as I had been maintaining.

'God Zo, I'm sorry — I just —'

'I'm not.'

She kissed me again. And this time I was well beyond self-control.

#4

★ CARELESS WHISPER ★
GEORGE MICHAEL (1984)

I woke first, which was hardly surprising given the extent to which Zoë had self-medicated with the contents of my parents' liquor cabinet. I lay there for a while, my arm around her, and my brain churned away as I tried not to wake her. One one level, it was wonderful to wake up with her in my arms. But it was also exactly what I'd promised myself I wouldn't do. When she had needed a friend most of all, I'd failed her.

I tried to work out what would happen when she woke, sobered up, and came to terms with what we'd done. Would there be a scene? Or would there be coldness, formality and agonising awkwardness, resolved only when she escaped into a cab?

Feeling a growing sense of dread, I gently removed my arm from around her and went to the bathroom. I splashed some water on my face and stared at myself in the mirror. Yesterday had been a dream come true, but I'd happily have undone it to avoid paying such a heavy price today.

When I returned to bed and gingerly slipped in beside her, her eyes opened and she smiled at me. I propped up my head and tried to talk to her.

'Hey Zo, can I just say that —'

She suddenly placed her finger across my lips.

'Don't say anything,' she said. 'Not now, anyway. Let's go back to sleep.'

I nodded and collapsed into the pillow, not touching her. She grabbed my arm and returned it to its earlier position around her waist.

'Much better,' she said. More proof, as if I needed any, that she was always right.

★ ★ ★

We finally woke at around two-thirty, and it wasn't until four that we finally walked upstairs, desperate for something resembling food. The intervening period — let's just say it was all very pleasant. As opposed to, say, finding my parents in the kitchen after we had wandered in, dressed only in bathrobes.

They were as embarrassed as we were. And my lame attempts at trying to pretend we'd just been swimming only made it worse.

'Paul, we don't have the slightest issue with this, but I think you should probably know before you go any further into the details of your little swimming party that it's been raining – which is why we came home early,' my father said. 'At about one.'

'Oh,' I said.

'Anyway, we were just going to pop down to the supermarket, weren't we Helen?' he said. 'We'd better get moving.'

'Thanks guys. I'd bet against us being here when you get back,' I said.

They retreated with almost indecent haste, and Zoë, who had been silently blushing, burst out laughing.

'Well, so much for keeping it to ourselves.'

'Yeah, my stance on living at home isn't looking so flash right now,' I said. 'And you know, while we don't have to get into it this instant, we will have to talk about this, I'm afraid.'

'I know,' she said dejectedly. 'I think I took advantage of you.'

'Don't be ridiculous. If anything, it was the other way around. I don't want to hurt our friendship.'

'Don't worry, this has happened before, remember?' she said. 'We survived.'

'How could I forget? Although it wasn't *quite* the same in every detail, was it?'

'Good point. OK, I'm going to go and get dressed, and then we're going to go and have a nice meal together and totally avoid this whole issue,' she said.

'Sounds perfect.'

'And then you can drive me home, and we'll leave it all for another time. I'm done – I don't want to think about anything at all today, least of all this. No, second-least of all this.'

'Sure.'

So we went to Bill & Toni's for old times' sake – old times like, say, the week before. Things seemed almost back to normal as we joked around, but then she grabbed my hand and held it tightly.

'I know we still have to have this awful discussion and everything, but I just want to say thanks,' she said. 'I've hardly even thought about Josh.'

'Glad I could take your mind off it. Although I could have found a better way of distracting you than embarking on a whole new disaster.'

She laughed, and told me I wasn't allowed to start the chat yet.

'But just so you know, I'm not feeling in any way disaster-stricken,' she said. And squeezed my hand even more tightly.

I smiled back at her. All day I'd been telling myself that she had just been in a strange place the previous night, and I was preparing myself to be a gentleman about the whole thing – good old Paul, dependable friend and romantic no-hoper. But it occurred to me as I was sitting there with her hand in mine that this was exactly what I'd been looking for. And I found it impossible to suppress my optimism completely.

★ ★ ★

No – what suppressed my optimism was arriving back at her place and finding Josh sitting on the doorstep, grumpily reading the newspaper. In the haste of his departure, he apparently hadn't taken his keys.

'Ah, so that's where you've been,' he said. 'I should've known.'

Zoë suddenly ran up to him and started shouting. 'What the fuck are you doing here?'

'I live here, remember?'

'No you don't, you piece of shit. You're out of here.'

'Well, I need my laptop and some suits, at least. But we can get to that. I'm more interested in Paul right now. Spent the night at his place, did you? And most of the day, it seems.'

'It's none of your damn business. I needed somewhere to go that didn't remind me of *you*.'

'Look, I think it's probably good — makes things even. And we should be able to at least be civil, since we've both moved on.'

'*Even*? Moved *on*? What the *fuck*?'

I thought it best to interject at this point. 'Look, this isn't really any of my business, so I'm gonna go.'

'Yeah, that'd be best,' Zoë said. 'Thanks Paul. I'll call you.'

'Just tell me something mate,' Josh said. 'You do owe me an apology, don't you?'

I didn't even know how to answer that question. Fortunately, before I did, Zoë butted in and started furiously jabbing her finger into his chest.

'*Him* owe *you* an apology, when you haven't even made one to *me* yet?'

'Um, guys,' I said, backing away. 'This is for you two to work out.'

My attempts at a dignified retreat were somewhat ruined, however, when Zoë gave the game away.

'And hey, Paulie, thanks for last night. You were amazing. Josh, you should take some tips from your friend — maybe you'd have a better chance of satisfying that stupid little speck of dirt you picked up —'

By now, I was walking rapidly away, but not so quickly that I didn't hear Josh shout out, 'Thanks a bunch, Johnson. Great thing to do to a friend.'

And I really wished I hadn't felt like he had a point.

★ ★ ★

I spent the rest of the day at home, unsuccessfully trying to distract myself with the television. It had been all too clear there on the porch that Zoë still had strong feelings for Josh. Of course she would – you don't go from wanting to marry someone to feeling nothing in a day. And people have forgiven worse. I might have been taking advantage of her, in one sense. But like she'd said, hadn't she also been taking advantage of me to get back at Josh? And as he'd pointed out, they were on a level playing field – well, levellish, since technically Zoë hadn't been cheating on Josh, just moving on very quickly – so they could try and negotiate a reconciliation. One thing was certain: Josh had been shown he could no longer take Zoë for granted.

It was probably just a rebound thing, and mine had happened to be the most convenient, willing body. The idea seemed intuitively correct, which brought me down. And my parents' attempts to give me advice – a thinly disguised attempt to get me to spill the beans if ever I've heard one – only made things worse. Mum claimed she'd always hoped Zoë and I would get together, and refused to believe that things weren't as simple as just telling her that it was what I wanted. Whereas my father seemed to be proud of me for getting some action, and thought there was no need to worry about committing to anyone just yet, what with being in my youthful prime and all. Then they argued amongst themselves over who was right. It wasn't exactly therapeutic.

Eventually they left me in peace – or alone with my thoughts, which weren't peaceful at all. To try and read the tea leaves, I texted Zoë that night, asking whether she was OK. But even though I checked my phone at five-minute intervals, there was no reply.

One was waiting in my inbox when I arrived at Morphett's the following day, though. An email, sent first thing that morning from her work address. I tried to interpret this – had she avoided her home email yesterday because she didn't want Josh looking over her shoulder? Had he been there *to* look over her shoulder? And perhaps stroke it, then massage it a little, then – well, everyone says make-up sex is the best, don't they?

I admonished myself for worrying about things I couldn't control, and just opened the darn message.

Hi Paulie,
Thanks for being there on the weekend. It meant a lot. Look, obviously I've got a lot of things to work through this week and although I know it's a lot to ask, can we just defer our chat until a drink or something later in the week? And don't stew the way you always do, OK?
x Zo

Which told me precisely nothing, other than that she was willing to at least see me again. It meant we were still talking at least, so I just replied, 'Yeah no worries, let me know what you want to do.' I was going to include a little witticism about stewing and peaches, but sensibly decided not to.

Over the course of the week, I kept turning things over in my head. Nige was no help – he just claimed she'd come begging if I left her to it. He also kept making sly jokes about us having already slept together, which quickly became annoying. He'd have been astonished to hear we actually had, but there was no way I was going to tell him.

I wanted to be with her. There was no denying it, and our night together had convinced me of it. But as this didn't seem possible, the bottom line was that we had to preserve the friendship – and Zoë had pre-empted this imperative before we'd done anything. We needed to be able to write it off as just a crazy night, fuelled by heightened emotion and vodka. Our feelings for one another were strong, and while that had made it easy to cross the line, it ought to make it easy to cross back. So I braced myself to be supportive about a reconciliation with Josh – or, equally probable, a decision that she just wanted to be single for a while and not get involved with me or anyone else. It'd be tough to forget our night together, and accept it wouldn't be repeated. But it would be far tougher not having her in my life at all.

#3

★ (EVERYTHING I DO) I DO IT FOR YOU ★
BRYAN ADAMS (1991)

I tried to focus on work, but I couldn't stop analysing that night. Was there something I could have done differently to make her think we should be together? I kept mulling over what she'd said and done, hoping to gather enough positive evidence to give me hope. But when I gathered together all the shreds, I still had little confidence. Ultimately she knew me too well to want to be with me. I thought back on all the times she'd gotten frustrated with me, and told me what to do with my life. I was a mess, and she had more than enough evidence to know that she could do better. I was a close friend, sure – but not boyfriend material, not for the likes of Zo. I'd be the Kevin Federline to her Britney Spears, and she'd get rid of me without even giving us the chance to film a humiliating reality show together.

By the afternoon, I realised that what I was doing definitely constituted stewing. I tried to focus on the letter I had to review, but even the boring banking words like 'commitment' and 'relationship' brought thoughts of her. Still, it would only be a little while until I saw her, and we worked it all out – for better or, more likely, worse. I'd been waiting so long, a few more days wouldn't hurt.

But on Wednesday, I got another email from her.

Dear Paul,

I've been talking to Mum – she knows everything now, including about us – and she thinks I should just take some time out until I get my head straight. She's a bit more experienced with breakups than me, given Dad and all that, and I'm taking her advice.

So, I know this seems sudden, but we've decided to go to Thailand for a couple of weeks, leaving on Friday morning. Her work's quiet, and I will bring some Ph.D stuff over with me – the department's been really nice about it. But mainly I'll be relaxing on the beach at Ko Samui. When I get back, though, we should have that talk.

Much love Z.

I sat back in my office chair in surprise, and immediately started writing a reply.

Hi Zoë,

That's a great idea. You'll have a lovely time. But please, so things aren't left hanging for weeks, can I just say what I wanted to say on Friday? Let's just forget about what happened. It was a mistake, we both know it. Don't worry about me — I just need to find somebody of my own. I think we both know that we work best as friends.

Bon voyage and all my love,
Paul

I couldn't bear to have this hanging over me for weeks when I felt it was probably a forlorn hope anyway. Plus, if I sent the email, Zoë would only have to worry about her situation with Josh, without the added complication of me.

I stared at the screen for a moment, my mouse pointer hovering over the 'Send' button. And I thought about the email I should have written, the one where I told her the truth. That what I wanted was to give her as much time as she needed to get her head straight, and when she did, I'd be waiting, because my feelings were more constant than George Michael's arrests.

But I didn't want to build up all that hope for weeks when I was convinced that disappointment lay ahead of me. Better to have her as a friend than nothing — that had to be my mantra. And so, after permitting myself a momentary sigh, I clicked 'Send'.

I felt I'd done the right thing. It was better for her, and it was probably better for me. I'd have to go cold turkey and overcome my feelings for her properly — it was the only way I'd ever be rid of them. So I quit the email program and got back to my legal work.

Later that afternoon, a one-line reply came.

Thanks for letting me know how you feel, but it doesn't get you out of the talk! Zx

She was right, of course. I couldn't simply hit the 'Undo' button this time, like I had in first year. But I'd cleared things up, I felt, and I was pleased about that. So I just replied, 'Sure. Have a Singha for me' and left it at that.

★ ★ ★

It wasn't a great night. Again I tried to distract myself with the television, but I kept wondering whether I'd done the right thing. Always sleep on an important email, that's usually my rule – and what could be more important than the reply I'd just sent? The problem was that I couldn't quite purge myself of my hopes about us being together, not yet. It just made so much sense to me. Surely the realisation would hit her like a flash when she was poolside at her Thai resort, and she'd reach for her phone to tell me she was coming back to be with me?

And then I scolded myself, saying that no matter how many fanciful scenarios I came up with, it still wasn't going to happen.

Shortly after two in the morning, I realised that sleep wasn't going to happen either. So I got up and walked into the room where I kept my guitar. I sat at my desk, pen in hand, thinking I should get down not the way I felt about Zoë, but the way I ought to feel. Whenever I sensed myself weakening, I could remember the words of the song. It had worked with Mel, when I'd written a song called 'Out Of Mind', and it might work again.

So, I asked myself, what was the right way to think about Zoë? And I set pen to paper.

Late on a crazy night
We made a call that wasn't right
And now you've taken flight, you've taken flight.

Best to keep the detail sketchy, I figured. I might want to perform this in public someday.

There's no way to defend
Going beyond just being friends
And I am sure it has to end, it has to end

I liked that, so I tried a chorus.

I know right now everything's strange
But things won't change, they won't change.
There isn't anyone to blame
So things will stay the same, stay the same.

It wasn't exactly Bob Dylan, but it said what it needed to, and I hadn't written anything I liked as much in over a year. My favourite Beck album, *Sea Change*, had been written after he broke up with a long-term girlfriend, and it was full of powerful, melancholy songs. Maybe I could transform my own disappointment into some half-decent music as well?

Some less mournful songs might be a good idea too, I thought. And I started thinking about a fun one based on the night I'd left MobyDisc and the *Croozr One*, called 'Harbour Cruise Girl', which lent itself to a whole heap of easy rhymes: 'booze', 'views' and, best of all, 'spews'. It'd be a bit of a pisstake, but if I could make it catchy enough, it might actually get played on one someday. Men at Work had gotten everyone rhyming 'Down Under' with 'chunder' in the '80s, so I'd be following in a rich vomiting party anthem tradition.

By the time I'd finished, I'd jotted down concepts for eight songs. In some cases a chord or a lyric or two, and in others just a title. But I felt I had the bones of something, and I was delighted. It was almost four, so I decided to call it a night, what with needing to be at Morphett's by nine. I collapsed into the same bed Zoë and I had shared, probably for the only time. But the notion didn't make me feel as sad as it had before. I'd just proven that there was enough happening in my life to fuel a whole bunch of songs, if I actually sat down and wrote them. Perhaps no one would like them except me, but that would be OK. Even if I packed it in and resigned myself to becoming a lawyer, at least I'd have tried — and finally produced something. I'd have a record, in both the musical and the historical senses of the word.

★ ★ ★

The next morning, I listened to the rough recording I'd made of the Zoë song. The effect was a little naïve, but I hoped it was in a charming, Kimya Dawsonish way. Zo had bought the *Juno* soundtrack like every other indie girl I knew, so it pretty much fit. I copied the track across to my iPod so I could listen to it again on the way to work.

Just before it swung down the ramp onto the Harbour Bridge to take us into the city, my bus passed The Oaks. I remembered my night there with Nige, just before I'd joined his firm. I'd enjoyed the months of working with him, and had even grown fond of some of our colleagues. But what with poker night and the regular sessions in pubs like that one, it wasn't like my life had been light on Nige and his buddies before. So, now that I'd ruled out Felicity, the only thing left to stay at Morphett's for was the work. And when I thought about it in those terms, I knew what I had to do.

Brent was great about my resignation. I told him I'd realised I had to be in or out, that there was no point in trying to juggle law work and the other things I wanted to do. Either Morphett's was going to pull me towards working more and I'd neglect the other projects, or I'd end up doing a half-arsed job in both areas. And he understood, and even apologised because the workload he'd given me had so far outweighed what I'd signed up for. So we agreed that I'd finish up in a couple of weeks, and catch up for a coffee in six months – after which, he clearly hoped, I'd have failed in my other endeavours and be keen to come back. Perhaps he would be proven right, but at least I'd know.

I'd expected him to be nice about it because it made good business sense. There's always a chance a disgruntled employee will end up crawling back, and they want to avoid that being humiliating. Plus, HR departments love people who've already proven themselves – they're so much less risky to recruit. And when people leave Morphett's, they often end up working in-house somewhere – so the firm wants its 'alumni' to remember it fondly when they need to hire outside legal advice.

The following day, I ducked my head into Felicity's office and she blushed before I even said anything. I smirked because I knew why – my tip that Will should bring over a bottle of champagne had been, shall we say, gratefully received by the lady. After the whole experience with Zoë, what I'd thought I'd felt for Felicity seemed the mildest of crushes. Not only were the feelings gone, but I really couldn't relate to them anymore; it was if they'd happened to some other person. So I made the conversation as painless as I could.

'Hey, I'm glad to hear about Will,' I said.

'Really? Because he said you'd be cool with it, and I dunno, I kind of believed him, and –'

'No, honestly – I think it's a great idea. He's a good guy, he'll treat you well. And besides, you know – I'll be out of here in a few weeks.'

She pouted a little bit and said she was sorry, but I thought she overdid it a little.

'I'm sure we'll still hang out,' I said. 'Especially if you keep seeing a good friend of mine.'

She laughed. 'Well, I'll be sure to keep you in mind for the next Morphett's party, then. Thanks a lot Paul.' And then, the coup de grace: 'You're a great friend, I'll miss you.'

The f-word was exactly what I'd been hoping to achieve. So I said I'd see her round, and went back to my office, feeling I'd tied up another loose end. It was becoming increasingly clear to me that what I needed to do was go back to square one. Before Emily, before Felicity, before Morphett's and – most importantly – before the night with Zoë. In retrospect, there had only been one thing wrong with my life before I started trying to change everything, and that had been my attitude to it.

Well, there was one other problem on my plate, of course – I had to find a girlfriend. But maybe the right thing to do was to stop worrying about it. I'd made a few big decisions, and if I kept on sorting myself out and focusing on the stuff I wanted to do, maybe I'd become fulfilled or even successful. That would make it easier to find a woman – or perhaps one might even find me.

#2

★ GROOVE IS IN THE HEART ★
DEEE-LITE (1990)

A week later, I still felt a combination of guilt and regret whenever I thought about Zoë, which was a lot. I knew that I wanted us to be together, and also that I'd definitively ruled out the prospect with my email. But I managed to stop feeling sorry for myself by spending a lot of time working on music. I'd finished my song about Zoë, after multitracking some vocal harmony parts and deciding late in the piece to replace the drum loop with some simple tambourine, making it feel a little like the Beatles' 'You've Got To Hide Your Love Away'. Which seemed appropriate.

The harbour cruise song was also close to finished – I'd downloaded a few genuine 1980s synth samples that wouldn't have sounded out of place on an a-ha track, and I had high hopes for their potential cheesiness.

Angela had followed up on the dinner plan, so I met her and Phil at a trendy Surry Hills eatery that was very literally named Bird Cow Fish. Phil insisted on ordering pork, just to be hilarious, but it was a lot of fun polishing off two bottles of wine between the three of us. I agreed to come back to MobyDisc on a higher wage after a break to work on my own music, and take on some additional training and management responsibilities. mDisc was a goner without me to champion it, but Angela had convinced Phil that if I helped him run the show, he could expand his operation, perhaps even doubling his staff.

'It won't be a backyard operation anymore,' Ange said. 'Phil's going to get an office somewhere central so that clients can come in and see what you've got. And so that next time you're stuck without the right CDs, you can let yourself in!'

'You're saying farewell to the garage, Phil? Wow, talk about the end of an era!'

'She's got a great business brain on her, this one,' he said, squeezing Ange's shoulder tightly. 'And it'd be good to upscale – we'll need the extra dough once we start popping out kids. Isn't that right honey?'

Honey laughed and squeezed back.

'He's got a point: I'm turning thirty-seven soon and we'd be crazy to leave it too much longer, to be honest. Watch out Paul, or he'll sign you up to be a godfather or something.'

It turned out they were already planning their wedding, and Phil paid me the greatest honour he knew how by asking me to handle the DJing duties at the reception. I was touched and said I'd be delighted – as long as I could bill the standard rate. For a moment, he took me seriously.

'Now you have to promise me something, Paul,' Ange said. 'You have to bring a date to the wedding. And not just that friend of yours Phil's told me about – what's her name, Zoë? I mean a real romantic date. You've got eight months, will that be long enough?'

'I can't promise I'll find a girlfriend in that time, but I can definitely commit to not bringing Zoë,' I said, laughing at an irony they couldn't appreciate.

'There are some lovely girls about your age at my work,' Ange said.

'Oh, there are always plenty at our work too, but he never goes for 'em!' Phil butted in. 'Now I'm off the market, you'll have a free run at the ladies Paulie!'

'To be frank, I'm taking a break from the ladies at the moment,' I replied. 'Things got a bit complicated recently.'

'Oh come on now Paul,' Ange said. 'You're quite a catch. And there are some really lovely, bright girls I could introduce you to. I'll make sure you're on the invite list for some of our client functions in the new year, and I won't take no for an answer.'

'Well, if I have no choice – sure, hook me up with all the cute brainiacs you've got,' I laughed. If they were half as cluey as Ange, they'd be well worth looking into.

★ ★ ★

When I arrived home, I had an email from Zoë. Its subject was 'Therapy', which sounded serious. I clicked on it, concerned that things had taken a turn for the worse, but she'd been joking: it was a photo of her lying on a deckchair on a Thai beach at sunset. She was holding up a cocktail made from a hollowed-out coconut and smiling at the camera. Also, she was in a bikini, which brought back a few memories I'd been trying to suppress.

The message was brief.

Hi Paulie,
As you can see, I'm feeling a whole lot better! I'll be back
Sunday week, so expect to see me shortly after that. Miss you.
  xox Zo

I was glad she was thinking about me. But what was important about her email, I thought, was what it didn't say. It was exactly the sort of message she'd always sent me when she was on holidays. I was hoping it was another sign that – as I'd written in the song as a way of reminding myself at precisely these moments – things didn't have to change.

I opened up the song again in Pro Tools and took another listen to the final version, which I'd mastered the night before. When I had a few tracks together, I decided, I'd use Zo's contact at FBi to try and get some airplay. And maybe I'd have a chat to them about doing a bit of on-air work as well. It made sense: if there's one thing I know about, it's playing records, and a radio audience had to be easier to deal with than the likes of Harris. I opened up the harbour cruise song and added another keyboard track. I scooted sideways to the synth and began playing, tweaking the levels to get exactly the right sound. And for the time being at least, Zoë was forgotten.

★ ★ ★

I'd been steering clear of my parents since the night I'd entertained my 'guest', but on Saturday we finally caught up over breakfast – eggs in the backyard, scrambled by my father in a rare moment of culinary artistry. It was a lovely morning and I was glad to see them, even though I knew I'd probably get grilled more thoroughly than the bacon.

'We keep hearing music floating up the stairs at all hours of the day and night,' Dad said. 'Are you working on anything in particular?'

'Not really, I guess I've just got a lot of ideas at the moment.'

'That's great, Paulie,' Mum said.

I hadn't told them about my job situation yet, so I thought I'd better do it while we all seemed to be in a good mood.

'I feel like I really need to pursue the music stuff,' I said. 'So I've decided to leave Morphett's for the time being.'

'Oh?' my father said, raising an eyebrow.

'It's taking up too much of my time. So I talked to Brent, and I'm gonna give it six months. If it doesn't work out, I can go back.'

'Well, I think it's great to give music a proper try,' Mum said. 'Especially if the option's still open to go back to the law. That seems very sensible.'

'Yeah, and let's be clear on this,' Dad chipped in. 'We don't think you have to be a lawyer or anything. I'd like to think we're a little more open-minded than that.'

My smile gave my opinion away, and Dad acknowledged it.

'OK, it's probably fair to say that we've pushed you in that direction. But look at our careers – neither of us particularly values the corporate world. We just want you to be a success at whatever you choose to do, as long as you choose *something*.

And it's not because we care about achievements or anything for their own sake, it's because we know you well enough to know you're happiest when you're achieving things. You're no different from us, or your siblings in that regard.'

'Look, if you wanted to become a Buddhist monk, I'd – well, I probably wouldn't be delighted. But I'd at least be happy that you had a firm direction,' Mum said. 'That's all. Music's a great thing to pursue – and if there's anything we can do to help, just tell us.'

'There is something that comes to mind,' Dad said. 'I was wondering about getting that room of yours sound-proofed.'

'Oh sorry, I've been a bit loud, have I?' I said, feeling guilty.

'Well, perhaps once or twice. It's not just that, though. I was looking through some old med revue photos the other day, and I was thinking it might be fun to take up the drums again.'

'Hey Dad, that's great,' I said. I'd heard him play from time to time, and his drumming was as precise as he was in the operating theatre.

'As long as you don't mind me giving the skins a workout from time to time myself,' he said.

'Of course – and more than that, if you want to play drums on a recording sometime, I could really use it. Live drums sound a million times better than the samples I've been using.'

'I'd be happy to, if you think your old dad is up to scratch,' he said.

'Oh Paulie, you know he'd love that,' Mum said, smiling.

I smiled myself, because I knew my dad would rush straight out and buy a really snazzy drumkit. What's more, he'd probably call the builders about soundproofing first thing on Monday. He never did these things by halves.

'Now we know it isn't any of our business,' my mother said. My stomach lurched because I knew what was coming. 'But I just have to ask one thing: is everything OK with Zoë?'

'She had a fight with Josh,' I said.

'Yeah, we'd kind of assumed that,' Dad said. 'What's the story?'

'Well, he was seeing someone else, and let's just say it was a disaster.'

'Oh, that's awful! Poor thing!' my mother said.

'She hasn't been great, but don't worry too much. She's in Thailand with her mum, and they seem to be enjoying themselves.'

'Oh good. You know how fond I am of her,' Mum said. And I did – she'd already made it embarrassingly clear on several occasions that she was more than willing to have Zoë for a daughter-in-law if the opportunity ever arose, refusing to heed my insistence that it would ever happen.

'I haven't heard what's happening with them,' I said. 'She might take him back, she might not. I guess she'll decide when she comes back.'

'And I expect you'll be waiting at the airport with a bunch of flowers and a silly grin on your face, eh?' My father chipped in.

'Ha ha, very droll. Look, I want us to stay friends, and that's all I want. Really.'

'Fine, son, whatever you say. Just remember that if you happen to need one for any reason, I know an excellent florist –'

'Don't listen to him, Paulie,' Mum cut in. 'I think it's great that you're there for her. And if that turns into anything more, then that's lovely too.'

'It won't,' I said brusquely.

'Anyhow, are you doing OK?' Dad asked.

'Yeah,' I said. 'I'm fine, really.'

I don't have a great track record when it comes to talking to my parents about girls, but this time I was telling the truth.

★ ★ ★

Dad's new drumkit was a joy to play. Mum was pleased because the two of us hadn't worked on a project together in years, and Dad was stoked to have a chance to dust off his 'silky stickwork', as he put it. I found myself hurrying home from work each day to get in a bit of drum practice myself, and I couldn't wait to finish up at Morphett's and spend more time on it. The soundproofing was due to be installed in a fortnight's time, and the builder had promised we'd be able to play the kit at full bore without disturbing the neighbours. I was still a pretty useless drummer, and I'd promised Dad I'd stick to brushes to control the noise until the builder had finished, but it was still great fun practising to some of my favourite songs. I figured in a year or two, I'd be good enough for my own recording purposes, at any rate, but there wasn't any rush – Dad's first session had sounded great.

Zoë texted me on the Monday afternoon of my final week at Morphett's to say she was back, and to ask whether I wanted to come by her place for a drink on Friday. I was happy to agree – I'd been in the habit of dropping by for an after-work beer with her and Josh on the odd Friday I wasn't DJing, so it felt like another encouraging sign that things were gradually drifting back to normal.

#1

★ **ISLANDS IN THE STREAM** ★
KENNY ROGERS AND
DOLLY PARTON (1983)

When I told him I was leaving Morphett's, Nige didn't try to argue with me. He just shook his head in ironic sorrow and told me I owed him $2000 for the HR finder's fee he'd have to forego. He was prepared to be reasonable though, and offered me the chance to pay it off progressively, in the form of beers. I could start with a lengthy celebratory session on the Friday of my departure. I laughed and deferred him until the Saturday by explaining that I had plans to see Zoë on my last night, which opened up a whole new angle for taking the piss out of me.

And so, after I walked out of the office for the final time, I steered clear of the upmarket pubs that usually host Morphett's escapees'

281

departure drinks and wandered through Hyde Park towards Zo's terrace. The gardens are beautifully manicured these days, an oasis of calm in the CBD, but I needed more than just a park to relax me. I was impatient to see her again, but I was apprehensive about Zoë asking awkward questions about my feelings. I hoped the email had cleared everything up, but she'd always been a little too good at seeing through me.

As I walked past the War Memorial, I wondered what she'd decided about Josh. Given the scene the last time the three of us had been together, I assumed she'd have warned me if he was going to be at the house. But if she had forgiven him, he might have taken off for the night to give us a chance to work things out. I prepared myself to fake being cool about it if he was still in the picture.

I knocked on her door gingerly, but when she opened it, Zoë embraced me as enthusiastically as if she'd been overseas for years. Perhaps she clung to me a little more tightly than usual, but as we broke the clinch she gave me a little peck on the cheek, the same way she always did. It was the kiss of a friend, not a lover.

Her favorite Ella Fitzgerald record was playing as we wandered through to the kitchen, and she chattered away at a million miles an hour about her holiday, her Ph.D, the political situation in Thailand – anything, in fact, that didn't involve her, me, Josh, or any awkward combination of the three. And while she talked, she made tea using a little Japanese tea-set I'd given her for her twenty-first, another ritual we'd played out many times before. If I'd been given the option, I'd have chosen something alcoholic, but the tea's familiarity was comforting. It was genmaicha, the variety with burnt rice that we both love and Josh can't stand. If he'd left, I thought, we could drink it all the time.

Toting a little tealight candle, she led me out into the backyard. It was a tiny terrace courtyard but there was something lovely about it, with its ramshackle assortment of vines and potplants. It was her favourite spot to read, and normally there were few places I found more relaxing. But given the conversation we had to have, the cobblestones made me think of public squares and executions, with myself in the Sydney Carton role.

I wanted to get the whole thing over with. I didn't need to hear about how she was excited because part of her thesis might make it into the *Alternative Law Journal*. Well, I did, but not at that moment. So when she stopped talking about it momentarily to take a sip of tea, I figured it was time to rip off the Band-Aid.

'Look Zo, I just want to say I'm really sorry about what happened, OK? I was in a strange place that night,' I said, hesitantly. 'I'd had too much to drink, and I wasn't thinking.'

She immediately folded her arms and sat back in her chair.

'God Paul, I was so much enjoying not talking about it.'

'Yeah, but –'

'I know, it has to be done. OK, for starters, who says there's anything you need to apologise for? I needed companionship that night, and you gave it to me. As far as I can see, I should be thanking you, not fielding an apology. You were there for me, and it meant a lot. An awful lot.'

'OK, well, that's good. But really, it wasn't what I planned. I lost control.'

'I don't know that I displayed a lot of control either. I broke up with the guy I'd been living with, and immediately slept with my best friend. So hey – things were a little confused for me too. But I don't feel bad about it. Not at all.'

'Yeah, but Josh –'

'We don't use that word in this house anymore, actually. It's like in Harry Potter – he shall not be named. Bad things will happen if he is.'

I grinned.

'I'm happy to say, for reasons of personal vanity, that he asked me to take him back a few days later. As you can imagine, I quite enjoyed saying no.'

I laughed.

'And when I had time to think about it over the last few weeks, I realised it was the right thing,' she continued. 'I wouldn't have chosen for things to end, but now that it's happened, I'm fine with it, really.'

'I'm glad you feel that way.'

'I guess I thought that if I only believed in the idea enough, or tried hard enough, we'd come good. But it's kind of like Santa Claus. No matter how much you once believed in him, as soon as you discover there's nothing there, the charm's gone, and you're left with a fat guy invented by the Coca-Cola company.'

'I know what you mean: that's how I feel about Mel now. I'd started asking why she didn't want me anymore, and ended up asking myself why I'd ever wanted her.'

'As opposed to a certain wise friend of yours who *began* by asking why you ever wanted her.'

'Yeah, yeah. But look – it's great you could get away to think it through and everything. A clean break and then you can just take some time out from the whole relationship thing and focus on yourself for a bit. And that's why I'm so glad we're still friends despite what happened, you know? I want to be hanging out with you, not making things more complicated.'

'Mmm,' she said, looking at me quizzically. 'You made that pretty clear in your email.'

'I thought you'd appreciate not having to worry about me along with everything else.'

'That's sweet, but honestly, it'll take more than an email to stop me worrying about you!'

I didn't quite know how to take that, so she went on.

'But enough about me. How's the harem?' And she flushed with a hint of embarrassment. 'I mean, the other members – um, you know what I mean.'

'Uh, it's been disbanded,' I said. 'Emily's found someone more age-appropriate, and Felicity hooked up with Will, and that seems to be working out.'

'Aw, poor you! From an abundance back to the old drought, huh?'

'Yeah, it's a little ironic I suppose. But it's all right: Will's a better match for Felicity, and good luck to them. And before you say it – yeah, you were right about that as well.'

She nodded, and couldn't quite conceal a self-satisfied smirk. I continued.

'Whereas Emily – lovely girl, but except for a few moments when I got carried away with the novelty factor, neither of us ever really thought it was going to be serious. So, I'm back to no women in my life, but it's better than wasting my time with people who aren't right.'

'Hey, it's not like there are no women in your life. There's still me.'

'Yeah, well –'

'And your mum.'

I laughed, and she looked away for a moment, lost in thought. I slumped a little in my chair and stared at the table, wishing she hadn't immediately undercut her observation with a joke. After the best part of a minute, she turned to face me again and began speaking.

'Look, I understand what you said in that email – which, by the way, brought back a whole heap of *déja vu* from first year.'

'Ha, me too.'

'And that's fine – as far as I'm concerned, our friendship only comes out of this stronger. We can hang out a lot now, like you said, now we're both swinging singles.'

'Yeah, and that's why I wanted to clear things up immediately, you know? I didn't want to damage what we have, and I thought it was best to have some clarity.'

'Sure, and I don't want to damage anything either. There's no need to, as far as I'm concerned. But just do me one favour, OK?'

'Sure, anything,' I said, expecting a quip about me promising not to set her up with any more of my friends.

'Just tell me one more time that it's what you want.'

And I realised that despite my best efforts, we weren't quite done with this topic yet.

Sometimes when you're at a crossroads, you only realise it in retrospect. But other times, it's abundantly clear, like when she'd asked me early in the piece whether Josh was a good idea. I'd told her he was a great guy, and she shouldn't worry about committing, all the while privately wishing that she'd decide not to.

This was another one of those moments. I could safeguard

our friendship, and destroy whatever hope I had. Or I could tell her the truth, and just hope she forgave it. Neither option appealed, but they were the only ones I had.

'Well, like I said, I don't want to lose you as a friend,' I began. 'I'd be left with only Nige to give me advice, and frankly, that wouldn't work at all.'

'When you put it like that, you're right – our friendship must survive at all costs,' she said, laughing. 'Given that his great prescription for your life was bringing you back to Morphett's.'

'Oh, and by the way, I've got some news on that front. Today was my last day.'

'Hey,' she exclaimed. 'That's wonderful. I want to hear the whole story –'

'OK, well I guess I realised –'

'Right after you finish answering my question.'

I laughed. 'Was I that transparent?'

'Uh, yeah,' she smiled.

'Fine,' I said. 'Here's what I've been thinking, while you've been away. We can go out to bars and stuff, and have a great time, like we did at the Loft that night.'

'Yeah, that was great,' she said.

'And then, while we're having fun, we'll meet a bunch of people, check that the other one of us approves of them, and then we'll both be happy. I've been looking forward to you coming back so we can give it a go – and if you feel like it, we can go out somewhere tonight.'

'That's a lovely idea but believe me, I'm not going to be doing any barhopping for a little while yet.'

I laughed, and went on. 'However, for that scenario to work, we'd need to have a really honest understanding between us, especially after what's happened. We'd probably have in the back of our minds the possibility that if we were drunk enough, or upset enough, we might end up crossing the line again. So I'm now wondering whether my plan was such a sensible one.'

'You're right. I don't want there to be anything unresolved between us. I couldn't bear it.'

She was probably expecting me to rule things out definitively, I thought. To purge our friendship of the ambiguity that our night together had introduced. But I realised that doing so would only mean signing up for more concealment.

'Here's the thing,' I said, my voice quavering. I pressed on. 'For me there's really only one way to achieve that resolution, and it'll probably only create more awkwardness, I'm afraid. The reality is that if we went out drinking, trying to be each other's wingman – wing*person* – I'd be sitting there the whole time, hoping you'd decide you were better off with me.'

I looked away, feeling like a fool. But when I dared look back, she was smiling.

'Thanks Paul. I'm really glad you said that.'

'Oh, I suspect it was hanging out there anyway. Nige is always telling me I've got a terrible poker face. He suspected it too, the bastard.'

'Well yeah, I guess I've occasionally wondered. But it seems so presumptuous, even when there's obviously some attraction, to think a friend might be seriously interested in you. Particularly when he keeps talking about all these other girls.'

'I hope you're flattered, at least,' I said, my cheeks burning.

'Oh, definitely. Even though you haven't shown much evidence of taste in women lately.'

'No,' I said, a little wistfully. I felt glad I'd told her because there were no more secrets: whatever we were left with after this would be real. But I felt horribly exposed, and it made me queasy in the pit of my stomach. Zoë must be feeling pretty sorry for me about now, I thought, and I didn't want to put her through the agony of letting me down gently.

'You know what? It might be best for me to go,' I said, thinking of resurrecting the plan for drinks with Nige and forgetting all about this for the time being.

'Go? You only just got here.'

'Yeah, but it's all turned awkward now,' I said, standing up. 'This is exactly what I was trying to avoid. I'm glad I was straight with you – but really, I've had enough painful honesty for one night.'

'Before you go, there's an obvious question you're overlooking.'

'No I'm not,' I said. 'You don't have to say it. I said it to myself in that email, remember? It'll be fine, but let's not go through it tonight, OK?'

'No way,' she said. 'You gave your answer, now you have to hear my response. It's only fair.'

I flopped down into the chair and looked at her with suddenly weary eyes.

'Thanks. And I'm glad you're prepared to listen because it took me most of a two-hour foot massage to figure it out, I'll have you know.'

'I appreciate the sacrifice,' I said, laughing with gratitude that she'd broken the sombre mood.

'I'm trying to be a bit analytical in my personal life – it's long overdue,' she said. 'I think I shut off that part of my brain with Josh, and I never want to do that again. So I decided to start by analysing the existing service-provider arrangement.'

Bloody law school girls.

'The way I see it, I've been providing you some pretty high-value services,' she said, as impassively as if she was explaining a constitutional principle to one of her tute groups.

'And I rather enjoyed some of those services.'

'Don't get seedy, kiddo. I'm talking about regular companionship and attention, even to the extent of being described by a certain jerk of an ex-boyfriend as, and I quote, being at your beck and call.'

'Ha!'

'Anyway, I've supplied hours of high-quality advice, even if it's rarely been acted on. And I've spent dozens of nights at seedy pubs, listening to you and Nige and a bunch of other law firm wankers crapping on about yourselves, without ever once making you come to one of the bars *I* happen to like until the other night.'

'What about that time last —'

'That was my *birthday*! You're not getting a shred of credit for that.'

'OK, fair point.'

'Next, I would like to put on the record that I've never once complained about your endless prattling on about cricket.'

'I thought you liked cricket!'

'You thought I liked a sport that goes for *five days*?'

'OK. Well, for what it's worth, remember how we used to watch *Sex and the City* together? I hated it. Doesn't that count for anything?'

'Bullshit. You just pretended to hate it so Nige wouldn't question your masculinity. Quite as much.'

'Darn.'

'Come on, we couldn't have *dragged* you away. You had the hots for Charlotte – which is a terrible reflection on me, come to think of it. Anyway, what I'm getting to is that for the past few years, I've been putting up with virtually all the downside that I presume is involved in being your girlfriend while receiving none of the upside.'

'And you're going to sue me for restitution?'

'Of course not, don't be ridiculous. You know as well as I do: never sue when you can reach a settlement. Now, I did some preliminary calculations on the plane,' she continued.

'Oh god,' I said, laughing.

'And I've worked out that you owe me – let's see – roughly fifty-four bunches of flowers, eighty-five romantic comedies you've no interest in seeing, twenty-four sessions of buying me cocktails while listening to me complaining about my work and–or thesis, and eleven foot massages – not counting the one I needed to work all of this out, that one's on me –'

'I'm sure you've overcalculated.'

'Shut up, it's called compound interest. The rest of the debt you may repay by cooking delicious meals, assuming you learn how, or – well, a little more of what we did that night at your place might also suffice.'

'So what you're saying is –'

'My offer of settlement is that until these debts are repaid, you're going to have to serve as my boyfriend. Fortunately, there's been a recent vacancy.'

I was grinning uncontrollably, but she wasn't done yet.

'Before you respond, I'm putting a few extra terms and conditions into the contract,' she said. 'The first is that you have to acknowledge that you were a total chickenshit in first year, and that you didn't really think it was a bad idea like you said.'

'I admit it unreservedly. So you mean you might have been willing to –'

'Hey, *you* were the one who started off that morning-after conversation by saying it was a mistake, remember? Before I could even express an opinion. Just like you tried to do with your stupid email.'

'Yeah, OK. I admit, I didn't view what happened as a mistake, that time or this one. I guess I just assumed *you* would, so I wanted to be the first to say it.'

'For the record, at the time I was more than happy to try and save face myself, what with being an insecure eighteen-year-old and all. But let's just say if you'd taken a different stance, I'd have at least given it a try.'

I shook my head regretfully.

'But I'm glad we're talking about that,' she continued, 'because it leads me to my second condition. Don't ever try and assume what I'm going to think again. If I'm ninety, and incapable of coherent speech, you can decide what I want – but until then, you have to ask, OK?'

'Ninety eh? This contract's going to last for a long time, is it?'

'It's taken you seven years to have this conversation, so I suspect it's going to take you a very long time to make it up to me.'

'I'm sure you're right. But let me just backpedal for a moment here. Are you honestly telling me that all this time you've been interested?'

'God no, how much of a loser do you take me for? Oh, don't look so crestfallen; I don't think *you* were a loser for your moments of pining – well, maybe a little bit.'

'Thanks.'

'No, it was sweet. A little bit perplexing at times, but mostly sweet. Let's just say that all the while, I was comfortable with the friends thing, but it was in the back of my mind that if things didn't work out with Josh, you might be . . . an option.'

'An option.'

'Yeah, like a stock option. Something that might mature later.'

'Sorry that didn't work out for you!'

'I know. But I want to collect anyway,' she said.

'All right, so where do I sign?' I asked, taking her into my arms.

And as I kissed her, the song I'd written floated into the back of my mind. I still liked the melody, and the lyrics would serve as a precious record of a certain moment in my life. But I was going to need a whole new song about Zoë.

★ ACKNOWLEDGEMENTS ★

Thanks to the law firms who wisely rejected my clerkship applications, with the exception of Ebsworth's, whose response letter I'm still waiting for, nearly a decade later. Fingers crossed.

This novel began as an assignment for a creative writing course at the University of Technology, Sydney. Thanks to my teachers Jean Bedford, Brenda Glover and Debra Adelaide, as well as my classmates for their helpful feedback, in particular Brayden Yoder and Tiffany Hambley.

Thanks to Chas for allowing me to shamelessly trade off his bad name on the cover, and to the rest of the Chaser crew for their indulgence of the frequent absences that helped me get this finished.

Thanks to Dave and Roxy for their tolerance of our house being filled with piles of paper, and to the studio crew for their company and ping pong. Thanks also to the people who read early versions and tried to think of nice things to say about them, and especially to Justin and Nick for helping me over the finish line.

Thanks to all at Random for their willingness to accommodate prima donna behaviour from a lowly first-time novelist, and particularly Larissa, Bert, Jess and Jeanne. And thanks to Nadine for not letting me get away with anything. Thanks also to Jasper and Christabella for the delightful illustration and design.

And finally, thanks to all the people who encouraged me to write a novel – I hope you aren't now regretting it!

If you liked the book, or despised it and can't wait to send me an abusive email, get in touch at www.domknight.com.